The Lighthouse

T. James Reese

Veritas et Virtute
Media Production

ISBN 978-0615742533

First Edition

Stacy…there are more reasons than anyone could ever imagine as to why this book is for you, so I'll simply say *because* you are *my everything*…I love you.

"All my life I have tried to pluck a thistle and plant a flower wherever the flower would grow in thought and mind."

Abraham Lincoln

CONTENTS

1

Ashley couldn't help but smile as she stared at her reflection in the mirror. She'd only just finished applying the final coat of vibrant blue paint on the recently remodeled walls of her now nautical themed bathroom. But it wasn't the color that moved her. She looked adorable, her hair pulled up into a short pony tail, her white tank top marked with paint spatter in seemingly just the right places. But that wasn't the reason either. Her emotions clashed as both happiness and angst flooded her thoughts.

She looked down at her hands, the corners of her mouth curling into a quirky little grin. Slowly, she slid her finger under the side flap of the small pink box that she held in front of her and took a deep breath. The seal broke free easily. Ashley did her best to ignore her jitters and pulled the pregnancy test from the package, sorted through the contents, and began reading over the directions.

-Knock, knock-

Ashley nearly jumped out of her skin, the unfolded paper in her hand falling to the floor and settling next to her flip flop clad feet. Her focus was drawn to the whitewashed door reflecting behind her in the mirror as she heard the knob begin to jiggle. Frantically, she stuffed the pregnancy test and all of its miscellaneous wrappings into the top drawer of the bathroom counter, grabbed her still blue paintbrush from where she'd set it, and reached for the door, a look of forced calm creeping across her pretty face.

"You Ok?" Gavin asked as the door popped open.

"Yeah, baby, the knob sticks sometimes."

"I know, just add it to the list," he grinned.

"You bet," she said with an awkward smile.

"What's that?" he asked, noticing the creased paper on the floor.

"Oh, um," Ashley thought, grasping for anything that would make sense, "it's instructions for the paint."

Stupid! she yelled at herself, her teeth clenched as she continued to smile.

Gavin blinked and then laughed, "The paint came with instructions? Who needs instructions for painting?"

"I don't know," she replied, "some people, I guess?"

"Anyway," Gavin said, her cell phone in his hand, "it's for you."

She took the phone and let out a relieved sigh as he turned and clomped off down the stairs. Ashley headed into the bedroom and flopped down on the unmade bed.

"Hello?"

"Hey, Ash."

"Kayla! How are you?"

"I'm good, you?"

"Fine, just a little...*distracted*."

"Ok," Kayla laughed in a motherly voice, "I just hadn't heard from you in a couple of days and I wanted to see how things are going."

"A couple of days, huh? I'm surprised you didn't put out a missing persons report."

"Yeah, yeah," Kayla laughed sing-songily.

"So how's Ethan?"

"He's good, last night he discovered sweet potatoes, you should have seen his eyes."

"Really?"

"Oh yeah, he was amazed!"

"Is he walking yet?" Ashley grinned.

"He pulls himself up on the couch, then stumbles between it and the chair, but Jamie thinks..."

A raucous, burbly rumble cut Kayla off. Ashley looked up at the wall. One of her paintings was slowly inching its way off kilter as the noise vibrated the whole house.

"Kay, can I call you back?"

"Yeah. I'd better go. Marley and I were baking cookies and it looks like, yep, all over her face, flour, ok, bye."

Ashley ended the call, then made her way downstairs, through the kitchen, and out the door to the driveway. All she could do was shake her head. Gavin looked up at her, the biggest grin she'd ever seen. His arms were covered in grease; she could hardly make out his tattoos.

"WOO HOO!" he yelled, revving the throttle on his old, black motorcycle.

"I see you finally got it running."

"What?"

"I said, it's finally running."

Gavin motioned that he couldn't hear her, then let out the clutch, and turned off the engine, "It's finally running!"

"I hardly noticed," Ashley teased, her ears still ringing. "Do you think it's loud enough?"

"Nope," Gavin replied as he climbed off the bike and pulled a dirty rag from his tool box.

"I've honestly never heard a motorcycle that loud."

"Thanks," he winked.

With a smirk, Ashley smacked his backside and headed into the kitchen. Gavin cleaned up the mess of tools he'd been using, dropped them off on his workbench in the garage, then stopped to admire his handiwork one more time before chasing after her. The bike still needed a paint job and a little more tuning, but it was officially *among the living*, as he liked to say.

The backdoor clicked shut behind him as he stepped into the kitchen and flipped open a white cupboard door, then reached for a glass. Ashley stared blankly at the sink full of dishes.

"Everything OK?" he asked, pressing the glass into the water dispenser on the front of the refrigerator.

"Just thinking," she smiled

****

"Beautiful weather today, isn't it?"

"This is Los Angeles, it's always beautiful."

"Only in the movies, my friend."

Two men stood shoulder to shoulder, speaking just loud enough for each other to hear and engaging in unassuming small talk whenever there was the off chance that someone may walk by and overhear. They stared out from one of the terminal windows at LAX airport and watched as a British Airways 777 touched down on the tarmac.

"Is this man as good as you say he is?"

"Better."

****

"You just seem, distant," Gavin frowned, stepping up behind her, wrapping his dirty arms tightly around her.

"I don't mean to be," Ashley shrugged, "and you need a shower."

Gavin stepped back and raised his arm. Ashley's nose wrinkled as she watched him sniff at the air.

"Maybe."

She smirked at him as he headed upstairs, then turned and looked again at the sink. Ashley wasn't against having a baby and Gavin had hinted at starting a family; besides, they'd been married for five years now. Maybe it was time.

Oh, boy! she smiled.

****

The doors to the tunnel opened as a flight attendant stepped through, slowly leading the passengers out of the corridor. The men watched till there was no one left.

"This was his flight, right?" one of them scoffed.

Before the other could answer, a man appeared at the exit, a long black trench coat hung over one arm, the other wrapped around the waste of a pretty stewardess. They watched as he whispered something in her ear, followed by a kiss that sent her blushing back into the tunnel.

"Mr. Nelson?" he asked, his hand extended in greeting as he approached the men.

"Yes," the man on the right answered curtly, "and this is my associate..."

"Call me Franklin," the second man interrupted, "at least for now."

The man nodded, shaking Franklin's hand as well, then flicked his trench coat, sending it into a swirling blur as it fanned out around him, his arms suavely slipping into the sleeves. It settled across his shoulders, his new acquaintances staring in amazement.

"Shall we go then?" he smiled coyly, his British accent all the more beguiling.

****

Steam from the shower coated the mirror with condensation. Ashley closed the bathroom door behind her. Gavin sang to himself, his off-key melody echoing off the tub surround. Quietly, she undressed and slipped into the shower, resting her head on her husband's shoulder as she pulled the curtain shut.

****

The men worked their way through the crowded airport, stopping at the baggage return to pick up his luggage.

"So what do I call you?" Franklin asked, scratching at his receding hairline.

"The solution to your problem."

"And what is my problem?" Franklin grinned.

"Mr. Nelson contacted my employer who informed me that you required a consultation," the Brit answered smugly. "And in exchange for that service, my employer requested a certain form of remuneration, one that he believes only you have. Therefore, I *am* the solution to your problem."

****

Gavin dried off. Ashley gave him a quick kiss followed by a mischievous smirk as she wrapped her towel around herself. Sitting down on the edge of the tub, she grabbed a bottle of moisturizer, squeezed some into her hand, then rubbed it onto her legs as the smell of strawberries filled the room.

"I need to call Kayla back," she said, wiping excess lotion on her towel. "Love you."

"Love you too, baby," he grinned.

Ashley headed for the bedroom and opened her chest of drawers to pick out a pair of underwear, then slipped into her favorite jeans and pulled on a t-shirt, her hair still wet from the shower. Gavin stood in the bathroom, cleaning his ears with a q-tip. Picking up her cell from where she'd left it lying on the bed, she dialed Kayla.

"Hey, it's me," she said as Kayla answered.

"Ash," she said curiously, sensing the uneasiness in her sister's voice, "what's up?"

Ashley sat down on the edge of the bed, "Well..."

"Well what, Ash?"

"I *think* I'm pregnant," she blurted.

Kayla didn't speak for a moment. Ashley squirmed nervously.

"Have you taken a pregnancy test yet?" Kayla wondered, the phone in one hand, a baby bottle in the other.

"Almost."

"What does that mean?"

"It means I'm working on it," Ashley sighed.

"So what does Gavin think?"

"He doesn't know."

"You haven't, hold on," Kayla paused, "Jamie, get her down from there, Jamie..."

Ashley shook her head, a smile on her face.

"Ok, sorry Ash, I'm back."

"No problem," she said, still smiling. "That's quite a little zoo you have there."

"Yeah, it's Marley," Kayla laughed, "my invincible four-year-old. So what was I saying?"

"Something along the line of asking why I haven't told Gavin."

"Oh yeah," Kayla continued. "So why didn't you talk to him yet?"

"He's got a lot on his plate; work is really stressing him out."

"How's that going anyway?"

"Good. He makes a great supervisor. The toy store has never done so well. All the employees love him."

Kayla held Ethan in her arms, feeding him the bottle, coaxing him into a nap, the phone held between her chin and shoulder. Jamie ran through the living room, a makeshift blanket-turned-cape tied around his neck, Marley giggling, hot on his heels, her curly hair bouncing as she chased after him.

"How long has he been there," Kayla asked, "three years?"

"Yeah, almost four. He really wants to move up, but the company is dragging their feet. The last manager they hired was from outside the company, which is stupid. Gavin isn't the only supervisor there capable of moving up. They practically run the store for the managers anyway."

"It must be tough for him," Kayla said, Ethan's eyes growing heavy.

"Yeah, he has so much potential."

"I mean giving up a life of freedom and excitement, the danger of being a demon hunter, and now trying to live a normal life with a normal job. Moving from the big city to a small town is a severe change of pace, Ash."

"He's doing his best. I know he's frustrated, but this was his choice. He's trying, you know?"

"Sounds like it. And how about you, how's the museum?"

Ashley smiled, she, on the other hand, loved her job.

"I'm teaching a painting class for kids at the art museum. It's great. Plus, I'm still doing restorations on the side. I'm working on a Rembrandt now for the Cleveland Museum of Art, very nice."

"So big museums send you pieces and you fix them up?"

"Yeah, museums, private collectors, investors...well, they don't send them to me actually, they ship them to Cleveland and I go up there, it's more secure than shipping a million dollar painting to a house, you know?"

"Sounds good," Kayla smiled proudly, knowing that her little sister was all grown up. "Well, no matter what, pregnant or not, it's all in God's hands."

"I know," Ashley sighed, "I know."

****

A large black sedan pulled to a stop at the curb. Mr. Nelson opened the rear door as Franklin and their guest slid into the leather seats. The heavy door closed with a solid *thunk*.

"We've set up an apartment for you, downtown," he explained settling into the passenger seat. "You can use it as a base of operations for as long as you like."

The car lurched forward as the driver merged into the exit lane. Franklin fastened his safety belt.

"That's very kind of you."

"Welcome to Los Angeles," Mr. Nelson smiled.

****

"Honey, have you seen my wallet?" Jamie asked, his face red from playing.

Kayla glanced from the living room to the dining room. Marley sat at the table, the wallet flipped open. His credit cards, driver's license, and other miscellaneous clutter were all spread out in front of her.

"Come play store, daddy!"

"Not now, sweetie," Kayla said, picking up the wallet and sorting its contents. "Daddy has to get back to work. Lunchtime is over. Go play dolls."

Marley slumped down off the chair and ran for the family room. Jamie gave Kayla a kiss as she handed him the wallet.

"Was that your sister on the phone?" he asked, slipping the wallet into his pocket and adjusting his tie.

"Yeah," Kayla smiled wistfully, "and, ready for this?"

"What's up?"

"She might be pregnant."

****

The sedan stopped in front of a tall building. The Englishman stepped from the car and looked up approvingly at the luxury high rise.

"Your suite is on the tenth floor," Franklin informed, handing him a set of keys on a fancy ring. "You'll also find a car in the underground garage. The valet can retrieve it for you."

"Thank you, Franklin."

"We'll be in touch." Mr. Nelson added firmly.

The man gave them a nod as the car pulled away from the curb.

"Home sweet home," he smiled, raising his cell phone to his ear.

****

Gavin, his face covered in shaving cream, watched in the mirror as Ashley stepped into the bathroom and readied to dry her hair.

"So what did you want to do tonight?" he asked, shaving his right cheek, then rinsing the blade under the tap.

"Well," she thought, "we could see a movie? That new wizard one is in the theaters."

"*Harry what's-his-name?*"

"No," she laughed, "it's been years since those movies were new."

"Ok then, little miss know-it-all, how about food, then?"

"I don't care. You pick."

****

The man slipped off his trench coat and laid it delicately over the back of a very modern brown leather chair. A large picture window at the far end of the living room immediately caught his interest. From there, he looked out at the city. Sunlight poured in.

Methodically, he emptied his suitcase, sorting the mundane contents onto the coffee table where he made a neat pile of perfectly folded undershirts and boxer shorts on one side, then organizing his dress socks on the other, then finally pulling out a travel grooming kit and a small zippered bag. He unzipped the bag and checked its contents. Satisfied, he closed it back up and set it aside as well. For a moment, he paused, staring at the empty suitcase, then leaned in close, carefully running his finger across the inner seam till he heard a click. Expressionless, he pulled away the bottom to reveal a hidden compartment. A brief smile swept across his face as he looked over the components, all resting safely in the foam-lined case. He began removing the parts, carefully assembling them piece by piece.

As he finished, he relaxed into the soft cushioning, admiring his handiwork. He stood and walked to the window, then raised the rifle and peered through the scope. He panned the street below, watching people pass in his crosshairs. With a smug look of satisfaction, he turned and rested the gun on the couch, then headed for the bedroom to lie down.

****

Gavin took Ashley's hand as they headed out the theater doors, "It's later than I thought it would be."

The sun had set. Fireflies flickered in the parking lot as they headed for their car.

"I love summer," Ashley grinned.

They stepped up to an age-worn 1971 MG B convertible. Gavin

unlocked the doors, then started folding back the manual roof. Ashley leaned against the side, glancing at the roadster's lack of rear seats.

"Maybe we should trade this in?" she asked, trying to sound completely innocent.

"Why? You love this car."

"I know. I guess I was just thinking, since I drive it to work every day, it might be nice to have something a bit...bigger?"

"Ash," he protested, "I put off my motorcycle project for three years so that you could have this car instead of the old van. It gets great gas mileage *and* it's fun to drive."

"The van wasn't even running?"

"Don't argue semantics," he grinned.

"Well then maybe we could get a second car, something not-too-expensive, but nice; something a little better suited for Ohio winters?"

Gavin sat down in the driver's seat and turned the ignition. Nothing happened.

"This car is a classic," he grunted, trying to start it again, "and besides, it is just the two of us."

"Yeah," she said, smiling as it finally sputtered to life.

****

The man woke with a start from his nap, his eyes fiery, the Sig Sauer 9mm in his hand trained at the door. He calmed himself and stood, undoing the buttons on the cuffs of his dress shirt, then loosening his tie.

"Hello," he smirked, opening the door, the stewardess he'd left at the airport now standing in the hall.

She stepped into the apartment, her heels clicking on the hardwood floor. Turning back to him, she let her hair down from the bun she wore on her head, her golden blonde locks sweeping across her shoulders. With a smile, he kissed her neck, his hand gently sliding up her thigh, disappearing beneath the hem of her skirt.

"Mr. Killion..."

"Please, love, call me Terry."

****

Ashley laid down next to Gavin. He'd already fallen asleep. She looked at his arms, his tattoos, remembering when they'd first met, how heroic he was. Rolling onto her back, she stared at the ceiling. Her mind was racing with every last detail concerning a baby. She pictured which room they could turn into a nursery, the color of the walls, the furniture. Diapers, onesies, and teddy bears: nothing escaped her.

Slowly, her eyes grew heavy, her thoughts drifting into the darkness. Gavin stirred, turning, wrapping his arm around her. She snuggled in close to him, pulling the covers up under her chin, safe, at peace.

2

"So as we leave this place and go our separate ways, find joy in knowing that our Lord is with us. Let's pray..."

Reverend Harlow McNamara closed out his sermon. The congregation bowed their heads as the organ swelled, wailing its appeal for repentance.

"...Amen," he said, raising his arms high, the choir behind him smiling stoically as they opened into an energetic chorus, the people standing on cue, shifting towards the end of their row, and shuffling out like herds of well-managed cattle. "Oh and don't forget your checkbooks next Sunday. It marks the kickoff of our annual outreach rally with our surprise key note speaker. Have a blessed week!"

The massive congregation began its slow processional out from the sanctuary and into the crowded, noisy lobby. Running children weaved in and out of the clusters of adults engrossed in conversation, catching up on the latest he said-she said.

In the sound booth, the technicians powered down the equipment, saved computer files, and burned audio CD's of the Reverend's sermon to sell at the coffee bar. Above in the balcony, video operators flipped off their cameras then double checked the lens caps, finally hanging their headphones from hooks on the tripods.

Rev. McNamara slinked into his office, taking off his suit coat and loosening his tie. His young wife was already there, sitting on his fine jade-green upholstered sofa.

"You left out a part in the middle of your sermon," she chastised, a tumbler in her hand, scotch swishing around the glass as she spoke, "the part about the gift of God being eternal life."

"How would you know what I didn't say?"

"Because," she replied snidely, "that's the fourth time I've heard it in as many years."

"It's a good sermon," he huffed in defense.

"Yes, but all your sermons are good. That's why you host the largest syndicated religious hour on TV, not to mention a decade's worth of bestselling books and that little endorsement deal with Larry Otto's car dealership."

"Yes, Otto's Autos," he chuckled aloud, the catchy jingle from his friend Larry's commercials playing in his head.

He was interrupted by a knock on the door. Mrs. McNamara stood and emptied her drink into a large potted plant that flanked the sofa and tucked her glass away in the cushions. She sat down on the edge of his desk, her young, slender frame posed as innocently as possible.

"Come in" he said, his furrowed brow quickly smoothing into a forced smile.

"Sir," a young man grunted urgently, short of breath, "I may have discovered a potential issue."

****

"Good morning," Killion whispered, gently caressing the stewardess's soft, naked skin as she stirred next to him in bed.

The bright morning sun blazed through the window. She stretched; blinking as her eyes adjusted to the light, then sat up, pulling the sheets up under her arms.

She leaned in for a kiss, then slipped out from under the covers and eased down on top of him, "I think I'm falling in love."

"I know."

****

"So what are you telling me?"

"Again, Sir, let me explain," the young man said flustered, "As you know, every Saturday, I receive weekly email updates from our agents in the field. Yesterday, Las Vegas and San Antonio checked in with details regarding the progress of our campaigns in those cities."

"Ok?"

"Well, I was filing them away and reviewing dates on some of the reports in their respective folders Chicago, Toronto, Charlotte, the list goes on; they were all up to date except New York. When I realized NYC was missing. I dug deeper, searched the records on the computer and found that the reports from that agent have been sporadic at best over the last five years. And what's worse, he hasn't checked in now in over six weeks, even though I have a bank statement that shows a monthly withdrawal against our investment. I don't know why I didn't notice sooner, but sometimes the agents in the big cities do miss a week here and there and I suppose I just assumed that was the case with New York."

"So what do you think this means?"

"I think it means he's M.I.A."

****

Killion stared at his naked reflection in the mirror as he flipped on the bathroom faucet. Soaking a wash cloth with hot water, he wiped the stewardess's lipstick off his face and neck, his lips curling in disgust.

"Do you want to order breakfast?" she asked from around the corner, still lying in bed, her cheeks flushed. "There's a place not far from here that delivers. It's greasy, but good. I get it every time I fly into L.A."

He leaned against the counter, a smug, slightly irritated scowl on his face, "I'm not hungry. Order whatever you want, breakfast for one."

Quickly, he walked through the bedroom and into the living room, glancing over to see her picking up the phone from the bedside table and poking away at the numbers. Killion flipped open his suitcase and pulled out his 9mm handgun, then removed a silencer from the little black zippered bag and screwed it onto the end of the barrel.

The stewardess hung up the phone as Killion stepped though the bedroom door. She turned and smiled at him, but before she could speak, he pulled the trigger.

****

"What do you mean M.I.A.?" Rev. McNamara blurted. "How do we lose track of one of our men?"

"I'm not sure, perhaps he's still on the job, just reclusive?"

"Or perhaps he's gone rogue?" his wife added, a twinkle in her eye.

"Stop thinking like your stupid soap operas, Barbara."

"So what should we do then, Sir?" the man asked.

"Either way," McNamara grunted, "it's bad. Send someone out there, make contact."

****

Killion wrapped her limp, naked body in the blood soaked sheets, then quickly dressed. He tucked his gun into the back of his trousers and headed out the door, locking it behind him. Carefully, he studied the hallway and found what he was looking for, down at the very end, right beside the stairwell.

All clear, he smirked.

But the killer froze as he turned back to his apartment. A young skinny teen stood knocking at the door, his knobby elbows bent awkwardly, a brown delivery bag in his hands.

That was fast...

"Excuse me," Killion smiled congenially, his English accent hidden behind a southern drawl," is there somethin' I can help you with, boy?"

"Um, I have a delivery for a Ms. Brown," his voice squeaked nervously.

"Well, there's no Ms. Brown at my place I'm 'fraid."

The delivery boy looked at the apartment number on the door, then at the address written on the green and white receipt, "But this is the address she gave us?"

"Hmmm?" Killion replied coolly, "I haven't lived 'round here long, just moved in from Georgia, matter of fact, had a peach farm but I had to sell it on account of havin' no peaches growin' on ma' trees, you see? But now that you mention it, there *is* a pretty blonde 'bout two doors down from me. I've never talked to her but she's real easy on the eyes."

"But the address says..."

"And I told you, boy. There aint no Ms. Brown here," Killion said firmly, a hint of threat echoing in his voice as he took an intimidating stride towards the apartment, "understand?"

"Ye...yes, sir," the boy said hanging his head sheepishly.

Killion watched with bated breath as the boy moped down the hallway and stopped in front of another door, knocking softly. Slowly, he reached around his back, his hand grasping the grip of the gun. After a second knock, the boy shook his head at Killion and mumbled something that sounded like *thanks anyway* as he headed for the elevator.

He relaxed, sliding his key into the lock and turning. Quickly, he raised her body onto his shoulder and peeked back out the doorframe.

Still clear.

Killion made his way to the end of the hall and stopped in front of a three-foot-by-three-foot stainless steel chute on the wall marked *garbage*. With his free hand, he pulled open the door, then dropped her down into the darkness, a certain look of satisfaction as he listened to the sound of her body thudding as it tumbled down the aluminum chute.

****

"Rocco?"

"Yeah, Jimmy?"

"Are you busy?"

"Not today. Why?"

"McNamara needs you to go to New York City."

"Why?" Rocco asked, looking out his window at the gold-domed capitol building in downtown Boston.

"It's Gavin," Jimmy answered.

"Yeah, what about him?"

"We think he's gone underground. Find him."

"And when I find him, then what?"

"Eliminate him."

****

"So what did you think of that church?" Gavin asked Ashley, pulling from the parking lot and into the traffic on the street.

"The pastor was great, but the music was awful," she frowned. "The keyboard player couldn't keep up with the guitar player and the lady singing soprano sounded like she was choking a rooster!"

"So I take it we're not going back there then?"

"I don't know? It's just so hard to find a good church."

"Yeah," Gavin agreed.

"And that old man that greeted us, I thought he was going to stop us and lay hands on you and pray or ask you to leave or, I don't know....*something*...when he saw your tattoos."

"Well, that goes without saying."

"I don't know if we'll ever feel at home anywhere, Gavin."

"What we need to find is a church that is welcoming, not judgmental, with just the right mix of forward thinking and honest biblical teaching..."

"...and good music," Ashley added.

****

"So is Rocco going to take care of this Gavin issue then?" Barbara asked, playing with her long golden curls as she stared across the desk at her aging husband.

He ran his fingers through his slicked-back, graying hair, "Yeah, but I can't feel at ease yet. Gavin could be a real liability. He never truly bought into The Order. I guess I have his mentor, Joseph, to thank for that."

"So you think he took off with this Joseph and now he's in hiding?"

"No. The old man is dead. Triton saw to that. If this goes too far, I'll have Franklin breathing down my neck."

"Why don't you tell him the truth?" she asked, retrieving her glass from the couch and pouring herself another drink.

"Because, Franklin is the head of The Order and he'd excommunicate me, or worse..."

"Then tell him to mind his own business. You're an equal partner in this whole thing."

"Triton was the only man who kept Franklin in his place," Harlow frowned, "since he's been gone, Franklin's become a different person, controlling, secretive. He cares more for himself now and less for The Order."

"Then I think you need to take care of this situation and quick. Handle things right, and Franklin will never be the wiser."

****

"I'll take a number six combo, large, with a diet soda and..."

"...a...um...small number one with cheese," Ashley decided.

"...a small number one with cheese," Gavin repeated into the speaker at the drive thru.

"Wha...d...you <*skkrsshhh*> to drink with tha..." the voice from the other end responded.

"Um, iced tea," Ashley grinned, "and can I have some chicken nuggets too?"

Gavin finished ordering, then pulled around to pay the rather hefty looking man at the window. As Gavin handed the food across to Ashley, she checked the bag to make sure it was all there and then nodded her approval.

"Hungry?" he asked, pulling away from the restaurant as he watched her nibble on a nugget.

"I'm a growing girl," she said with a pout.

****

The elevator stopped at the parking garage. Killion stepped out and looked down at the key ring Mr. Nelson had given him. A key fob for an Audi rested in his hand. He hit the panic button. The horn beeped and the lights flashed, drawing his attention to the aisle on his right. Grinning, he approached the silver car and pressed a small button on the fob, a key flipping out from the remote. Then, he spotted a red S8 emblem on the chrome grill and smiled even bigger.

3

S cree...scree...scree...scree...

Ashley rolled over, swatting groggily at the alarm clock on the bedside table, her eyes adjusting to the faint, early morning light. She looked at Gavin and shook her head. He lay sleeping, his mouth open, a wet little puddle on his pillow.

"Get up," she nudged.

"Ugghh...is it seven already?"

"Unfortunately."

Ashley pulled off the covers and made for the bathroom. Gavin followed reluctantly.

"So do you work today?" he managed to ask through a yawn, slumped over at the counter, running water to splash on his face.

"I always work on Mondays," she said, a hint of irritation ringing in her words.

"Is there time for breakfast?"

Ashley shrugged, flipping on the shower. Gavin pulled a bath towel off the rack on the wall and hung it over the shower curtain rod for her.

"It's going to be one of those days," he sighed as she undressed and slipped into the shower.

"What was that?"

"Nothing," he replied, pulling the bathroom door shut behind him as he left the room.

****

The sun slowly peeked from behind the trees, the rays inching across the green-grassed estate, the shadows growing smaller with each passing moment. A man stood in his white gravel drive, a vast Tudor manor sprawling behind him.

He watched the sunrise, a black mug of coffee in one hand, the other thrust in his pants pocket. His navy pinstripe suit was tailored perfectly, not a hair was out of place. Taking a sip, he turned and headed for his multi-car garage.

The man stopped at a small digital keypad and punched in the code, followed by the press of a button marked *Door 1*. As it opened, he looked once more at the sun, then strode into the garage and looked down the row of cars. Red Ferrari, yellow Lamborghini, green Aston Martin: his collection read like a who's who at an exotic auto salon.

He pulled a set of keys from a rack that hung on the back wall of the garage, just above a stainless steel workbench surrounded by perfectly organized matching cabinets and expensive shelves neatly filled with automotive odds and ends. His tools were immaculate, not a speck of dirt or grease to be found. He slid into the leather seat of his black Porsche and turned the key, the engine growling to life. Slowly he pulled out from the garage bay and headed off down the long drive.

****

"So I'll see you this afternoon, then?" Gavin smiled, trying to lighten the oddly hostile breakfast mood as he picked his motorcycle helmet up off the kitchen counter and readied to leave for work.

"Yeah,"

"Think about what you want to do this evening."

"Alright."

"Anything you want to do, we'll do it."

"Let's go out tonight," Ashley decided, "I don't feel like cooking."

Gavin grinned, "I want to take you someplace nice then, maybe Italian?"

"Ok, the *olive place*."

"The olive place it is."

****

The Porsche whipped around the twisty turns. Light filtered through the dense trees that lined the brim of the road, casting odd patches of light and shadow on the pavement. The engine screamed as he held the throttle high in the RPM range, pushing the car to its limit with each controlled flick of the wheel, the whoosh of the turbo whistling with each gear change. He hadn't seen anyone for miles. The road wound deep through the mountain forest, his home far from any real civilization.

As he cruised around a sweeping bend, he came upon a small gas station. Its windows were covered in dirt. Ivy grew over its old cinderblock walls. Two old fashioned pumps stood in the lot like faded red statues. A black and white Ford Crown Victoria sat facing the road, a gold star emblazoned on its door, a thin row of red and blue lights garnishing the roof. The man pulled into the station and stopped at a pump, his tires running over a black rubber chord. The faint jingle of a bell came from inside the building.

The door to the cruiser opened and a sheriff's deputy stepped out, his tan cowboy hat shading his face. Gold framed aviators rested on the tip of his nose. A toothpick hung from the corner of his mouth.

"Going a little fast there wouldn't you say, friend?" he grunted, pulling his thick black belt up as he walked towards the sports car.

The man stepped away from the pump as a young boy, no more than thirteen, ran up to the car, wiping his hands off on his already dirty, blue coveralls.

"Premium, please."

"Yes, sir," the boy acknowledged as he grabbed the nozzle and started filling it up.

"What brings you out here today, Moe?"

"Nothing really, Michael, just some spooked folk out here."

"How so?"

"Well, the Thompson farm reported some missing cows, the Conner family's barn burnt down, and the coup de gra: crazy old Lucy Devinshire claims she saw bright flashing lights in the woods last night and now there's a circle the size of a football field in her corn crop."

"All in one night, huh?"

"Well," Moses thought, "within the last week."

"Any leads?"

"Shoot," Moses laughed, "of course not. I mean who would burn down the Conner's barn 'round here?"

"I don't know, Moe."

"And you know how Lucy is. She's telling everyone it's," he lowered his voice as if he were embarrassed to say the next word, "*aliens!*"

"Well," Michael smiled, "I'm sure it's not other-worldly visitors."

"Yeah, but don't you remember back a few years ago when farmer's were finding their cattle dead, the blood drained, the brains gone," Moses continued seriously, "out west somewhere, remember that?"

"No, Moe, I don't."

"Well I watched a show on T.V. on a, like a, discovering history channel or somethin' like that and they said it was aliens that did it."

"And what does that have to do with this?"

"The Thompson's cows, of course!"

"You said they're missing, not butchered."

Michael stopped. His attention was drawn away from the trooper. An old man was sitting on a rickety bench in front of the building.

"What is it, Michael?"

"Did you see where that man came from?"

Moses turned around to see where Michael was pointing, but no one was there.

****

"Ma'am, please, no, I didn't raise my voice. Ma'am, all I said is that you need a receipt for any returns or exchanges...ma'am?"

Gavin hung up the phone at the customer service desk. Two of his coworkers stood next to him, their faces red as they held back their laughter. Their nametags read *Thomas* and *RJ*.

"What was that all about, boss?" Thomas asked.

"The usual, 'I want to return this but I don't have a receipt,' routine," Gavin grinned mockingly.

"She sounded mad, boss," RJ added.

"Yeah well, some customers just think the louder and angrier they get, the more likely I am to give them what they want. But the first time they swear at me, I'm done. I've already made up my mind: *no* means *NO!*"

"I know exactly what you mean, boss."

"Stop calling me boss," Gavin frowned, "it's creepy. Call me *master.*"

The three of them burst into laughter as the automatic entrance doors slid open. A man stood in the doorway, a big green duffle bag in his hand. The scowl on his face told Gavin one thing, he meant business.

****

"I'll talk to you later, Moe. Good luck catching your aliens."

Michael ignored the deputy's confused response and pushed past him. The old man on the bench stared ahead blankly as he approached. The closer Michael got, he could see that the man's eyes were glazed over, a hazy white film covering them. Michael looked away as Moe pulled out into the road, dust kicking up from his tires as he sped off. Then, turning back to the man, their eyes met.

The old man stared at him, not so much with his sightless eyes, but with his thoughts. Michael could feel it, like the sensation of being watched when you're all alone.

"Who are you?' Michael demanded.

"You know me," he said, his toothless mouth opening into a smile.

"I know you?"

"Well, maybe not like this, but you know me."

"Sorry, I don't hang out with blind old-timers that appear out of thin air at gas stations in the middle of nowhere."

"I'm sure," the old man chuckled, his voice changing slightly, a deep reverberation present as he spoke, "but there's someone here to see you, *Thirteen*."

****

Gavin leaned against the customer service desk. Thomas and RJ flanked him, their chins raised defiantly. The man stepped up to the counter, the door closing behind him. He looked around at all the shelves, toys as far as the eye could see. He cast a suspicious glare in the direction of the video game department, eyeing the locked glass cases filled with games. Slowly the man drew closer, then paused, his hand disappearing into the satchel.

****

Michael stepped back from the old man. He wasn't sure what to say.

"No one's called me that in years," he finally said, his mouth dry, "I left that life behind."

"You can forget the past, Thirteen, but the past never forgets you."

****

"So," Gavin said, keeping his cool, "what can we do for you today?"

The big man grunted, clearing his throat. His baggy jeans draped over his filthy shoes, the fraying cuffs dragging on the floor as he walked. A faded t-shirt covered his large frame, a little tight, like it was a size too small. A worn logo stretched across the chest, but the name of the band it advertised was long gone. He tilted his head to the left, his greasy hair falling away from his eyes.

"I'd like to return this, please," he said, his voice deceivingly higher than they expected from his appearance and demeanor, "I have my receipt."

He pulled his big hand from the bag and removed a broken action figure, its arm off, snapped at the shoulder. Thomas smiled with relief.

"Sure thing," Gavin sighed. "RJ, take care of him, will you?"

"Gotcha, *boss*."

****

"What do you know about my past?"

"I know you killed a lot of people."

"No, not me."

"You're only fooling yourself, Thirteen. You know you miss us."

"Miss who?"

"Us," a voice called from around the side of the building.

A clutter of sound filled the air, a chorus of whoops and hollers followed by the stomping of feet. Something only described as an electrical hum buzzed from above. Michael could feel the tips of his fingers tingling as he looked around the corner. No one was there, just a trash dumpster, some old, empty beer cases piled on top of broken delivery pallets, and the woods, dense and dark.

Michael stared hard into the trees. The voices had subsided. All was quiet. He turned to head back to the car, but stopped cold. The old man was gone.

A rustling in the brush pulled his gaze back to the trees. He looked again, searching for movement. That's when he saw it; a set of red glowing eyes and a toothy, shark-like grin peeking out from among the leaves.

4

Ashley adjusted the angle of her work lamp then leaned in for a closer look. She held a small clear cup filled half-full with a special cleaning solution in her left hand. With her right, she delicately dabbed a thin coat of the watery, yellow concoction onto the canvas with a cotton swab which slowly turned brown as she removed years of dirt from the painting.

It was a Rembrandt, recently donated by a wealthy family; a wealthy, chain-smoking family. Little by little, the portrait grew more alive, the color restoring to its original vibrancy as she wiped away the layers of smoke.

"Ashley."

"Yeah?" she mumbled.

"*Ashley!*"

"What?" she huffed angrily, answering the voice that called from over her shoulder, quickly turning to see who was disturbing her work.

No one was there. Ashley stood and set her cup down on the table next to her easel, then tossed the cotton swab into a trash can.

She stepped to the door and peeked around the frame. The hall was empty. To the left, at the end of the hall, a fluorescent light flickered in the ceiling. A door clicked shut quietly somewhere on her right. Slowly, she peeled off her latex gloves and tossed them into the trash before stepping into the hallway. The muffled sound of hammering and other construction echoed from far above her.

As she made her way towards the door she thought had closed, she touched her index finger to her lip nervously, but pulled it away sharply as soon as she tasted the bitter chalky residue left behind by her powdered gloves.

Gross.

Ashley stopped in front of the door and peeked through the window. The lights were off. Silhouettes of easels and stools blended in with the dark shadows. Cautiously, she took the knob in her hand and turned.

****

A big, black Cadillac Escalade wound its way through the congestion in New York City, its windows tinted like a limousine. The thumping of its sound system rattled cars as it passed and echoed off the buildings on the boulevard. He pushed his way closer and closer to the docks. Finally reaching the harbor, he scanned the addresses, signs, any markings he could find, on the facades of the old warehouses. Freighters blasted their ship horns. Seagulls cawed from overhead. The SUV pulled to a stop, its oversized chrome rims glistening in the sun and the driver's door slowly opened.

****

"Hello?" Ashley called into the darkness of the room.

Two twelve-foot tables were set up in the middle of the floor, chairs neatly tucked under at each place. A row of empty easels lined the far wall.

She tried the switch on the wall. Nothing.

****

Rocco stepped from the SUV. He took off his sunglasses and set them on the dash, then reached under his seat and pulled out a nickel revolver. Flipping open the .44 Magnum, he checked the rounds, then flicked his wrist, the cylinder clicking back into place. He tucked the gun into the waste of his trendy pre-ripped jeans and stepped around the front of his truck.

The warehouse seemed empty. A rust-red steel container sat in front of the loading bay. Cautiously, he made his way to the entrance, looking left and right, making sure no one was watching.

He stopped, standing where a door should have been. He ran his fingers down along the frame and looked at the broken jam. The hinges had been torn clean from the steel upright. A rusty bolt-lock lay at his feet, half covered in dirt and debris.

"What the..."

****

Ashley flipped the switch back into the off position and slowly backed out of the room. Nothing seemed suspicious.

She turned, pulling the door shut, and came face to face with a sweaty man in baggy, gray coveralls, the name *Winston* embroidered on his left chest.

Naturally, she screamed.

"Hold on, lady," he said, his hands raised innocently, "I'm a worker, I came down to check the lights on this floor."

"What?" she asked, gathering what little composure she could.

"I'm from upstairs. One of the guys was running new electrical line, and *ZAPF!*" he explained, making an odd noise with his mouth to describe the sound. "We lost a breaker. I'm checking what areas in the building were affected by the outage, then replacing the breaker and opening up new channels for power to the rest of the museum."

Ashley smirked, *see you idiot, nothing to worry about!*

"Were you in there when we lost power?" the worker asked, wiping sweat from his brow with a dirty handkerchief.

"No, my work room is down the hall, but I heard..."

"Yes, ma'am, go on."

"Nothing, I heard nothing. I have to get back to work. Good luck fixing the power," she said, faking a smile as she headed off to finish her restoration.

****

Rocco's boots crunched as he walked across the cracking cement floor of the old warehouse, the beam of his flashlight sweeping in an arc. He paused in the center of the room. A dark black oil-like substance stained the floor, broken furniture littered what looked to be a makeshift living room.

Cozy.

Quickly, he turned, pulling the revolver from the waist of his pants. He scanned the darkness, his flashlight following the shuffling noise as it skittered past him. He stepped towards the spot where the sound had stopped. An old refrigerator stood against the far right wall, the door hanging open, the bulb flickering faintly. Dusty cabinets created a little, decrepit nook of a kitchen. A set of small piercing eyes stared at him from beneath the dirty fridge.

Rats...I hate rats.

Lowering his gun, he headed back to the main room, then pulled a cell phone from his pocket, "Hey. It's me. Yeah. No, he's not here. Uh huh, looks like he's been gone a long time. Ok. Don't worry, I'll find him."

****

"Elizabeth..." he mouthed, staring blankly into the darkness, the unblinking red eyes staring back at him.

Michael turned and raced back to his Porsche, cranking the ignition as he hurriedly fastened his seat belt. The rear tires squealed in a burst of bluish smoke as he whipped the tail of the car around and sped back to his mansion. Each second was agonizing. With every bend, his imagination twisted, thoughts of what he might find when he made it home: an image of his wife taking a last, labored breath froze in his mind, and then, he thought of his son.

****

Ashley sat back down at her work station and stared at the painting. It was a beautiful Rembrandt, the face in the portrait stoic, yet its eyes hinting at whimsy, as if the woman in the painting was in on a secret. Ashley couldn't gather herself, no matter how hard she tried. All she could think of was the voice. It polluted her mind. Where had it come from?

****

Michael pulled into his drive, the car kicking up dust and gravel as it passed beneath the giant stone archway, the automated iron-gate closing behind him. He slowed as he reached the front entrance. Everything looked fine. He edged around the corner of the house and headed for the garages, scanning the windows as he drove. Nothing seemed out of place.

He parked in the empty bay and stepped from the car. The door from the garage led through a mud room, then into the kitchen.

"Hello?" he called, flipping the switch on the elaborately decorated wall.

Nothing happened. No one answered.

"Elli?"

A faint moan echoed down the main corridor. The house creaked as wind beat against its exterior. A storm was coming. The sky was growing dark.

"Cain?" he whispered.

Michael pulled a flashlight from a drawer and pressed down on the switch. The bulb flickered for a moment, then faded. A candle sat on the ledge above the sink. A box of matches lay beside it.

Slowly, he walked down the hall, the heels of his shoes clicking as he made his way towards the library. Eerie shapes danced across the walls, cast by the candle's soft yellow glow. Again, he heard the moan as he neared the end of the long hallway, though now, it was more like laughter.

Michael pushed the wooden library doors open. Flashes of lightning burst through the tall window on the left side of the room. His desk sat straight ahead, behind it loomed a throne-like high back chair. The room itself was shaped like a giant horseshoe, the arch wrapping around on the right, the enormous window on his left, the opening on the shoe. Books were shelved starting way down at the darkly-stained wood floor and stretching all the way up to the richly copper plated coffered ceiling. An immense black iron chandelier hung overhead.

"Michael," a familiar voice called from the chair that sat behind his desk, "it's been a long time."

He raised the candle higher, but the darkness of the room seemed to swallow the light.

"Who are you?"

"You know who I am," the man's deep voice replied.

"But you're dead, I..."

"Yes," the man said, standing as lightning briefly lit his face, "you killed me."

Michael watched as Triton stepped from behind the desk. Lightning flashed again. A cool draft crept through the open door. The candle went out, a wisp of smoke rising from the wick.

Blackness engulfed the room. Michael waived his hand past the top of the candle, but nothing happened.

"I see you've lost your powers." Triton grunted, his voice drawing near.

"I haven't needed them."

"No, I guess not." Triton smiled in the darkness, his tone changing, his words more raspy and guttural. "You've neglected us, after all we did for you, you forgot us, forgot where you came from."

Michael felt something brush against the back of his leg, then a finger trace the length of his arm. The candle flared to life.

He jumped back, a demon's face inches from his own. It laughed, sulfurous smoke escaping from behind its jagged teeth.

"You're not Triton."

"And you're scared; the great Thirteen, meek as a schoolgirl," it exclaimed, flailing its arms with exaggerated gusto.

"Where's my family? What did you do with them."

"I didn't do anything, *we* didn't...we swear."

Michael suddenly became aware of the innumerable eyes that blinked at him in the darkness. Again, he felt something against his leg. Hot, panting breath warmed his hand. A jet black hound sat beside him, wolf-like, but the size of a full-grown man, its eyes red, its teeth stark white and razor sharp.

"Then what are you here for?" Michael questioned, the evil around him calming, natural, like an old friend returning home.

"You forgot us, but we never forgot you. We came to serve you, to remind you that in your darkest hour, as your family has been taken from you, we are here."

****

"Where are you taking us?" Elizabeth cried, clinging to Cain as she looked out from the window of a helicopter.

Trees blurred by, partially from the speed, mostly from her tears. She tried to clear her vision, tried to make out the face of the man who sat across from them.

"I promise I won't hurt you," he smiled cunningly, his hand extended, holding out a fine cotton handkerchief, "or the boy."

"Then what do you want?"

"It's not what I want, Misses," he replied, his English accent charming, seductive, "it's what my employer wants."

5

Gavin pulled his motorcycle into the driveway, its tires thumping over cracks in the cement, and parked next to the white picket fence that enclosed their backyard, the rumble of the exhaust reverberating off the houses. Slipping off his helmet, he made his way for the back door. He was just glad to be home and ready to get out of his work clothes. All day, something had been eating away at him and he knew exactly what it was: boredom. His job was great, even easy. As a supervisor at the local big-box toy store, he made decent money and had minimal responsibility. But that wasn't what he really wanted. There was no excitement, no thrill, but most of all, no challenge.

He pulled off his red work polo and tossed it on the bed, then switched out his khakis for some age-worn jeans. Gavin opened a drawer on his armoire and flipped through an assortment of t-shirts. Picking the one he wanted, he slipped his head through the neck and pulled it down over his tattooed frame. The shirt was a faded shade of navy blue. Cracking white screen-print stretched across the chest: *NYPD*; a gift from Jamie, one of his old shirts from when he was a New York cop. Gavin stared at the letters in the mirror, his heart aching for the life he once knew, but he'd made a promise. He was no longer a demon hunter, no longer under the heel of The Order. His love for Ashley drove him away from that life. They'd disappeared; traded the big city for a small town. Gavin had done everything he could to assimilate: find an average job as he blended into a semi-rural urban environment in a mostly quiet, completely quaint town in Ohio. But he was struggling. How do you stop being who you are? How do you give up everything you know, everything you love, your passion, maybe even your calling, for love?

The questions were driving him mad. But he did know one thing: he loved Ashley, more than anything, even more than the life he'd left behind. He tried to remind himself that their move was to protect her, to protect her from his old employers, unsure of what they may do when they realized he'd gone off the grid.

****

"Is it done?"

"Yes, I have them: we're in route now."

"Good," Killion grinned. "Call me when you reach the safe house."

"I will," the man replied over the sound of the helicopter's beating rotor.

Killion removed the Bluetooth from his ear and slipped it into the inner pocket of his suit coat. Slowly, he wound his Audi through the congested streets of Los Angeles. Easing to a stop as a streetlight flicked from yellow to red, the booming bass of a car stereo rattled his windows as rap lyrics flooded the street. A charcoal gray Yukon pulled up on his left, its windows tinted dark, freshly polished twenty-two inch chrome wheels shining. Killion watched as the front passenger window rolled down. A man stared out at him, the bill on his L.A. Raiders cap pulled down low, hiding his face. Killion's hand disappeared into his jacket, finding the grip of his 9mm. Quickly, he slid the gun from his shoulder holster, then pulled out a silencer and twisted it onto the gun's threaded barrel. The back door of the SUV popped open and another man jumped out, pistol in hand. Killion readied his aim.

"Get out the car, man!" the guy yelled.

Killion rolled down his window, his gun just out of view, "I'm sorry, what did you say?"

"I said get out of the car!"

"No," Killion smiled coyly, raising his gun, the barrel trained at the gang-banger's face.

"You're dead, man!" the thug grunted.

Just as Killion readied to squeeze the trigger, he caught a glimpse of blue and red flashers flickering in his rearview mirror. The would-be carjacker jumped back in the SUV as the driver stepped on the gas, the big V-8 roaring off and around the corner. Two police cars sped past Killion and out of sight, hot on the trail of the SUV. A third vehicle sat right behind the Audi. The officer stepped from the cruiser and made his way to Killion's window.

"Good day, Officer," he said, his British accent once again masked beneath a slow, Southern drawl.

"You alright?" the cop asked, eyeing the expensive sedan.

"Oh, yes, Sir," Killion schmoozed. "I don't know what I'd have done if ya'll hadn't shown up when you did."

"License and registration, please."

"Gladly," Killion smiled as he reached awkwardly into his right-rear pants pocket and removed his wallet, handing his driver's license to the cop, "but I'm not in any trouble, am I officer?"

"No, no," the officer replied, looking over the ID. "Atlanta, Georgia; you're not from around here, are you?"

"No, Sir. I'm in Los Angeles on business."

"And what kind of business is that, Mr..." the officer glanced again at the license, then handed it back through the window, "Rodgers, is it?"

Killion took the license back with a smile. The officer tilted his head curiously.

"The kind of business that's all mine and *none* of yours," he replied, his fake accent gone, a flash bursting from the muzzle of his gun.

Killion pulled away as the officer's body fell limply to the ground. He twisted off the silencer and holstered his gun as he merged into traffic, disappearing into the hustle of the city.

****

Gavin stood at the top of the basement stairs and flipped on the light switch. The soft hum of florescent bulbs hung in the air. He made his way down the stairs and across the poured concrete floor. A rolling tool chest stood on the far wall, a work bench on either side of it.

He looked at his watch: 4:30pm. Ashley wouldn't be home for at least another hour. Gavin pulled the chest out from its place and stared for a moment at the whitewashed cinder block wall. Placing his shoulder against it, he pushed. With a creek, a whole section of the wall slowly began to swing open. Gavin stepped through the opening he'd created and into total darkness, then let the hidden door close behind him with a soft thud. Reaching up, he pulled a string that hung from a light on the ceiling.

It took a moment for his eyes to adjust to the sudden burst of 100-watt illumination, but he quickly smiled as he looked about the small room. To his left, a polished metal shelving unit stood against the wall, its contents made up of army-surplus ammo cans and various other miscellaneous aluminum cases and stacking plastic bins. On that same wall, hung long ways, was a 4'x8' panel of white pegboard displaying several shotguns and large caliber rifles. Below the guns was a workbench that started on that wall and made a *U* as it turned onto the front wall and continued on the right where it dead-ended at a set of very nice red, anodized rolling tool chests and a very large antique safe. Another sheet of pegboard hung on the right hand wall as well, just above the bench top, this one filled with gunsmith's tools and punches, differing sizes and types of knives, a bundle of heavy duty rope, and lastly, tactical slings, harnesses, holsters, and Kevlar vests. The wall directly in front of him was home to his varied pistols, a few revolvers, and his collection of assault rifles. Two sets of drawers beneath that work bench protected his gun-cleaning supplies, extra magazines, and box after box of ammo.

Gavin walked across the cement floor and pulled out an aging leather, rolling office chair, then sat down, looking around the room. Turning back to the wall in front of him, he reached up and took down his favorite rifle from amongst his collection of AR15s, bullpups, and SBRs: a suppressed HK MP5 sub-machinegun. He pulled back the cocking handle to verify that the chamber was empty and ejected the empty magazine, laying it on the bench. He then took hold of the silencer and twisted it free from its 3-lug mount, removing it from the barrel and placing it next to the magazine. He clicked on the holographic sight and raised it to his shoulder, aiming at a spot on the wall, stopping to adjust the collapsible stock, then looking again at the green, glowing crosshairs.

Perfect.

He turned off the sight and reinstalled the suppressor, then slipped the magazine back into the receiver with a click, stood, and gently returned the gun to its place on the wall. Turning, Gavin stepped up to the safe.

Slowly, he spun the dial first to the right, then to the left, then back to the right, the tumblers falling into place. Once unlocked, he paused as he took hold of the large brass wheel that opened the safe, then took a deep breath and turned, the door swinging smoothly, though its hinges were rusty, corroded with age.

The interior of the safe was divided into two sections; one half, a series of equilateral shelves; the other half, open from top to bottom. The side with the shelves was packed with neatly stacked bundles of twenty, fifty, and one hundred dollar bills, each denomination on its own shelf; a small fortune by most people's standards. The other side was empty except for an oddly shaped object, thin, but over three feet long, tightly wrapped in an old beach towel.

Gavin ignored the money and reached for the well-wrapped object, then made his way back to the work bench. He laid it out on the bench-top and opened the towel in a slow, respectful manner. Inside was a sword, safely in its sheath. He took hold of the ornate black handle and slid the blade partially from its resting place. The sword's steel was black as well, the edge lethally sharp. The further he pulled the blade, the more he noticed an odd ringing in his ears. Suddenly, the light flickered. For a moment, Gavin thought he'd heard whispering followed by a breath on his neck. He turned. No one was there. The light continued to flicker, like the bulb was loose in the socket. He reached up and tapped at the bulb, but it was solid. Gavin slid the blade back into its sheath and everything stopped: the ringing, the whispering, the flickering light; everything. Confused, he wrapped the sword back up, set it in the safe, then closed the door securely and spun the dial. Finally, he turned out the light and reopened the secret door.

In the basement again, he let the door close, then maneuvered the tool chest back into its place. Thunder rumbled. Gavin peered out from one of the windows. The wind was whipping through the trees in the backyard, bending the branches like they were straw.

"Big storm coming," he said aloud.

He tried to reason away his questions about what had just

happened. Maybe it was just the storm? Maybe it was an electrical hiccup? Either way, he was spooked; a feeling he hadn't felt since before he'd met Joseph.

✳✳✳✳✳✳✳✳✳✳✳✳

Ashley was still a bit shaken as she made her way across the second floor of the museum's parking deck. Thunder echoed between the cement floor and the low ceiling, but oddly enough there was no rain. She settled into the front seat of her convertible and pulled her cell phone from her brown leather art satchel.

"Hey," she smiled, happy to hear Gavin's voice on the other end, "remember I have a class tonight, so dinner will be late."

"Sure thing, babe. Actually, I was going to head to the shooting range anyway. So, I'll see you later then."

"Ok," she paused, the strange voice still on her mind, "do you ever hear...*things?*"

"What?" he laughed.

"Like voices."

Gavin thought for a moment, considering what he'd experienced only a short while ago in his hideaway, "Honestly, I haven't heard any definite voices since New York. I feel things now and again, catch something in the corner of my eye, but it's not like it *was*. Why?"

"Just curious. I love you"

"Love you, too."

Ashley hung up and put her car in reverse. She left the CSU campus and wound her way through the streets of Cleveland. Merging on to Interstate 77, she began the tediously long drive home to Massillon. She'd have plenty of time to ponder what had happened that day.

✳✳✳✳✳✳✳✳✳✳✳✳

Michael sat down in the throne-like chair that stood behind the

42

ornately engraved desk in his office. The darkness, like his anger, consumed him as the storm outside raged on, heavy rain drops pelting the enormous window. Two demons flanked his chair. A third demon perched atop the high wooden back as others scurried amidst the flashes of lightning. The hell hound rested at his feet.

"We can give you back your powers," one of the demons hissed.

"We will give you everything you need to avenge them," another added.

"And what do you want in return?" Michael asked.

"Don't you remember your agreement with the Dark Lord?"

"Dark Lord?!" Michael laughed. "My agreement was with Franklin. He wanted Triton out of the picture and I wanted money. Done and done. My agreement was not with the devil."

"But Franklin speaks for the Dark Lord and you forgot the most important part," another demon reminded. "You may have killed Triton, but Franklin also requested his trinket and you failed to deliver."

"That stupid key," Michael replied, "is just a myth. I held it myself, it was nothing; just one of Triton's delusions."

The demons cackled with laughter. Michael remained still, brooding and confused.

"Triton didn't tell you everything."

"No and neither did Franklin, apparently," Michael guessed.

The demons laughed again. Michael grew impatient.

"So Franklin wants the key?" he huffed. "That's why he took Elizabeth, for a stupid relic?"

"Not exactly."

"There's a loose end, a threat that still exists."

"The Order has other assets, let Franklin use one of them."

"Oh, I promise, he is. But he still needs you."

"And Franklin has Elizabeth?"

"No."

"Then who took her?"

"Can't say," a demon laughed.

"Why not?" he asked, clenching his fist angrily.

"Because that's not part of the game."

"So then, what is this loose end?"

"The hunter lives."

"The tattooed hunter," two more demons added in unison.

Michael thought for a moment, sure he'd witnessed Gavin die in the explosion as New York General Hospital collapsed down around them, "That's not possible. I saw him burn."

"You saw what his guardians wanted you to see."

"I'm not sure I believe you, but I'll play along. You're saying the demon hunter is alive and that he has the key, so now Franklin wants him dead and I'm the only one who can kill him?"

"Go on," the demon on the back of the chair prompted.

"And if I kill this man, then Franklin will give me back my family?"

"Can't say for sure," a big demon snorted, "but that's where you should begin if you want to see them again."

"Where is he, the hunter?"

"Can't tell you," the big demon snorted again, "unless you agree. So are you ready to play the game?"

"If this is what it takes to save my family, then yes," he conceded.

"Excellent!" they cheered in a demonic chorus. "We will serve you again, Thirteen."

"And my powers?"

"We will restore them to you."

"No," he growled. "I want more!"

"Anything else, Master?"

"Yes," Michael said, standing and walking to the window, lightning illuminating his solemn face, "get me my mask."

6

Gavin stared at his target where it hung thirty feet down range, a 9mm HK USP in his hands, raised and ready, big red earmuffs adorning his head, his yellow tinted shooter's glasses reflecting the dim fluorescent lights. He steadied his feet, exhaled, and pulled the trigger.

BANG!

The bullet pierced the paper target dead-center in the head portion of the outlined body. He pulled the trigger again, the second bullet marking just next to the first. Gavin cycled through the rest of the magazine, two shots at a time: the first to the chest; the second, quickly to the head.

He ejected the empty magazine and turned from his stall, heading for his range bag for more ammo. He glanced to the left. A man was firing a long-barreled .357 magnum, the gun booming much louder than Gavin's 9mm. On his right, a father was instructing his teenage son on smooth, short trigger pulls. It brought a smile to his face.

The room was long and a little dreary. The walls were gray cinderblock, the floor cement and cold. Divided stalls separated the range into twelve lanes, each with a cable that ran from the stall to the far wall, about fifty feet away, and back, targets dangling from the line. The ceiling was old, the once-white fiber-board tiles now dingy and faded. The sound of the range's ventilation system roared constantly in the background.

Gavin reloaded his gun and stepped back to his stall. He flipped a switch on the divider and the cable shook to life, moving the target further away by ten more feet. He pulled back on the slide, chambering a round, and focused on the target. He pulled the trigger, but the gun didn't fire. Instead, the lights flickered, then went out.

"Must be the storm," he mumbled, more concerned about the misfire.

Gavin peered at the other stalls, but they were empty. The father and son had disappeared. The man with the .357 was gone as well. He slipped off his earmuffs and quickly dug in his bag for a flashlight. He clicked it on and a bright blue beam cut through the stale darkness. Spent casings skittered across the floor as he cautiously stepped towards the door. Something moved on his right. He scanned the range with his flashlight, the targets casting odd shadows against the walls, but nothing stood out.

With a loud bang, the lights kicked back on. Gavin stood with his ears ringing, his eyes adjusting to the light. The father and son stared at him questioningly.

"Earmuffs," the dad said, shaking his head, "safety first!"

Gavin turned, watching smoke rise from the magnum's silver, seven -inch barrel. The cylinder turned, the hammer slammed forward, and the gun boomed again. Gavin snapped back to reality and slipped his earmuffs on, his eardrums aching.

Quickly, he packed up his gun and ammo and headed out of the range, setting his gear bag down on the cash wrap's counter as he slipped off his earmuffs. The owner of the range cashed him out.

"Everything alright, Gavin?" he asked as he handed him his receipt.

"Yeah, Bill..." he hesitated, "heck of a storm though, huh?"

"Is it?' Bill wondered, peering out the front of the shop. "Looks like it's raining a little."

Gavin stared out at the dark clouds, "I meant the power. The lights in the range went out."

"Really? Everything's fine out here," the owner replied, reaching beneath the counter and pulling out Gavin's motorcycle helmet. "Better get going before it really gets bad."

"Thanks, Bill," Gavin smiled stuffing the receipt into his pocket and slinging his bag over his shoulder, then taking the black helmet and heading for the door.

Gavin swung his leg over the bike and settled down on the seat. He pulled the helmet on, turned the key in the ignition, and kick started his Harley, the exhaust rumbling as it idled.

"What was that all about?" he grunted, twisting the throttle, the bike lurching forward.

****

Ashley had only just pulled into the driveway as the rain really started coming down. She parked in the garage next to Gavin's old van and smiled, his motorcycle was wet, he must have been out too. She peered at the house from the garage. Lightning flashed, it was pouring. She'd have to make a run for it.

****

"Department of Motor Vehicles, how can I help you?"

"Mary?"

"Yes..."

"I need a favor," Rocco spoke into his cell phone, "I'm trying to find somebody."

"I could lose my job," she answered.

"Come on, I'll give you a hundred bucks."

"Five hundred and we have a deal."

"Five hundred?!"

"Do you want my help or not?"

"How about I come pick you up and make it worth your while?"

"We broke up, Rocco. Remember? Five hundred or nothing!"

"Ok."

"Fine. Text me the name and I'll text you the address."

"Thanks, babe."

"Shut up, Rocco."

****

Ashley pulled the door shut behind her as she raced in from the rain. She'd fumbled with her keys as she'd hurriedly tried to enter. Now she stood staring at Gavin as he sat at the kitchen table, his pistol disassembled in front of him, gun-cleaning supplies spread out. She pulled her wet stringy hair from her eyes and gave him a sad little pout.

"I missed you today," she smiled.

"Me too," he said, setting down his bore brush, the chair beneath him grating against the hardwood floor as he slid back and stood. "We still doing dinner tonight?"

"If you're up to it," she teased.

"Well," he said, backing her against the counter as he unbuttoned her jeans, "we'll have to get you out of these wet clothes."

"Alright," she smiled, kissing him.

Gavin lifted her up and set her on the counter. Ashley quickly loosened his belt and undid his jeans.

"I love you so much," she whispered, "*so* much!"

****

Rocco leaned against the bar, a vodka shot in his hand. He smiled unsuccessfully at two beautiful women as they walked past, oblivious to his presence. He threw back the drink and slid the glass across the wooden top, back to the bartender for another pour.

"One more, my man."

A moment later, Rocco readied his drink. But as he raised it to his lips, he paused, the obnoxious ring of his phone almost lost under the thumping bass of the nightclub's music.

"Good girl," he mumbled as he pulled his phone from his pocket.

He smiled as he read the text message and then threw back the shot, slamming it down on the bar when he'd finished. Dropping a twenty dollar bill next to the glass, he turned and headed out the door. Rocco dialed Rev. McNamara's number as he walked down the sidewalk towards his SUV.

"I found him," he said smugly.

"Where, is he in New York?" McNamara asked.

"No, Ohio. I'm leaving now."

"I'm sending you a team," McNamara said. "There can be no mistakes."

****

Gavin finished his plate of manicotti and dropped his green cloth napkin on the table in utter satisfaction. Ashley sat across from him, nibbling on a breadstick.

"Can I get you guys anything else," the waitress offered, "maybe our triple chocolate cheesecake or our signature tiramisu?"

"Oh boy," Gavin smiled, gesturing at his stomach and puffing out his cheeks like a blowfish, "I think we're pretty stuffed, unless you want something, Ash?"

Ashley thought for a moment but then shook her head no, a slight look of disgust on her face, "no thanks."

"Alright, I'll be right back with your bill. Thanks for coming in tonight, guys."

"You ok?" Gavin asked as the waitress disappeared into the kitchen.

"Yeah, I'm fine," Ashley replied, still a little green in the face. "I just started thinking about all the ingredients in the dessert and then thought of what color cheesecake is and it made me think of chunky, old butter. Gosh, I could even smell it! It made me so nauseous. I'm really nauseous!"

"I'm so nauseous," he mimicked in a nasally voice. "Oh, chunky butter! I'm so nauseous."

Ashley erupted with laughter. Gavin leaned back in his chair, grinning from ear to ear.

"Maybe you're pregnant," he joked, chuckling to himself, no idea how close to the truth he may be.

"Ha, yeah," Ashley said, calming down, wiping a happy tear from her eye, "wouldn't that be funny..."

****

The sun sank deep into the West as the sound of crickets chirping filled a little New Jersey backyard. Somewhere, a dog barked in the darkness. Paul Kemp stood on his deck, a before-bed cigarette hanging from his aging lips, his sun-spotted arm around the waist of his wife, Nancy. The dog barked again, this time followed by a menacing growl.

"You hear that, Paul?" Nancy asked. "He sounds mad. Is that the Rosencrantz's dog, what's his name, Pepper, or Pablo, or something with a *P*? He's a collie, right?"

Paul took a long drag on the cigarette, then exhaled slowly, watching the smoke swirl into the starry sky, "It's Petey, they call the dog Petey. Petey, the *German Sheppard*, sounds mad."

"What do you think it is Paul?"

"Not sure, Nancy...kids, maybe a skunk, hell if I know!"

They stood together, watching the little yellow blips of fire flies blinking in the yard. The dog barked once more, this time followed by a yelp and then a scampering retreat.

"Did you hear that, Paul?"

"Yeah, I did…" he said thoughtfully, "can't think of much that would scare a German Sheppard."

A rustling in the bushes at the back of the lawn pulled their eyes away from the neighbor's fence. Paul put his cigarette out on the porch railing and stepped down onto the grass. The bushes shook again.

"Be careful, Paul," she whispered scratchily.

He motioned for her to quiet down as he cautiously approached the bush. An odd clicking sound came from somewhere deep beneath the branches.

Paul knelt down, his hands and knees sinking into the well-manicured turf. He peered under the branches, but couldn't see anything.

"Too darn dark," he mumbled gruffly.

He crept closer, his eyes searching. The bush moved again. Paul edged back uncertainly, bracing himself: something was coming out. A tiny black and white kitten pranced from beneath the shrub, its paws dirty from the mulch. Nancy screamed.

"What is wrong with you woman," Paul cried out, startled by her outburst, "it's just a cat."

He turned just in time to see her fall limply backwards. Forgetting about the kitten, he raced to the deck.

"Nancy? *NANCY?*"

He clomped up the stairs and dropped down next to her body. Her eyes were wide open, fearful. Her mouth hung agape.

"What's wrong, Nancy?" he asked, shaking her gently.

She tried to speak; but instead, her eyes began to well up. Slowly she raised her wrinkled hand and pointed at the tall oak tree that shaded their yard. Paul scanned the branches slowly, trying to see what she saw, but he couldn't make out anything unusual. The sound of her hand thumping against the wooden deck planks pulled him back to her, her eyes now closed, her body limp.

"Nancy," he asked, beginning to cry, "you alright?"

He shook her again. Her head rolled to the side.

"Nancy..." he sobbed, checking for a pulse, but finding none.

Paul flopped down onto his backside, tears blurring his vision. Something touched his shoulder, but he shrugged it off. Again, something brushed against him, this time more persistently, as he became suddenly aware that something blocked out the moon's light. He stood cautiously, afraid to look over his shoulder. Is this what his wife had seen?

He gathered his strength and spun on his heel, ready to face whatever it was. Nothing was there. He studied the yard, everything looked fine. But Paul was suddenly aware of how deadly silent the world had become. A pain began in his fingers and tingled all the way up his arms till finally it settled in his chest. His heart began to race.

Clutching at his chest, he stumbled back around, his ears ringing. He was met by a pair of red glowing eyes, sunk deep into the head of a massive shadow. Everything went black as he collapsed to the floor, settling next to Nancy, his arm resting around her waist.

"Was that really necessary?" a voice questioned.

"No," the shadow replied, its opaqueness lessening as a demonic figure began to take shape, "but it was fun!"

Two demons emerged from the darkness of the garden, their red eyes bobbing against the shadowy backdrop. They met the third on the deck and paused a moment to savor the smell of the recently deceased.

"Let's get what we came for," one of the demons urged, looking around at the beautiful flowerbeds and quaintly decorated lawn, the kitten playing happily with a bug it had caught, "this place gives me the creeps."

The demons moved towards the house, their physical forms evaporating into wispy, smoke-like, black masses, allowing them to pass through the outer wall of the house and into the kitchen. Their shadows then began to solidify as they returned to their true shape.

"Where is it?" one wondered.

"I can feel it," another said, snarling through his shark-like teeth.

They moved fluidly, almost as if floating, down the dark hallway of the single-level ranch home, passing by a guest bedroom, a bathroom, a play room filled with grandchildrens' toys, and finally coming to the master suite.

"It's in here," the murderous demon chuckled.

They went to work searching through dresser drawers, the closet, under the bed, till finally one called out, "This is it!"

The demon grasped the drawer pulls with its clawed fingers and slid open the drawer. A pile of blue polo shirts lay neatly folded; the words *J. & L. Construction* embroidered on the left chest. White undershirts filled the rest of the drawer. The demon closed its eyes and reached under the stack of polos, its fingertips finding a soft piece of cloth. It raised it up triumphantly, holding it out for the other demons to see. The stitching on the black cloth was unmistakable: Thirteen's hideous mask.

7

Ashley finished brushing her teeth and turned off the faucet, then placed her toothbrush back into the holder on the bathroom counter. She could hear Gavin in the bedroom, opening and closing the drawers of his armoire.

Maybe I could take the pregnancy test real quick, she thought.

But just as she reached for the drawer she'd hidden it in, Gavin walked into the room, clad in only his boxer shorts, and stepped up to the toilet. Ashley grabbed a brush and ran it through her hair innocently.

"So what are you up to tomorrow?" he asked.

"I have to finish up a painting in Cleveland," she explained, "then I was going to head home and clean a bit, the dining room is a mess! When do you work?"

"I close," he said, flushing the toilet, then turning and standing next to her to wash his hands. "I like that tank top on you."

Ashley looked at herself in the mirror. She wore an orange ribbed tank and a cute pair of white boyshorts adorned with navy blue stripes. She smiled: he was right.

"See you in bed," he said, patting her on the behind as he headed out into the hall.

Tomorrow, she decided, standing at the mirror, looking herself in the eyes.

****

Michael paced in his study. The storm had subsided. Moonlight now shone through the towering window. The hell hound watched as he walked back and forth, then yawned and rested its head on its enormous front paws. Michael tried to remain calm, but with the passing of every moment, with every image of his wife and son that tormented him, he grew more and more impatient. He stepped to his desk and opened the bottom right drawer, removing an old brass key from beneath a stack of file folders.

"If only you were the key that Franklin seeks," he said aloud sadly, looking at it in his open palm.

He turned and approached an ornately engraved antique china cupboard, the shelves filled with relics from all the far reaches of the world, some ancient, others rare. Michael slipped the key into the lock on the top drawer and turned it with a click. He pulled open the drawer and smiled. A pair of stainless steel Desert Eagle .50 caliber pistols greeted him. He caressed the barrel of one of the guns fondly before taking hold of the grip and lifting it up from the red, pillowed satin that lined the drawer.

"I will find you, Hunter," he promised.

****

Ashley tossed and turned as she tried to fall asleep. She couldn't stop wondering if she was pregnant. She wanted to take the pregnancy test, but at the same time, she didn't want to either. What if she took the test and it turned out she wasn't pregnant? She was so excited; it would be such a letdown. But, how great would it be if the result was positive.

"Ashley," a voice called, trying to rouse her.

She had just finally drifted off, what now?

"Ashley," it said again.

"Gavin?" she whispered, still half asleep. "What is it?"

"Ashley..."

"What?" she asked, sitting up.

Gavin lay sound asleep, a spot of drool on his pillow. She looked around the room, the furniture foreboding in the darkness. The room was silent. Ashley lay back down, confused and uncomfortable as she drifted back to sleep.

****

"You have it then?" Michael asked.

The demons stood from where they knelt. The one with the mask held it out for Michael to take.

"Here it is, just as you requested, Thirteen."

Michael took the mask and held it tightly. He sighed and closed his eyes, raising it up to his face. Slowly, he pulled it down over his head and began to laugh uncontrollably as he felt his power return, the energy coursing through his veins like a drug.

****

"Can I get you anything, Misses?" the man asked, rapping gently on the heavy oak door to the room.

He waited a moment, but heard no response. He knocked again. Still nothing.

"If you change your mind then, use the telephone in your room to dial down to the desk. They'll get you what you need."

Elizabeth listened as the man's footsteps faded down the corridor. Her face was red from crying. Cain seemed less concerned. He stood in front of a large flat-screen television, his arm swinging a video game motion controller in a big sweeping arc, his character on the screen moving in correlation, rolling a digital bowling ball down a digital lane towards ten digital pins.

She had no idea where they were. She'd stood at the window staring hopelessly at the city below. All she could gather was that it was a high-rise penthouse in an upscale city somewhere very far from home.

The helicopter seemed to have flown forever crossing over fields and farms, cities and suburbs. At one point, she'd managed to fall asleep. She wasn't sure how much time had passed, but when she woke, it was dark and the ground below seemed to be desert. The bright lights of a city could be seen off in the distance and it occurred to her that it might have been Las Vegas. The flight lasted another hour, or so she figured. The helicopter touched down on the roof of a tall building and she could see the ocean to the west.

"Strike!" the television announced, startling her.

"Look, mommy!" Cain shouted, jumping up and down on the finely upholstered couch. "I got a strike!"

"Very good," she encouraged, smiling the best she could.

She stood and walked to the bedroom. Two suitcases were lying open on the floor, neatly packed full of clothes for her and her son. Whoever had abducted them had also taken the time to gather up some of their clothes. This confused her. Who would go to such trouble and be so courteous to his prisoners?

****

Rocco's phone rang to life as he cruised along the interstate. With a yawn, he flipped open the phone and answered.

"What's up?"

"Barnett here, we're on the plane. We should be at the airport in a few hours. Where should we rendezvous?"

Rocco hadn't thought of that. They needed a place to meet, a place to sleep before attempting to apprehend Gavin.

"I'm getting a hotel room," he decided quickly. "I'll text you with details when I have them."

"Roger that," Barnett answered. "Over and out."

Rocco hung up the phone and shook his head, "I love these ex-military guys, always focused on the mission."

****

Michael hadn't felt this way in a long time. He was stronger, faster...invincible. He stared into the mirrored back of the china cupboard and smiled, his mask wrinkling.

He turned and made his way to the grand staircase in the cavernous foyer of his mansion, then bound up the stairs effortlessly. It was like walking on air. How had he lived without this?

Tossing the mask on the bed, he quickly changed out of his navy suit and headed for the giant walk-in closet. He undid his tie and hung it on an empty hook on his tie rack, then took off his white dress shirt and dropped it to the floor, pulling another crisp, freshly pressed shirt off a hanger and slipping his arms into the sleeves. Michael pulled on a finely tailored pair of black slacks and took down his solid black tie. He buttoned up the shirt and cuffs, completed a perfect Windsor, and reached for one last thing before putting on his black suit coat.

In a box that sat on the shelf above the clothes bar, Michael found his leather shoulder harness. He pulled it down and slipped it over his shoulders, adjusting the straps for a perfect fit. The harness had four holsters: one on each side, tucking the guns just under the arms above the elbow, and two more on the back, specially designed for his twin Desert Eagles, easy to conceal, easy to reach. Four Velcro pouches flanked the ribs on each side, just below the holsters, meant to carry extra magazines of ammunition. Michael put on the suit coat and checked himself in the mirror. The harness was completely hidden. He grinned and sat on the edge of the bed, tying up the laces on his expensive black Italian shoes, then stood, tucking the mask in an inner coat pocket.

The demons cheered as Michael reentered the study, begging for him to put the mask back on. The hound howled, joining the evil chorus.

"Welcome back, Thirteen!" one bellowed.

Michael grinned as he made his way to his guns. He picked up the Desert Eagles and secured them in the holsters on his lower back, then placed four full .50 caliber magazines in the one side of pouches. Closing that drawer, he opened the next one down and pulled out two Glock 17

9mms and slipped them into the side holsters, again placing extra loaded magazines in the remaining four pouches.

"What will you do now?" the demons asked.

"I'm going after the hunter."

"Will you kill him?" they hoped.

"If I must," Michael answered, a hint of reluctance in his voice.

"Where will you find him? We haven't told you yet?"

"No need, I know where he is," he replied, smiling as if all the world's secrets had been revealed to him, "Massillon, Ohio."

****

"Has she eaten?" Killion asked, watching Elizabeth and her son on the monitor.

"No," the man answered, looking up at Killion.

"Alright, Edward," he replied. "I'll see if perhaps I can persuade her. You get some rest, it was a long flight. Good job, brother."

****

Michael stepped down into his garage and slid into the seat of his Porsche. He turned the ignition and raced out into the darkness, his power consuming him.

He had a long drive ahead of him. Michael would travel through the night, find Gavin, and make him turn over the key. And when that was complete, he'd find Franklin and get his family back. Everything was falling into place.

****

"Mrs. Laurent?" Killion asked, knocking curtly on the door.

"Please, Elizabeth, open up. I have news regarding your husband, Michael."

He stepped back patiently. After a moment, the lock clicked over and the door opened cautiously.

"Thank you for speaking with me, Elizabeth," Killion smiled. "May I enter?"

She nodded *yes* uncertainly, "Why have you brought us here?"

"Would you care for a glass of wine?" he asked, coyly dodging the question.

"No, thank you," she replied.

"I would love a glass."

Killion disappeared into the kitchenette and returned with two goblets and a chilled bottle of chardonnay. He handed her a glass and poured, then filled his as well.

"Please..." Elizabeth paused, "tell me what is going on. Why have you taken us from our home?"

"My dear woman," he smiled enthusiastically, leading her to the dinette table and pulling out her chair for her to sit, "I have only been asked to do what I have done. And it is your husband who asked me to escort you here, to the safety of this hotel."

"What do you mean?" she asked, watching him take the seat across from her. "Where's Michael?"

Killion leaned back in the chair and crossed his legs, then took a sip of his wine, "He's on his way, I can assure you. Something arose that he must take care of and, fearing for your safety, he requested I look after you. Isn't the wine lovely?"

She had yet to take a drink. His explanation was a surprise to say the least.

"Did my brother take good care of you and tell me, how was your flight? I was told you slept for most of it."

"The flight was fine," she replied flustered, "and your brother was kind enough to pack our suitcases, but..."

Killion watched as she set her glass down on the table. He did the same and leaned forward, placing his hand reassuringly on her knee.

"Can I speak to Michael?"

"I'm *so* sorry, Mrs. Laurent, but your husband gave me explicit instructions not to contact him, that he would contact us when he believed you were safe."

She looked down at his hand, still resting on her knee. She felt a little better; at least it all seemed to make sense.

"What is he doing that I'm in danger, does this involve my father?"

"No, no, Elizabeth," he replied softly, standing and finishing his glass of wine, "I don't know any details, only that this was necessary to protect you and your son. I'll let you know as soon as I hear from Michael, I promise. Now, thank you for sharing a drink with me, but I must take my leave."

"Thank you, Mr…" she started to say, reaching out her hand to shake his, realizing she didn't even know his name.

"Killion," he smiled, taking her hand and raising it to his lips, "but you can call me Terry. If there's anything I can do to make your stay more…*pleasurable*, please let me know. Goodnight, Mrs. Laurent."

She watched him as he walked out the door, then turned to see Cain fast asleep on the sofa, the video game still on, vivid colors flashing across the screen. Elizabeth turned off the television and the gaming console and gently took Cain up in her arms, careful not to wake him. She entered the bedroom and laid him down on the bed, first pulling back the covers and then tucking him in.

Elizabeth searched her suitcase and found a change of underwear, a nightshirt, and her toothbrush and toothpaste. Whoever packed her things was very considerate. She stepped into the bathroom and flipped on the shower, then stopped and examined herself in the mirror. She was tired, but otherwise uninjured. The room was nice, her luggage was filled with everything she needed, and Killion seemed a very accommodating, albeit forward host. Perhaps there truly was an emergency, hence the rushed helicopter flight and the feeling of desperate urgency.

"Oh, Michael, if only I could hear your voice," she whispered aloud.

She checked the temperature of the shower and got undressed, then pulled down a plush-looking hotel robe from a hook on the back of the door and slipped into its fleecy sleeves. It was warm, comforting. She stepped from the bathroom and checked on Cain, then picked her wine glass up from the dinette table before returning to her hot shower. Maybe it was as Killion had said.

8

Killion leaned against the front fender of his Audi, a trendy coffee shop cup in hand, his eyes fixed on the rolling surf. It was early. The sun hadn't been up long. Joggers traveled along the boardwalk. A few sunbathers were out already, laying their towels out on the sand and applying sunscreen. The ringing of his cell phone interrupted his focus.

"Killion," he answered, activating his Bluetooth earpiece.

"It's Mr. Nelson," came the reply, "where do we stand?"

"I was beginning to worry," Killion smiled coolly, "I hadn't heard from you since my first day in L.A."

"We are well aware of how you've *spent* your time. Have you made any progress?"

"You'll be pleased to know that I have his wife."

"Have you asked a ransom or made contact, told him what we want?"

"No."

There was silence for a moment, then Mr. Nelson replied, "What are you planning then? Franklin wants to know when you will have a solution."

"Michael will come to me. It's very simple. I took what is of value to him in order to get what is of value to me; in this case, what's of value to my employer."

"You seem to be taking your sweet time," Mr. Nelson scoffed. "We're paying you very well. There will be consequences if you don't deliver."

Killion was amused by this, "I'm sorry, mate, but is that a threat? You came to me to accomplish what you could not. And I do not see how time applies to this situation. Franklin has waited his entire lifetime for this, I think he can hold out a few more days. You Americans are all so focused on instant gratification; now, now, now, everything is *NOW!*"

"That's fine and all," Mr. Nelson replied, "But we're paying you for results, not your philosophies."

"What would you like me to do, then?"

"Go speak with McNamara. He's taking care of our missing agent."

"Oh right, the one who assumes he hunts, let me get this right, demons, actual, physical demons?"

"There are things I can't divulge; confidential corporate secrets that must remain unspoken. This is one of those things. Clearly you don't fully understand who you're working for."

Killion thought for a moment, distracted by a beautiful woman in a bikini, "Can you answer this then, why does a man like Michael Laurent, or Thirteen, or *whomever*, who appears to have incredible, even supernatural, powers in fact work for the same organization that funds these alleged demon hunters?"

"I don't know that I'm the man to answer that," Mr. Nelson stammered.

"And do these so called demon hunters actually hunt demons or is it all a game?"

Mr. Nelson looked to the chair next to him. Franklin glared back, his brow furrowed angrily.

"Take control," Franklin barked.

Mr. Nelson nodded, "Listen Terrance, we brought you in to complete one job, no questions asked. Can you handle this task?"

"That is not in question," Killion answered, lowering his voice, "but I've done my homework and Michael Laurent was, if not still is, one of the most dangerous marks I've ever accepted. And without proper leverage, I have nothing to offer in exchange for what he has, if he has it at all."

"What does that mean?"

"What if your missing agent is the one who possesses the key, what then? I will have awakened a sleeping monster, for nothing!"

"I would be more afraid of your employer than some masked freak," Mr. Nelson huffed.

"Freak? Hardly. I've read the notes on what he did in New York. This man could tear an army apart without taking a single scratch."

"I thought you were the best?"

"I am, but only within the bounds of reality. There are accounts that this man could manipulate physics, nearly fly! It's documented that he could vanish without a trace, not just stealth, but literally disappear! Whatever Dr. Triton did to him was a success. This man wasn't an agent, he was a weapon."

"Give me the phone," Franklin ordered, watching Nelson's frustration get the better of him. "Mr. Killion, this is Franklin. Is there a problem or can you complete this task?"

"Finally," Killion grinned, "the man with the answers."

"Is there something more that you need, anything that would help you along?"

"Thank you, but no. I have Elizabeth. Michael will come to me. Away from his home, out of his element, I believe I will have the advantage."

"Don't underestimate Thirteen," Franklin said matter-of-factly. "He will be your greatest challenge."

"Without a doubt," Killion replied.

"And I do not disrespect your desire for knowledge in this matter," Franklin continued, "but now is not the time. You deserve to know the truth, but I promise, when you hear what I have to say, it will change everything you know forever."

Killion shifted his weight and stepped away from the car. Something in Franklin's voice concerned him.

"Fair enough," Killion conceded.

"Good. I don't believe I need to remind you of how great your reward will be when you succeed. Now, are we on the same page?"

"Yes, Sir."

"Excellent. Get me my key."

****

Gavin spread honey mustard across the top half of a wheat bagel, then flipped it over, placing it onto the bottom half to make a sandwich. In the middle was thin, deli sliced turkey breast tastefully smothered in a medley of balsamic vinaigrette, finely shredded mozzarella cheese, and crushed red pepper seeds. He placed his masterpiece on a napkin and then put it in the microwave, cooking it on high for forty-five seconds. He turned and pulled a soda can from the fridge and smiled, the delicious smell wafting from the microwave pulling his attention back to the conglomeration he was about to enjoy. He watched as the timer counted down: *five, four, three, two, one...BEEP, BEEP, BEEP!*

With a hungry grin, he popped open the door to the microwave and carefully removed the hot sandwich. Cheese bubbled out the open whole in the top of the bagel. Gavin transferred it onto a plate and added a handful of potato chips to his lunch, then grabbed his pop and headed for the family room. He flopped down on the couch and began eating, mindlessly watching a show about a man who travels around the country taking on food-eating challenges in an attempt to see who will reign triumphant: man or food.

Nothing like eating while watching a show about eating, he thought, happily chewing.

****

Ashley finished swabbing the last spot of residue from the aged canvas and leaned back to inspect her work. The Rembrandt once again looked the way it had over three centuries ago. She smiled, imagining the artist himself, sitting in his Amsterdam studio as he finished his final masterful stroke.

She was snapped back to reality by the grumbling of her stomach, *Time for lunch...*

****

Killion pulled his Audi into the parking lot of the Sunrise Chapel. The church was huge, impressively expansive. He was reminded of a military compound, but with stained glass windows. The church's outer wall stood tall, intimidating, like a stone fortress. The roof arched high above the top of the walls, sunlight refracting off of glass panels. At the rear was a tall glass tower which overlooked the area like a spire battlement, a cross standing on the outer edge, searchlights on each of the four corners. He could also make out a helipad and several communications dishes.

"Is this a church, or an army base?" Killion laughed, stepping from the car and into the vast, shopping mall-like lot.

He approached the tall front doors and crossed over a giant rubber welcome mat in the grand entryway. The inside was just as confusing, though richly decorated, the walls felt cold. Killion decided to explore. The building intrigued him. The entrance funneled into a luxurious fellowship hall, a coffee bar on one side, the church nursery on the other. Pillars stretched high above his head, supporting the glass ceiling. He watched as passing clouds momentarily shaded the room and then allowed the sun to break from its cover and shine down in all its glory, the stainless steel accents throughout the room glistening proudly as if the sun shone only for this purpose: to illuminate Reverend McNamara's church.

Killion left the fellowship hall and strolled casually down a dark corridor that led to the sanctuary, his hands in his pockets as he whistled a soft, indistinguishable melody. He knew very little of his employer, Franklin, and even less about Rev. McNamara, only that Franklin had wanted to buy Tri-Corp after Triton's death, but was outbid by a European investor. McNamara was even more curious to Killion; an esteemed preacher and evangelist who seemed better suited for life insurance sales than a pulpit.

"But isn't that what religion is all about, life insurance?" he chuckled, approaching an impressively large set of wooden double-doors that led into the sanctuary.

A small placard was posted on the wall to the right of the doors. Killion took a moment to read it before taking hold of the fine brass door pulls.

"Occupancy: 20,000," he sighed.

The sheer scope of the room was breathtaking. This was like nothing Killion had ever seen and that was saying something, he himself having experienced the most historic and beautiful cathedrals and churches in Europe. In his opinion, Notre Dame in Paris paled in comparison. There was no old gray stone, no weathering or damage from the elements and war, no dark foreboding ceilings. Just as in the fellowship hall, bright sunlight shone down from above, giving the impression of a greenhouse, the warm sun ready to nurture, grow, those inside. The seats raised around him like plush, upholstered bleachers, row after row, innumerable, they went to the left, right, and straight down for what seemed forever, right to the foot of the stage. Two levels of balconies wrapped around the sanctuary. His eyes were drawn upward as he walked towards the pulpit area. A P.A. system more befitting a concert hall hung from above. Light rigs and scaffolding flanked the stage. Video screens the size of city busses stood on the left and right. This wasn't a church, it was an arena, or better yet, a fully fledged stadium.

Killion stepped up onto the stage and planted himself behind the transparent, glass pulpit. He looked out at all the seats, the vastness of the sanctuary, and tried to imagine addressing a packed house. But something didn't seem right. He was not a religious man, not remotely, but there was something missing. He pictured the great cathedrals of Europe, even the small chantries that filled the countryside. Lastly, he recalled his visit to the Sistine Chapel. He remembered standing in the presence of Michelangelo's masterpiece, staring up at the portrayal of the final judgment, and thinking that if there were ever a time he wanted to believe, that was it. He could still envision the figure of Christ, strong, muscular, bold, His hand raised as He stood among the clouds. That was a Jesus Killion could relate with, one in control, feared, the way he thought of himself. But this was not the case at the Sunrise Chapel. There were no awe inducing paintings, no elaborate sculptures, not even a cross. No, this wasn't a church, he decided, it was a celebration of man.

His heart sank as he walked off the stage and back to the fellowship hall. In a way, he hoped to find something there, maybe just calmness. But that sanctuary was nothing more than a reminder of why he'd never believed in all the religious nonsense that had been thrown in his face as a boy.

We are alone. And, we are meaningless. We choose our destiny and, at the end of the day, I know which end of the barrel I want to be on, he reminded himself.

Killion followed a sign down another hallway which led him to the church offices. Pushing through the door at the end of the hall, he spotted a pretty receptionist sitting at an arching desk, only then realizing that she was the first person he'd seen in the building. Now, that fact seemed strikingly odd.

"Good afternoon," she smiled, "and welcome to the Sunrise Chapel, how may I help you today?"

"I'm looking for Harlow McNamara. I need to speak with him."

"May I ask as to what this is regarding?"

"We have business with a mutual friend and it was suggested I catch up with the reverend face-to-face."

"Alright, let me call up to him. What's your name, please?"

"Killion, Terrance Killion."

She picked up the phone and dialed an extension, "It'll be just a moment, sir."

He turned and studied the lobby. It was decorated nicely, almost better than the church. The ceiling was low, typical of an office. A restroom was visible on the left, to the right was an elevator. Perfectly placed chairs and potted greenery made the space inviting, but it felt very much like a reception area at a corporate park.

As he paced, Killion took a closer look at the elevator. There was no button pad on the wall, no up or down arrows, just two glass doors framed by decorative mirrored panels.

"Rev. McNamara will see you now," she smiled.

"Thank you," he said, nodding politely as the doors slid open on their own.

Killion stared for a moment. The inside of the elevator was also glass. He could see the inner workings of the shaft.

"What floor?" he asked.

"Go ahead inside," the receptionist prompted. "Security will call you to the proper floor."

Something didn't feel right. No controls on the elevator and security, what kind of church has staffed security? This elevator was designed for one purpose: lockdown. And he'd seen it before, at an MI6 facility in London.

****

Ashley finished her peanut butter sandwich and tossed her used plastic baggy in the lunchroom trash. Taking a last sip from her plastic water bottle, she threw that away as well as she looked at the clock on the wall. She'd finished that painting sooner than she had expected.

Maybe I'll walk around and view some of the exhibits, she decided.

****

The elevator ascended smoothly. A small modern low-watt light illuminated the dark shaft from inside the elevator car. Killion watched as cables, wiring, and cinder block walls slipped by. After a few moments, he was blinded as the elevator passed the roofline of the church and traveled up the glass tower, the sudden change in light intensity coming without warning. He covered his eyes, trying to adjust, and was rewarded with a spectacular view of the city, the Pacific Ocean visible on the horizon.

The elevator slowed. Killion assumed he was near the very top. The doors behind him slid open and he stepped out into another lobby. Two men greeted him warmly, but Killion saw them for what they really were. Shaking hands with the first man, he glimpsed a Beretta holstered under his suit coat and both men wore a tiny black earbud for wireless communication, discreet, but no match for Killion's trained eye.

71

Armed guards at a church?

9

Ashley stopped for a moment, staring into the large room that housed the collection of medieval arms and armor at the Cleveland Museum of Art. The walls were lined with glass cases, each one displaying intricately crafted pieces, some weapons, others helms or breastplates. Several fully assembled sets of armor stood proudly in attention, greeting any visitors who graced their hall. In the very middle of the room was a fascinating armored horse, its knightly rider saddled on its back. She'd seen this exhibit before, still impressive, but not as exciting as the first time she'd walked through. Ashley loved the colorful tapestries. Gavin was much more into the weapons and suits of armor. After their last visit, he'd talked about it for days, recalling every detail and musing at the early technology. He had noted that on the left side of the room were the bows and crossbows, on the right, early muzzle loaders and pistols. The exhibit marked the transitional era between the feudal past and modern warfare; knights trading their swords for guns.

Ashley smiled, picturing Gavin's excitement, *Get him talking about the right thing and he'll never shut up*.

She could hear his voice in her head, rambling on, his hands waving in exaggerated explanatory gestures.

Of course guns of this day were more beautiful than lethal. They were notoriously inaccurate and typically only fired one small, unstable round. And just imagine reloading, you'd need a powder horn, bore rod, and of course your lead shot...give me a ten-round magazine and a semi-automatic any day!

Ashley wandered through more of the exhibits, mostly old paintings, many by artists she only recognized from her college books, not particularly famous, but still excellent all the same. She lingered at the Van Gogh's and Monet's. The Degas was unimpressive, as were the Picasso's. She skipped the contemporary and modern art rooms, having glanced briefly into the next room and observed a large black and white canvas entitled *Homer*, which curiously resembled a certain bald, fat, yellow, beer swilling cartoon character. This exhibit wasn't worth her while.

Her last visit, she'd focused mostly on the paintings. This time Ashley wanted to make sure she walked the early-Christian Byzantine collection and the Egypt exhibit. She stepped into the first room of medieval art and viewed the displays, pausing briefly at an intricately engraved 13th century Bible and then a reliquary believed to hold a skull fragment of John the Baptist. The next room housed more sculptures and engravings, as well as another reliquary, this one of the true cross, that is, the cross on which Christ hung. Ashley had heard this before:

Legend dictates that the actual cross used in the crucifixion disappeared after Christ's death and resurrection, but resurfaced centuries later in the year 326 AD; discovered in Jerusalem by the Empress Helena, the mother of Constantine the Great. The suspect cross supposedly healed a sick woman and raised a boy from the dead, its healing power evidence of its authenticity. The wood was at some point separated, a piece traveling with the empress to the palace in Constantinople, the other's fate unknown. Since the middle ages, pieces of the true cross were hardly rare, with knights from the crusades often claiming that they carried such a relic. Some merchants even sold them from their carts, right alongside linens and jewelry.

Ashley laughed to herself, *Reliquary of the True Cross, if only people knew that salvation and healing comes from our faith in Jesus Christ, not relics, legends, or the bones of saints!*

She continued on, turning the last corner of the Byzantine collection and heading for the Egyptian exhibit. The space opened up into a wide bright room, not dark and cramped like the Middle Ages exhibit. Sarcophagi took center stage in the middle of the room, sculptures stood on pedestals, beautiful art hung on the walls. Ashley studied the intricate carvings, astounded at the amount of fine detail.

Just imagine, she thought, *chiseling out hieroglyphic text, only to make a mistake and have to start over!*

She stopped at a tall sarcophagus that stood towering in the very center of the room, marveling at how the colors had retained their brilliance even after tens of centuries.

She'd never seen anything like it.

Hours felt like minutes. Ashley glanced at her watch: she'd lost all track of time and needed to head home. She turned and headed past displays filled with Greek artifacts, but didn't stop to look, only glancing in the glass cases. The exit to the stairs was right around the corner.

Ashley.

She stopped. Had someone called her name?

Ashley, it called again, this time much louder.

To her left, a small school group was touring the museum, their teacher talking with the guide as the kids wandered in a tight cluster. On her right was the exit. But straight ahead was a stone relief, ancient Assyrian, spanning from wall to wall and floor to ceiling. The image was of a man, bold and strong, his muscles massive. A wreath of flowers rested on top of long flowing hair. His face was hidden beneath an impressive beard: a prominent nose and a glaring eye was all that could be seen. On his back was a set of feathery wings. Across the middle of the relief was an intricately carved text.

Ashley.

No one else seemed to hear the voice. And then, everything went black.

****

"Welcome to the Sunrise Chapel," Reverend McNamara smiled warmly, his arms outstretched in an exaggerated greeting. "What can I do for you, Mr...Killion, I believe you said?"

"Yes, Sir, Killion, Sir," he replied coolly, "but call me Terrance, please."

"Alright, Terrance," the Reverend repeated. "To business then?"

"Please, Sir," Killion answered.

"I assume you work for my associate?"

"Yes, Reverend. Consider me an independent contractor in the employ of one Mr. Franklin. He sends his regards, but was not capable of accompanying me on this visit."

"I'm sure," McNamara replied, hiding his suspicions.

"In regards to the matter which interests Mr. Franklin..."

"The key?"

"Yes, Reverend. Our mutual friend has conscripted my help in locating his property as well as seeing to its safe return."

"*His* property? Tell me, son, are you familiar with the name Dr. Maurice Triton?"

"Of course. Dr. Triton was brilliant. The world most definitely misses his contributions."

"Did you know the key was in fact his, not Franklin's"

"I wasn't aware."

"The key disappeared just before Triton's death. He searched tirelessly for the trinket. His desire consumed him and he only trusted one man with the task, a man who we also believe to be dead."

"Thirteen?" Killion asked, already knowing the answer.

"Yes," McNamara shrugged.

"If I may, Reverend, please tell me of what value the key holds? I would not normally be so bold, but my employer has been reluctant to tell me why he so desperately wants something everyone considers rather trivial."

Killion paced the perimeter of McNamara's office, studying every detail of its layout, searching for clues to what the Reverend was hiding in this fortified tower. McNamara eyed the man, then, against what he thought might be his better judgment, he motioned for his security to exit, the next part of their conversation meant to be in private.

Before McNamara spoke, Killion paused at a photograph in an ornate frame: a beautiful young woman. She could easily have been a model, maybe was.

"Is this your daughter?" Killion asked, picking up the picture, admiring her pouty lips and large beckoning eyes.

"Gracious, no," McNamara laughed, "that's my wife, Barbara."

"My apologies," Killion said matter-of-factly as he placed the frame back where it stood on the Reverend's desk. "She's quite beautiful. You're a very lucky man."

"No worries," McNamara assured with a wink, "she's beautiful, but she's also trouble; all women are!"

"However *she* looks like she'd make the trouble worthwhile," Killion laughed. "But my Apologies, we've digressed, Reverend. Now please, you were about to tell me about the key."

"Oh yes," McNamara remembered, pouring scotch into two tumblers and handing one to his visitor, "the key. Its origin is of course shrouded in mystery and history has not proven helpful in the knowledge of the truth. However, Franklin and Triton both came to believe the same thing."

"And that is?" Killion urged.

"The key unlocks a door which leads to great wealth. Some say riches, others knowledge...some would even say the supernatural. Regardless, Triton had it and Franklin wants it."

"So it *is* valuable?"

"It's valuable because people have made it so."

"One more question then, Reverend, and I'll be leaving."

McNamara nodded.

"Do you know the whereabouts of this key?"

"No," he shrugged, swallowing the last of his scotch, "but if I did, I'd tell you. Franklin knows I am loyal to him. We're partners: his gain is my gain and vice versa. I do have one lead however."

"Yes?" Killion asked, growing bored with the old man's story.

"One of my associates, the man we believe responsible for killing Thirteen, he has disappeared. We believe Thirteen may have given this man the key. But we'll find him."

"No, you won't," Killion said, setting the glass he'd been given down on the Reverend's desk.

"What?!" McNamara asked confused. "What do you mean?"

"Thank you for your time," Killion replied aloofly, "I know the way out."

****

"Alright, well I love you and I'll see you tonight when I get off work," Gavin said before placing the handset back on its cradle where it hung on the kitchen wall.

He'd tried calling Ashley several times, but she hadn't answered; so he decided to leave her a voicemail. Cell reception was terrible inside the thick-walled museum and he was aware of the fact, having had trouble reaching her before.

Gavin looked at the clock as he placed his dirty plate in the dishwasher.

"Time to get ready for work," he groaned.

He climbed the stairs and made for the bedroom. His red work shirt and khakis were neatly folded, resting on Ashley's hope chest that had become a bench seat at the foot of the bed. He changed his pants and then pulled the shirt over his head, tucking it in, zipping up, and fastening his leather belt. Slipping on his tennis shoes, he hastily tied them and readied to leave.

∗∗∗∗∗∗∗∗∗∗∗∗

"How dare you...who do you think you are," McNamara barked at the man on the other end of the phone, "sending that man to question me? It's insulting. We've known each other for a long time, long enough for you to know that I'm loyal to The Order, to our goals!"

Franklin puffed on his cigar before answering, "I just needed to see if you had made progress."

"This Killion said you'd hired him to find the key. But that's what I'm doing. I already have a plan in place. I'll find it: The Order will have it soon!"

"Consider him my insurance policy. I trust you are doing all you can, but I would be a fool not to search my own avenues, just in case."

"In case of what?" McNamara growled.

"In case you cannot locate the artifact, that's all."

"This is unacceptable, Franklin. I'm calling a meeting with the Elders. They'll hear about this. The Order will assemble at midnight tonight."

∗∗∗∗∗∗∗∗∗∗∗∗

Michael scanned the houses, looking for the right address. He passed by Gavin's property slowly, recognizing it instantly, his instincts guided by his returning powers. Then, he glimpsed movement. It had been five years since he last saw Gavin, the two of them bantering in that dark hallway on the third floor of New York General Hospital, just before Gavin set off the charges, reducing the old hospital to rubble.

"You're mine," Michael grinned, watching Gavin head to the garage and open the door.

Quickly, Michael sped off around the corner, circling the block and parking at the end of the street just in time to see Gavin rumble down and out of his driveway on his motorcycle.

"All mine..."

****

Rocco sat across the table from Barnett. The waitress came, bringing the men their second round. Rocco thanked her for the beers, then stared at her backside as she walked away.

"So what's the plan?" Barnett asked, pulling Rocco's attention away from her well-fitting jeans.

"I'm going after his wife. I'll surprise her at home. You go after Gavin at work. He has no idea who you are. If he sees me, he knows his cover is blown. Make sure your team is ready, don't underestimate this guy."

"We'll be ready," Barnett promised confidently, "I brought my best men."

"You'll need them."

"Do you think he'll come quietly?"

"Well, quietly, no," Rocco laughed, sipping the head off the top of his frosted glass. "He'll be cracking jokes the whole time, might put up a fight..."

"But as soon as he knows we have his wife..." Barnett followed.

"He'll cooperate," Rocco finished.

****

Michael stood at the locked back door of Gavin's house. He raised his hand, the lock clicking open. Cautiously, he turned the knob and peered into the kitchen. He'd waited patiently in his car for several hours, and now that the sun was setting, he made his move, hidden by the shadows cast by the sun's fading orange glow.

He quickly checked the first floor. The coast was clear. Michael returned to the kitchen, opening and closing drawers, scanning their contents. He then searched the living, dining, and family rooms in the same way, careful and precise.

The stairs creaked beneath him with each step. He headed into the master bedroom and looked around. There was a dresser on one wall, an armoire on the other, each one filled with clothes. Michael knew it would be difficult to search the entire house. He closed his eyes and concentrated, all his will bent on finding the key, hoping that its energy would draw him to it, lead him to its hiding place.

He opened his eyes with a sigh. It wasn't there. If Gavin had the old key, it wasn't in this house.

Michael turned and found the bathroom. He stood at the toilet, relieving himself, then flushed and faced his reflection in the mirror on the wall behind him. Washing his hands, he felt an odd connection with Gavin. Here, in his enemy's house, he suddenly felt alarmingly sorry for his prey. But he would do what he had to do to save his family, even if it meant killing Gavin and Ashley.

He searched for a hand towel, looking left and then right, but found none, just bath towels hanging on a metal bar. Reaching over, he dried his hands then decided to search the drawers in the bathroom, just in case the key was there.

Opening the top right drawer, he paused, his weight shifting to his heels. Michael reached into the drawer and removed Ashley's pregnancy test. He felt sick to his stomach, then pushed the thought from his mind.

Even if she's pregnant, it doesn't matter, he reassured himself, *you'll do what you have to do, for Elizabeth, for Cain.*

The sound of breaking glass startled him. He dropped the pregnancy test back into the drawer and reached into the chest pocket of his suit coat, quickly removing his mask and pulling it down over his face. Quietly, he slipped away into the shadows.

****

"Attention shoppers, the store is now closed. Please bring your items to the front of the store for checkout and have a pleasant evening."

Gavin smiled as he heard the automated closing announcement crackling from the overhead speakers of the store's intercom system.

He grabbed his walkie-talkie off its belt clip and radioed to the front of the store, "Let's get the front doors locked and ready to roll. Any customers left in the building?"

A cacophony of voices squawked back at him with replies of *no*.

"Great," he answered. "I'm heading to the stockroom to lock up the back door, then I'll be upfront and you guys can head on out. Good job tonight!"

He reached into his pocket and pulled out his store keys. Quickly, Gavin locked the back door, checked the trash compactor to make sure it was locked as well, then glanced at the trailer doors on the loading dock. They were locked too.

Awesome, he thought, *we'll be out in no time!*

Gavin turned the corner and headed back through the double doors that led to the sales floor. Suddenly, the lights went out. All throughout the store, motion sensing toys beeped, clicked, and chirped in response. An aisle full of interactive baby dolls came to life, a whole wall of giggling, cooing voices. It was very creepy.

"Thanks to whoever got the lights," Gavin said into his walkie.

No one responded. Instead, he heard an odd sound. Footsteps creaked on the steel roof. He looked up, trying to place the noise as one of his associates ran up to him, fear in her eyes.

"There's a guy at the front door, he looks like he's trying to get in."

"The doors are locked," Gavin said calmly, the sound on the roof stopping. "He's just a last minute shopper that didn't make it in time."

"But he's got a gun, I saw it," she stammered, "and I think he's trying to rob us."

Gavin thought for a moment. Was she right? Did this guy have a gun or was she just exaggerating? Maybe he had a cell phone in his hand and in the dark, it was misidentified?

"Are you one hundred percent positive of what you saw?"

"Yes!" she replied.

"Ok, get everyone away from the front as quickly as you can. Head back to the break room and lock the door."

"What about you?" she asked.

"I'm going to call the police."

"Thomas is in the cash office counting down drawers," she added.

"I'll get him, you just get everyone else safe!"

****

Thirteen watched as a gaudily dressed man ducked from room to room, a revolver in his hand. This was an unexpected inconvenience. Apparently he wasn't the only one looking for Gavin.

He stalked the intruder through the house, waiting till the moment was just right and then, when the man paused to listen at some distant sound, he struck.

Thirteen emerged from the shadows, took hold of the man's head and twisted violently, snapping his spine, the lifeless body collapsing to the floor. He checked the man's pockets and found a wallet tethered to his belt by a chain. Thirteen ripped it free and flipped it open.

"Rocco," he chuckled, staring at the picture on the driver's license, reading the name aloud, "better luck next time. The hunter is all mine."

****

Gavin raced into the cash office and locked the safe, "We've got trouble!"

Thomas looked up from the desk, a till full of money in front of him, "What's up boss?"

"Do you have your phone on you?"

"Yeah," Thomas shrugged.

"Head for the break room, call 9-1-1," Gavin ordered, "tell them we're being robbed."

Thomas pulled his phone from his pocket and ran out of the

office, doing just as he was told, making his way to the safety of the break room. Gavin poked his head out of the doorway and tried to spot the man at the door. No one was there. Cautiously, he stepped from the office, careful to avoid a direct line with the possible danger outside the large front windows. Soon the police would be there, soon they would be safe.

10

Thirteen drug Rocco's body to the back door, knowing that would be where Gavin would enter the house, distracting him as he arrived home, making him an easy target. But one thing unsettled Thirteen: where was Ashley?

He wanted to handle them separately. He'd hoped she would be home first, but even so, he knew he was more than a match for the both of them.

His trap was set, his plan, albeit improvised, was going to work. Once again, Thirteen slipped away into the security of the shadows.

****

Gavin tried to focus, to stay calm, but his heart was racing, as was his mind. What if this wasn't a simple attempted robbery? What if someone was after him?

But who?

Thirteen wad dead, killed in the blast at New York General. Had his old employers found him?

No, he decided, *this has nothing to do with me.*

He glanced again nervously at the door. No one was there. Maybe the robber gave up? The glass was thick, difficult to break, and the locks on the doors were a heavy-duty industrial type.

Gavin took a deep breath, beginning to relax as he sat alone in the dark. He began to feel a bit foolish. But the silence was broken by the sudden crash of glass and the crack of machinegun fire. Gavin slumped down behind the counter and peeked over the top of the register. In the store's roof were six skylights, the glass now shattered as shrouded men rappelled from above, their faces hidden behind masks and night vision goggles, assault rifles in their hands, the red beams from their laser sights glowing in the darkness.

It had been years since he'd faced anything like this. He had to shake off the rust, and quickly! Gavin glanced at the front door. There was a man there now, a gun in his hand, but all Gavin could make out was his silhouette. The man stood in front of a car, its high-beams on, aimed right at the entrance to the building.

"That's no good," Gavin whispered.

He couldn't escape through the front and decided he only had one option, but he had to be quick. Staying low, he ducked around to the back aisle of the boys department and headed for sporting goods. He stopped at an end-cap displaying spy toys. He pulled a pair of night-vision binoculars from a peg and ripped into the package, flipping the switch to on. Nothing happened. He checked the battery compartment: empty. Gavin left them on the floor, watched as one of the gunman crept past the far end of the aisle, then continued once the coast was clear.

Gavin turned the corner leading into the sports equipment aisle and grabbed an aluminum baseball bat from a rack, but as he did, the other bats on the display clinked together. Gunfire erupted all around him as the assailants zeroed in on his location.

He raced from that aisle and down a section of fashion dolls across the main walkway. The attackers' shots followed, the bullets tearing through the boxes on the shelves, raining down a confetti of shredded cardboard and random doll limbs. Gavin rounded another display and came face to face with one of the men, catching him by surprise. The bat thumped against the man's body armor as Gavin swung it as hard as he could into the man's chest, sending him stumbling backwards, the wind knocked out of him. Gavin then kicked him in the knees, dropping him to the ground, and swung the bat again, the impact against the attacker's head rendering him unconscious.

Gavin quickly stripped him of his rifle and slipped the night-vision goggles of his bloodied head. The odds were looking a little better, at least now he was armed, but more importantly, he could see.

****

Thirteen waited patiently in the dark, his chest moving slightly with each breath. But in the back of his mind, the question was beginning to bother him even more, where was the girl?

"You there, *Watcher*," he called out, "show yourself."

Silently, a demon appeared from within a dark corner of the living room, its glowing eyes floating ominously.

"Yes?" it hissed.

"The girl, his wife, where is she?"

"Not here."

"Obviously," Thirteen grunted.

"She's been taken by another."

"The dead man?" he asked, gesturing at Rocco's corpse.

"No," the demon answered, its voice turning to a whisper as it faded away into nothing, "but he knows you, you know him. And he, like you, is one of us."

****

Gavin knew he only had one shot to escape. If he didn't time it just right, he'd never make it out alive. He ducked low and wound his way around racks of apparel. There it was: an emergency door. He used the night-vision goggles to scan the room, his view washed in shades of green.

From here, he could see the attackers; they were near the aisle where he'd overtaken one of them. By now they knew he had the goggles and a gun. They would be extra cautious. He would use this to his advantage.

Quickly, he stood and pushed against the crash bar, sending the emergency door wide open, the alarm screeching in protest. But rather than run outside, he headed for the back of the store, careful to remain hidden by the round apparel racks.

Just as he'd hoped, the men were drawn to the alarm. He slipped into the stock room as the men searched around the exit and in the parking lot outside. As quietly as possible, Gavin made his way to the back door. Unlocking it so the alarm would not sound, he gently opened it and scanned the lot. Once he was sure it was empty, he sprinted away from the building and into a small wooded area. He knew the employees would be safe. The police were surely on their way, if not there already. It was most definitely not a robbery, the men had come for Gavin. Now his thoughts turned to Ashley. He had to get home, had to make sure she was alright.

Gavin's motorcycle was parked out front of the store, right in the middle of all the chaos. Knowing that was not an option, he decided to ditch the machinegun and the night vision goggles and began to run, exiting the trees and using the surrounding businesses and doctors' offices as cover. He knew of a bus stop he passed nearly every day on his route to work. That, he decided, was his best bet.

The wail of sirens flooded the area. Emergency vehicles were on their way. He was careful to remain in the shadows as much as possible so as not to draw attention to his position. He made it to the bus stop, looked at the schedule on the small covered waiting area, and then checked his watch. His ride was five minutes away.

Please be OK, please, please...please, he thought as he pulled his cell phone from his pants pocket and dialed her number.

No answer, only her voicemail.

A car passed, its headlights illuminating the bus stop. Gavin looked down at his red work shirt, a big red target. Hastily, he pulled it off over his head and threw it into a trash bin that stood at the end of the bench. He straightened his black undershirt and took a seat, again using his cell, this time texting Ashley.

Leaving work now...things are crazy, he typed, tapping away on his phone's touch screen, not wanting to say the wrong thing and send her into a panic, *too crazy to believe...you ok?*

He hit send. Leaning back against the bench, Gavin closed his eyes, half in frustration, half in prayer. The wait for her response was excruciating.

Gavin checked his watch again, the bus's headlights illuminating a bend in the road, *come on, come on!*

The bus squealed to a stop, its airbrakes protesting against the weight of the vehicle. Slowly, the doors opened. Gavin rushed onto the nearly empty bus, paying the fair, then taking a seat. He was going crazy; staring at the phone, wishing for a response with all his being.

The phone beeped. Quickly, he opened her text message and sighed.

I'm sorry work was crazy. I'm fine. See you soon :)

****

The bus lurched away from the curb leaving Gavin about a block away from home. He walked down the main street then turned the corner onto the road where their house was located.

Almost home.

The street was dark, quiet. He cautiously made his way down the sidewalk, watching the shadows for the slightest movement. Gavin paused. Parked two houses down and across the street was a black Porsche, rather auspicious in this lower-middleclass neighborhood. More peculiar, the car had New York plates. More confusing was the black Cadillac Escalade parked in front of his house, it having plates from Massachusetts.

The neighbors across the street always seemed to have company, someone visiting from out of town. Perhaps the owners of the vehicles were there?

Gavin looked up and down the street. Nothing else seemed out of place. He went on, still leery: he couldn't shake the feeling welling up in the pit of his stomach. Gavin made it to the end of the drive. A light was on upstairs: their bedroom.

With a relieved smile, Gavin jogged up the drive and headed for the backdoor. He couldn't wait to see her, kiss her, tell her that he loved her.

He pulled his keys from his pocket and began to unlock the door, but stopped, his face growing pale as his hands began to shake. The bottom right pane of glass was broken out. The door was already open. Gavin peered into the pitch black kitchen, but couldn't see a thing.

Slowly he opened the door, careful not to make a sound. Stepping into the kitchen, he was tripped up. Something lay on the floor in the dark. He scrambled to his feet and pulled a flashlight from one of the drawers. Flicking it on, he cast the beam on the spot where he'd fell. A body lay hidden in the dark. Gavin recognized the man instantly.

Rocco.

Gavin checked the body for a weapon, but found nothing. Why was an unarmed demon hunter lying dead on the floor in his house?

"Ashley?" he called out. "You upstairs?"

He heard a creak in the ceiling above him: the bathroom. Maybe she was in the shower?

Why would she be in the shower, dummy? There's a dead man in the kitchen...maybe she defended herself and she's cleaning up? He argued with himself.

Gavin quickly scanned the living room as he turned and headed up the stairs. Nothing else seemed disturbed. He checked the bathroom and the second and third bedroom, but they were empty. The door to the master was closed.

Gavin quietly grasped the knob and turned, then slowly entered the room. The light was on, but Ashley was nowhere to be found. He quickly dropped down and pulled a lockbox from under the bed. Entering the combination on the lid, he popped it open and pulled a USP .45 from the box. He checked the magazine and chambered a round, then tucked the pistol into the waist of his khakis, his black t-shirt falling over the black polymer frame.

"Ashley?!" he shouted heading back down the stairs.

The sound of a gun's hammer clicking back stopped him in the living room. He raised his hands in surrender.

"It can't be," he said in disbelief, "you're dead! No one could have survived that blast!"

"You did," Thirteen replied coyly, his gun trained on Gavin.

Gavin didn't know what to say. He'd miraculously survived the explosion at New York General, carried to safety by an angel. But how had Thirteen made it out alive?

"Where's my wife," he finally managed to ask, "where's Ashley?"

"I don't know," Thirteen answered.

Gavin stared at him, analyzed his every move, "Why are you here?"

Thirteen lowered his gun. Gavin watched as the brutal killer's demeanor changed.

"I came for Triton's key: the one you took from his office in the Tri-Corp building."

"That's a lie! What have you done with Ashley?"

"Nothing. She was not here when I arrived."

"What about Rocco?" Gavin prodded, gaining confidence now that Thirteen seemed to have dropped his guard.

"He came to kill you and your wife."

"How do you know? He was a friend."

"Here," Thirteen said. "This is his cell phone. Read his messages. He was definitely sent to kill you."

Gavin cautiously took the phone, his gaze never trailing from the glowing white slits in Thirteen's mask. Now was his chance. Thirteen was preoccupied, Gavin could tell.

With one hand, he opened the text message program on the phone. The other hand slowly reached behind his back, his fingers finding the grip of the gun. Quickly, he whipped the USP from beneath his shirt and flipped off the safety. Gavin had Thirteen in his sights, at point-blank range. He couldn't miss.

Gavin squeezed the trigger and the .45 auto boomed in his hand, the slide gliding back as the spent casing ejected to the floor and the next round fed into the chamber. He pulled the trigger again, felt the recoil as the second shot fired. Thirteen stood in front of him, unnerved, unflinching. The hollow-point bullets lay crumpled at his feet. Gavin hadn't missed.

Somehow Thirteen had stopped the bullets, "Don't take me for a fool. I'm still as powerful as I ever was and yes, I came here with every intention of killing you, whether you gave me the key or not. But, I had a change of heart."

"You have no heart," Gavin scoffed, his gun still aimed at Thirteen's face. "In New York, when we fought in Triton's office, you said the key was unimportant, that it was Triton's foolish obsession. But now here you are, five years later, standing in my living room and asking me about the very key you basically threw away. Why?"

"Lower your gun and I'll tell you," Thirteen requested calmly.

"No."

With a sigh, Thirteen reached up and pulled off his mask, revealing his face to his enemy, "Please, Gavin."

This was not what Gavin had expected. In an act of concession, the greatest threat he'd ever fought had not only shown him his true face, but the man looked very similar to Gavin himself, so much in fact that Gavin felt like he was looking in a mirror. Their hair was very different but the faces, the structure, the shape; their jaw lines were nearly identical.

Gavin lowered his gun, "Who are you?"

"My real name is Michael," he replied, "Michael Laurent. And I believe the people who took your wife have also taken mine, as well as my son."

11

"So tell me, Killion, what did you discover in your visit to McNamara's Sunrise Chapel?" Franklin asked, picturing how indignant the Reverend must have looked as Killion walked out on him.

"Well, he wasn't very fond of me, or at least of my judgment in his inability to locate your key."

Franklin grinned, "Too many years growing fat off the wealth of his misguided flock have made the old preacher pompous, forgetful of his humble roots. What else?"

"He has a beautiful wife."

"Ah yes, the brat," Franklin sneered. "She was in diapers when Harlow became a member of our board."

"You say that like you've known her for the entirety of her life?"

"Practically. She's the estranged daughter of one of our previous partners."

"How old is she?" Killion laughed.

"Not yet thirty," Franklin smiled.

"And how'd she end up with the old man?"

"Money, power...who knows? Maybe she actually loves him?"

"I doubt that very much," Killion replied, his tone growing serious. "I do have my suspicions however."

"Oh?"

"I believe that if the Reverend were to find the key, he'd keep it for himself."

"Interesting. Well, regardless, you have him flustered. He's called a meeting of the board for tonight. Are we covered on your end?"

"Yes," Killion answered proudly. "Everything is going as planned."

****

"Wait, so you have a wife?" Gavin laughed, the thought seemingly absurd to him.

"Yes, Elizabeth, and a son: Cain."

"Tell me then, Michael, or Thirteen...why should I trust you?"

Michael set his gun and mask down on the coffee table, then took a seat on Gavin's sofa, "Because, if I wanted you dead, we wouldn't be talking."

"But if I knew where the key was and I managed to help you find it, then how do I know you won't just kill me and use it to exchange for your family?" Gavin reasoned.

"You don't. But, I need your help. And if you want to find Ashley, then you need mine as well."

Michael had a point. Reluctantly, Gavin sat down in an armchair opposite the man and scanned through the messages on Rocco's phone. Michael was right. Rocco had been sent to kill Gavin. The orders were all sent from one number, the name stored in the contacts was *Big Mac*.

"Who do you suppose Big Mac is?" Gavin wondered.

"If he's the one giving the orders, then he must be of importance. Perhaps the man I killed is his partner?"

"Rocco? He was a demon hunter like me, but out of Boston. We worked together on and off."

"So the angel, Joseph, trained this Rocco as he did you?"

"Joseph trained me, as well as several other hunters who were killed in the field, killed by men like you, but not Rocco. He was from California, L.A., I think."

"So who gave Joseph his orders?" Michael asked.

"Well, Joseph was part of, in his words, a network of recruiters, or handlers. There's one for about every five hunters. They each were responsible for monitoring the reports of demonic activity within their regions. They then assigned their hunters to investigations based in their cities of operations. A large city, like New York, would have up to five hunters, Cleveland would have three at the most, and so on, in relation to the size of the city. A small town like the one we're in, wouldn't even have a hunter. The hunters from the larger cities also sheriffed the smaller towns. At least, that was my understanding. I only met the other men Joseph trained. Besides Rocco, the existence of hunters outside of New York City was never confirmed. But from what Joseph had said, I always assumed our numbers to be around one hundred hunters, nationwide, a select few who fought in the name of righteousness."

"And who do the handlers answer to?"

"I don't know," Gavin shrugged. "Joseph never told me. He would receive emails outlining possible targets, potential threats, then he would set one of us to task."

"So you never asked, never wondered, where your paychecks came from?

"Not really. I trusted Joseph, trusted that he was a good man. As long as the checks cleared, I continued to do what was asked."

"Are you still a demon hunter then?" Michael asked, amused that Gavin had accepted so much at face value.

"No," he grinned. "You could say I retired. With Joseph gone, I had no one to give me my assignments personally, everything came by email, well that and I married Ashley."

Gavin stared at Michael, the man he'd known only by the name Thirteen. Could he be trusted? Joseph had trained Gavin to fight evil, to track down and destroy the work of sleepwalkers and demons, of people like Triton and Thirteen, and now, this man, the most dangerous, most sadistic killer Gavin had ever known, was offering not only peace, but apparently friendship in exchange for Gavin's help. The thought was almost maddening!

"Do you suppose that is why the man was sent to kill you, because you *retired*?"

"Well," Gavin admitted rather sheepishly, "they didn't know I had quit, in fact, they've still been paying me. I had continued to respond to emails for a few years, acting as if I had completed the jobs, all the while withdrawing against Joseph's account. As long as it remained active, and the emails kept coming, I had money. Besides my name, the people sending the emails knew nothing else about me, nothing."

"How were they never suspicious?" Michael asked. "Didn't they see that your withdrawals were no longer being made in New York?"

Gavin grinned, "I would let the funds build in the account. I was smart, didn't take money out every month. About twice a year, I would drive out to New York and make huge withdrawals, then head back home."

"And the emails? Weren't you afraid they would eventually check to see where your IP address showed you to be?"

"Again, I was cautious there as well. I only accessed the email server through a network of proxies, my real location masked so as to appear that I was logging in from a hard-line in New York."

"You had it all figured out, didn't you?" Michael mused.

"I thought I did, but Rocco still found me."

Michael laughed, "Perhaps they did not come for the key after all, simply payback."

"But there are several references to a key in Rocco's correspondence with Big Mac."

Michael thought for a moment and then his eyes lit up, "So, Triton was obsessed with this ancient key, and in his absence, The Order, or rather the men now leading The Order, has become obsessed with the same artifact."

"Right?"

"Tell me, the dead hunter…"

"Rocco."

"…yes, Rocco, the *dead* hunter, was he paid in the same manner as you, through an account in his handler's name?"

"I would assume so," Gavin said.

"And you never met his handler?"

"No, I knew only Joseph."

Michael smiled coyly, "A man who was a known associate, with whom you shared an employer, came to kill you for a key that Big Mac, the person I would assume to be *Rocco's* handler, must be attempting to retrieve…"

"I think I follow."

"…retrieve for those who now seek it as did Triton, The Order."

"Go on…"

"I served Triton; therefore, The Order."

"So?"

"So?!" Michael asked, his expression extremely serious. "Do you know what this means?"

"Yeah, but there's no way, not a chance."

"The evidence says otherwise."

"Text messages between Rocco and this Big Mac guy are not enough evidence to suggest that we, you and I, both worked for the same person," Gavin argued, raising a hand in protest. "Joseph was not aligned with Triton. Joseph *opposed* Triton."

"Corporate espionage!" Michael realized, watching Gavin grow flushed with anger. "This makes so much sense. I was blinded by my ambitions when I followed Triton, but now, so far removed from him, I see clearly what I missed then. You may have been called a demon hunter, but you, your allies, men like Rocco, you were contract killers."

Gavin laughed, "No way is that true. My targets were always sleepwalkers. I never had a mark that wasn't involved in the occult. Joseph wouldn't have allowed it!"

"But that was Joseph giving you the assignments, not the person giving Rocco his assignments, or any other hunter for that matter. You said so yourself. Joseph did not train Rocco. Joseph was protecting you, maintaining your innocence."

"So how is that corporate espionage?"

"Triton was the head of an organization, an assembly of wealthy who's-who's with geopolitical aspirations. I thought they were a cult like many others, but this is different. Perhaps the head of the group you worked for, the one pulling all the strings, was on the same board as Triton, in essence, working together, meaning though we opposed each other, we were actually, in the end, on the same side. So Joseph, by training you, was in opposition to the wishes of the board, or The Order, as Triton called it, meaning that Joseph was sabotaging the plans that The Order was laying out. And you, Gavin, are that corporate espionage."

"Let me guess, Oswald didn't kill Kennedy either and we never landed on the moon," Gavin chided.

"No, Oswald did not kill Kennedy, but we most definitely landed on the moon."

Gavin couldn't believe what he was hearing. He felt like this was a crazy dream that he was incapable of waking from. But regardless, he needed to refocus on what was really important: finding Ashley.

✱✱✱✱✱✱✱✱✱✱✱✱

The members of The Order, or the Elders, as they referred to themselves, eighteen in all, each took their seat at a long, finely set table in the boardroom at the Casa del Mar hotel on the beach in Santa Monica. Franklin sat beside Mr. Nelson. The rest of the group was comprised of the top minds in many of their varied fields hailing from all across the country, They included several influential state senators and congressman, numerous CEO's of major corporations, more than a few spoiled heirs to aging legacies, and, of course, Reverend McNamara, slumped in his chair, glaring daggers at Franklin.

"Ladies and gentleman," Franklin bellowed, the minute hand on his wristwatch ticking from 11:59 to midnight, "thank you for joining us at such short notice. It's fortunate we are all privileged with private jets."

The group chuckled softly and raised glasses in a toasting fashion.

"But alas," Franklin smirked jovially, "to business. You all were not called upon so quickly for a matter as trivial as my jokes. The good Reverend deemed it necessary for us to gather, so I'll turn this meeting over to him. Let's begin."

McNamara leaned forward in his chair, his fingers clasped, his elbows resting on the edge of the table, "I also wish to express my thanks for you all agreeing to assemble like this. But I wanted to inform you in person of a breach of our code. Apparently, Franklin is dissatisfied with the job I have done in attaining the relic; so much so that he has hired another to secretly work at the same task, undermining my ability to complete the task you all so graciously allowed me to take on."

The room stirred, but their grumbling was not against Franklin. They knew he was powerful, a man who was capable of doing things they could not even imagine. But McNamara, he'd been a thorn in the side of The Order since he'd pledged his allegiance. The Reverend was a talker, not a doer. He wined and moaned about every little detail, anything he believed to be an infraction of their ancient code. And worse, he was insistent that he always be given opportunities to prove his worth to the other Elders, to convince them that he belonged. In truth, Franklin only tolerated McNamara's eccentricities because of the financial contributions his church granted The Order. They funded the *inner-city missionaries*, the nickname given to the hunters, The Order's assassins, their every need provided for. Lodging, food, clothing...weapons: the church unknowingly supplied it all. Yes, McNamara was a talker alright.

"In fact," the Reverend continued, "that very man working for Franklin had the audacity to come and question me, question my progress...at the Sunrise Chapel no less!"

A man cleared his throat and then spoke, his thick Israeli accent unique in the room of Americans, "Excuse me for speaking, Reverend, and perhaps this is a foolish question, but...have you an answer as to why Chief Elder Franklin would have cause to go to such lengths?"

"Leroy, my friend," McNamara gushed in response, "we've known each other a long time, since before The Order..."

"Indeed."

"And you know that I am quite capable to complete this task."

"Yes," Leroy nodded.

"Look," one of the senators interjected, "this is fine and all, but it's late. I have a flight to Washington in five hours and I'm growing impatient. Reverend, did you call this meeting simply to embarrass Franklin in front of us, to scold him for what you believe to be an intentional breaking of your trust, or do you actually have a point?"

McNamara grinned, his composure calm, his delivery planned and perfect. He took on the voice of a preacher, his words strong and convicting.

"This artifact is a breakthrough for The Order, beyond anything we have attained. With the power, the knowledge, the *wisdom* it will grant us, we can do anything. Senator, surely you hope to become President of the United States. Executives, if all your company's profits doubled, tripled...imagine the wealth. Leroy, you could even bring peace to the Middle East, once and for all!"

The Elders sat silent, contemplative. McNamara was right: the key could make such things a reality.

"Is this true," Leroy asked cautiously, gesturing at Franklin, "did you send a spy to Harlow's office today?"

Franklin stared long and hard at Leroy, his brow finally softening as he smiled, "It's because of the Reverend that you are a member of this Order, your ascension to these ranks is, without question, admirable. Your humble beginning would normally never have afforded you such an opportunity, but as each of us has our specialty, so do you. I understand your loyalty to McNamara, I do. But, as the head of this Order, I believe I am allowed certain *entitlements* befitting my position. The Order would not have known the key existed were it not for my knowledge."

"Knowledge stolen from Triton," McNamara interrupted.

"Yes, it was Triton who entrusted me with the secret, but with his death, I believe the key should be passed on to the new Chief Elder, passed on so that we can all benefit from its unimaginable power."

"So you're considering your man an entitlement, as well as spying on a member of The Order?" the senator asked.

"Not in so many words, think of him more as *insurance*."

Again, the room fell silent till a heavily botoxed woman spoke, the skin on her face taut, her cheekbones skeletal, "What is it you ask of The Order, Reverend?"

"I request that Chief Elder Franklin cease his investigation into the matter of the key. I will deliver it very soon, in fact my men carried out an operation this very evening to ascertain the exact location of the artifact. I'm simply waiting for confirmation. We may even have it already."

The moment of truth had arrived. But no one dared call for a motion against Franklin. His retribution would be ruthless.

"This meeting is over," the senator announced, standing and drinking the glass of brandy he'd brought in from the hotel's bar, untouched since the meeting had begun.

Franklin smiled victoriously at McNamara as the members all stood and headed for the door. Mr. Nelson pulled his cell from his suit coat and dialed a number, then disappeared into the crowd leaving the boardroom.

"Was it worth it," Franklin asked McNamara, "did you expose me to the Elders?"

"Just call off the watchdog," McNamara sneered. "I'll deliver the key."

12

"You're telling me that the people Joseph worked for assumed I was an assassin?" Gavin asked, lost in disbelief as he sat in his chair.

"I believe so, yes," Michael replied.

"But if Triton was head of a secret order and Joseph answered to a member of that group, wouldn't Triton have been aware of Joseph, known who he was? Joseph hunted Triton for centuries."

"You're assuming Joseph revealed himself to his employers in the same way he revealed himself to you," Michael reasoned. "But what if he used a different form, even name...wisdom teaches to keep your enemies closer than your friends. If he did indeed hunt my old master for such a long period of time, it would make sense to work just beneath his nose, secretly undermining him from within...that's what I did."

"You're not like Joseph, you're a killer," Gavin said cautiously.

"Was," Michael sighed, "was a killer, but the ends justified my means."

"But you killed for Triton."

"Wouldn't you if it was your task to earn his unwavering trust? A man as boundlessly evil as Triton would never allow a man with a conscience to join his inner circle. Serving Triton afforded me great power, but at a cost. In accepting that power, I had to give up a part of myself, in a way, I was like two persons, sharing one body."

Gavin listened intently. He was hearing things Joseph had never shared, maybe didn't know. To say he was excited by this sudden return to his forgotten life was an understatement. He wanted to hear more.

Solemnly, Michael continued, "The man you see before you is not the man you see as *Thirteen*. Without the mask, I am self-conscious, aware of my weaknesses, but with the mask, I am unstoppable, I am fearless..."

"God-like," Gavin mused.

"Yes...the ultimate deception. Was it not the serpent's way to tempt Adam and Eve with the thought of being equal to their Creator, as you said, *God-like*? Triton offered me the greatness I felt I did not deserve and I was too weak to refuse, in fact I welcomed it, something I have come to regret now, as I've been stripped of what matters most."

Gavin stared at the mask. Could it be true, that all of Thirteen's power, the power that Triton granted, was actually imbued by the mask? He studied the stitching on the mouth, the hollow eyelets: he was suddenly compelled to touch it, even try it on.

Michael recognized the hunger in Gavin's eyes and spoke, removing the mask from the table and hiding it away inside his suit coat, "My apologies, it was not my wish to tempt you. I would not wish it on anyone; the awfulness of duality, the tearing apart of one's self by the conscience and the inevitable darkness we all harbor."

Blinking as if waking from a trance, Gavin felt washed in guilt, "You're talking about sin nature, imperfection in man."

"Yes," Michael replied, "but enough about religion. It has and always will bore me."

"Right," Gavin conceded, still shaken by his lust for the mask, "So where do you suggest we begin?"

"Your *friend* who came to kill you this evening, where was he from?"

"Boston; well, originally Los Angeles."

"How fitting: the *City of Angels*," Michael grinned.

"Won't the kidnappers send a ransom, their demands?"

"Well, we both know what they want..."

"The key," Gavin concluded.

"Right."

"There's just one problem," Gavin admitted.

"Which is?" Michael asked reluctantly.

"It's not here, it's in Chicago."

****

The music in the nightclub was nearly deafening. Killion struggled to hear the voice coming through his cellular phone.

"Right," he confirmed, "as you wish, the Reverend will be dealt with."

He ended the call then slipped the phone into his pocket. Killion was less than enamored by this Hollywood hotspot. Though surrounded by celebrities, movie stars, and the like, this was not his scene. He'd come for one thing. The lion was on the prowl. He carried himself so differently than the rest of those who mingled; the stargazers desperate to rub elbows with the elite. No, he was the center of attention in his own private world.

It was then he chose his mark. He recognized her immediately. She was an actress, early twenties, an up-and-comer, but the object of nearly any teen boys' desires. She was surrounded by men, young and old, all ready to impress her with some exaggerated story of greatness and exploits, most likely of little truth.

Killion watched the way she moved, studied her curves, the perfect fit of her short, tight dress. She had the face of a model and the body of a goddess.

She'll do, he thought.

"Excuse me, miss," he said approaching her aloofly from behind, "I'm expecting a business associate within the hour. Could you show him to my table when he arrives?"

"I'm sorry?" she said turning to see who had made such an impetuous request of her. "What did you say?"

One of the surrounding men snorted a laugh. Who was this guy?

"My associate, love. Could you direct him to my table?" he smiled coyly, his English accent alluring.

"I don't work here," she blushed, not sure whether or not she should be insulted.

"My apologies. I mistook you for the hostess."

Killion turned and headed for the bar. He hadn't made it more than a few steps when he felt a hand on his arm.

"Don't you know who I am?" she asked, surprised that he had shown such little interest in her.

"Should I?"

"I'm an actress."

"You don't say?"

"I was in that vampire movie, the one where..."

"I'm sorry," he interrupted, "but I'm not one for cinema, I prefer the theater, and besides, you're much too young for me."

He turned away again. The hook had been bated; now to see if she bit.

"Too young?"

"You are hitting on me, aren't you?" he asked.

"No."

"Then why are you still talking to me?"

"So you weren't flirting with me?" she questioned.

"No. I came here for a drink. I'm in Los Angeles on business from London and the concierge at my hotel recommended the bar here. So I will have my martini and leave."

She was genuinely perplexed. This was the first man she'd met since her first starring role that hadn't gone out of his way to impress her.

"Order one for me as well," she decided, biting her lip innocently, her knees touching, her toes pointed inward like a little princess that just requested a pony from her father, sure that her cuteness would encourage him to oblige.

"On second thought," Killion replied, "this music is beginning to annoy me. I think I'll be leaving."

"Ok," she smiled, taking his hand in hers.

****

McNamara was fuming as he arrived home at his Beverly Hills mansion. His wife Barbara was already in bed, curled comfortably beneath silken sheets. He tried not to wake her as he undressed and readied for bed.

He used the restroom and flipped off the light, then pulled down the covers on his side of the bed and sat down on the edge of the mattress. Quietly, he slid open the top drawer of his nightstand and looked inside. An age-worn Bible sat amongst the clutter of odds and ends, on top of it, a .38 snub revolver. Reassured, he closed the drawer and laid down.

Sleep would not come easy for him. Every creak, every thump in the night, he imagined Killion standing at the foot of the bed, his gun drawn, ready to strike. He had called a meeting with the Elders and failed to accomplish what he wanted, only convincing himself of a need to watch his back.

****

As Killion and the actress exited the club, they were greeted by paparazzi, an overwhelming sea of flashbulbs and questions. They wanted to know if this was her new boyfriend or what her next role might be. But Killion was a man on a mission, confidently pushing his way through the gawkers, his prize following in his wake.

However, one photographer blocked their path, boldly standing between Killion and his car. His camera clicked away furiously as he snapped shot after shot.

"Excuse me, friend," Killion said politely, using his southern accent, careful that the girl did not hear him.

But the man stood his ground. The only thing worse for an assassin than being photographed was being photographed in the act.

Killion smiled, but his gritted teeth were visible as he spoke, "I'm only going to say this once, pal. Move or you'll have to learn to operate your camera with your feet. Your mangled fingers will be a souvenir of us making our acquaintance."

The paparazzi was used to threats, it was his job to invade peoples' personal space. But this was different than the usual celebrity reprimand. There was something in this man's eyes: cold, calculating, unattached. The photographer stepped aside, apologizing, not sure why, but apologizing none the less.

He watched fearfully as Killion's Audi raced from the parking lot, then looked down, noticing for the first time that he'd soiled himself, the urine stain dark on his khaki pants. Who was that man?

****

"So we go to Chicago, get the key and then make the exchange for our families," Michael continued. "But..."

"What?" Gavin asked.

"If Triton was right about the key, and remind you, I believed that it was just the fantastic ramblings of an obsessed fanatic, but still, I'm not sure I want The Order possessing that power."

"Wait a second," Gavin protested, "I'm no longer a hunter. I'm not looking for a fight, just Ashley."

"So if you had the chance to rid the world of their kind of evil, you wouldn't take it?"

Gavin's gaze fell on the door leading into the kitchen, Rocco's lifeless feet visible on the floor, "I've got a new life, a life with Ashley. I don't want to risk what we have now. My past is my past."

"As is mine," Michael assured, "but yesterday, my life was taken from me. Without Elizabeth and Cain, I am dead. My heart beats for them and them alone."

"*Ugh*..." Gavin sighed, rubbing his tired eyes. "You're right. I just wish this could be over."

"As long as The Order exists, this can never be over. Face it; you lived an uncomplicated life in New York. You completed your tasks as issued, a good little soldier. Any life you thought you could have outside of that was already in jeopardy. Your wife knew the risks when she married you."

"I just want her back."

At those words, Michael remembered the pregnancy test, "So it's just you and Ashley?"

"Yeah..."

"No kids?"

"Nope."

Michael couldn't believe it, Gavin didn't know. Maybe she hadn't had a chance to tell him; maybe she didn't want him to know?

"It's amazing, you know, being a father. It changed my life."

Gavin nodded sleepily.

"Let's get some rest," Michael urged, changing the subject. "We have a long drive tomorrow."

"We can't, at least, not yet," Gavin said, looking again in the direction of Rocco's body. "We have to get rid of him."

Michael shook his head, "An inconvenience to be sure. What should we do?"

Gavin thought for a moment. There weren't a lot of options and they needed something quick.

"There's a rundown, old, graffiti-covered building about twelve blocks from here," Gavin explained, "from there, we have access to the Tuscarawas River, but more importantly, dense foliage. Route 21 runs parallel on the east side of the river, but the brush in that area is so overgrown that no one could possibly see what we are doing."

"Can we get close with a vehicle?" Michael wondered, agreeing that this was possibly the most viable option considering their limited budget of time.

"We can pull right down off the road, use the old creepy building for cover and park directly beneath the bridge. In the dark, we'll be invisible. From there, we just need to cross a series of railroad tracks and dump him in the Tuscarawas."

"Sounds like a plan."

"Come on," Gavin said, rising from his seat despite his exhaustion, "we'll take my van."

Michael followed Gavin from the house and into the darkness in the backyard. Gavin opened the gate on the picket fence and punched the code into the security panel on the garage door.

"I remember that piece of junk," Michael reminisced, as the open door revealed the rusted old black heap of scrap metal, immediately recognizing it from their showdown in New York. "It still runs?"

"A little," Gavin smiled.

He climbed in the driver's seat and cranked the ignition. The starter whined as half-rotten fan belts squealed beneath the dented hood, the engine finally chugging to life. The exhaust pipe hung loose, no longer fully attached to the muffler, black smoke pouring from beneath the rear quarter of the vehicle as Gavin slowly backed out of the garage.

"See?" Gavin said, still smiling. "She runs like a top."

"Perhaps no one will see us, but there's a good chance they'll hear us."

"Sure, but I know just what to do," Gavin replied.

Together, they headed back to the kitchen and Rocco's corpse. Michael shook his head, the van's sputtering audible from inside the house.

"Grab his feet, will you?" Gavin asked, his hands already under Rocco's limp shoulders, ready to lift the lifeless torso from the floor.

Michael took hold of the ankles and they lifted Rocco up off of the ground, then carefully navigated out of the house and tossed the body into the back of the van.

The drive to the dump spot was short. Gavin had estimated twelve blocks, which, in a small city, pass by quickly, only two stoplights between them and the destination. The road sloped downward as they approached the bridge. Gavin switched off the ignition and the headlights and silently steered to the right, their vehicle making no more sound than the simple gravel crunching beneath its weight. Once off the road, a turn to the left brought them beneath the Tremont overpass. Crickets chirped from the underbrush as the locusts' rhythmic song flowed from within the trees. There were no lights beneath the bridge and they found themselves shrouded by the pitch-black night.

Michael was impressed. Everything was as Gavin had said. Crumbled bricks and rotting lumber lay scattered around the broken remains of an old building, a rusted lock hanging from a rusted chain which tethered shut a rusted fence that in no way impeded the aspiring artists that tagged every inch of the property with spray cans.

"And what's on the other side of the river?" Michael asked, his gaze now falling on the overgrown jungle that blocked their path.

"A post office, drive-thru convenience store, and oh yeah," Gavin winked, "the police department and city hall."

"Then let's get going," Michael urged.

They managed to pull Rocco from the van and began the slow walk to the river. The push through the thick overgrowth was difficult and Rocco grew heavier by the minute. Mosquitoes buzzed near their ears, landing when possible to sample their flesh. The lonely roar of the occasional semi passing on the highway beyond was a terrible reminder of just how much they risked being seen.

"You're sure they won't be able to see us from 21?"

"No," Gavin reassured, straining as they emerged from the tall grass, the trestle bridge visible, a massive steel silhouette emerging from its organic surroundings. "We're at the tracks."

They had an easier time now, this area being much better maintained. Trains used the tracks several times a day, so they were kept as clear as possible.

"We should hurry in case a train comes," Gavin encouraged.

After only a few more yards, the men reached the river. In unison, they swung Rocco's body out over the water and sent him tumbling down the high bank, splashing into the blackness of the murky Tuscarawas far below.

The moonlight illuminated their solemn faces. Whispers littered the wind. A foul odor filled their nostrils. Michael did all he could to restrain himself. Demons hiding amongst the surrounding growth hungered for death, begging for the blood of the hunter to be spilled. Gavin sensed it as well: Michael could tell by the look in his eyes.

"Let's go," Gavin said sternly, breaking the uncomfortable silence.

"I'm sorry, Gavin," Michael replied.

They quickly crossed the tracks and disappeared back into the brush. In the distance, a freight train's horn blew a warning as it crossed the trestle bridge, the ground trembling as the powerful engine and its long body of cars rumbled through.

"That was close," Gavin admitted as they settled into the van, starting it up with some difficulty and heading back to the house.

****

Killion finished his martini, the young actress at his side, a toothpick in her mouth that she played with teasingly. The bartender at the Sunset Marquis offered him another, but he declined.

"Well," he said to the girl, turning on the swiveling barstool to face her, "it's been an entertaining evening, but it's time for me to retire."

"Are you saying goodnight?" she asked, her brown eyes drowning in disappointment.

"My apologies, but yes," he replied coyly.

"Can I at least have a goodnight kiss?" she wondered with a half-smile, dropping the toothpick on the counter as she slinked off the stool she'd sat on and stood between his knees, her hands resting on his thighs.

He feigned hesitation, acting as if the deliberation was excruciating, then leaned in, his lips gently pressing into hers. She pressed back, her mouth slightly open, her tongue beckoning for his. Killion took her by the waste and pulled her close. She moved her hand up his leg, lingering at his trouser's inseam.

"Please," he said in a whisper, pulling his lips away from hers, "this shouldn't be happening."

"Why?" she asked, her hand egging him on.

"Because, I'm married," he lied.

"You're not wearing a ring..."

"No, I'm not. And this isn't love," he argued in hushed protest. "This will never work. Besides, I leave for London tomorrow. I can't stay with you."

She bit her lower lip, her beautiful doe eyes looking up at him, "Tomorrow, you can be a married man, but tonight, you're mine."

****

Michael watched Gavin as he slipped into sleep: he looked uncomfortable, slumped in the old leather armchair, his chin resting against his chest as his head hung low. In his mind, he formulated a plan, weighed his options, their chances. In the morning, they would begin, the eight hour drive west bringing him one step closer to his family.

"What are you playing at?" a voice hissed from the shadows.

"I know what I'm doing," Michael replied.

"You should kill him now, while he sleeps. He's told you where to find the key."

"Chicago is a big city."

"We'll help you," another slithery voice encouraged.

"Chaque chose en son temps," Michael agreed, closing his eyes, whispering in French, "all in due time."

13

Gavin woke with a start, the alert of an unfamiliar cell phone reminding him that the events of the previous night were more than just a bad dream. Michael woke as well, his eyes adjusting to the sunlight that streamed in through the living room windows. Gavin looked down at Rocco's phone, an icon on the screen marking the arrival of a new text message.

"It's from Big Mac," Gavin said excitedly.

"What's it say?" Michael asked through a yawn.

Why haven't I heard from you, Gavin read aloud, *is the job done?*

"He must mean *you*," Michael pondered.

Gavin hesitated, then began typing a response, a smirk accompanying the tapping of the qwerty keyboard, "I'm telling him that I'm dead."

Michael nodded his approval. Gavin sent the message. After a long moment, the phone beeped again.

Proof? the message said.

"He wants proof," Gavin frowned.

"Text him a photo, sprawl out on the floor, look dead."

"It's got to look convincing," Gavin said, handing the phone to Michael and turning toward the kitchen, "follow me."

****

The sun had not yet risen in Los Angeles. Killion stared out from the large windows of their suite at the Sunset Marquis. He looked back at the bed, the sheets twisted and disheveled from their escapades. There she lay, naked, flushed, exhausted, having finally just fallen asleep. He found his pants on the floor and dug through the pockets for his cell phone, then stood looking down over her young body, snapping several provocative pictures, mementos of their tryst.

He dressed, then returned to her, caressing her perfect round naval as she stirred, waking at his gentle touch. He bent down for one last kiss.

"You're welcome," he whispered, sweeping her hair away from her face to touch her cheek.

She smiled, "I'll see you in my dreams."

He looked her over one more time, committing every last inch of her to memory before pulling the sheets up to her chin. She cuddled up, warm and cozy, rolling onto her side. Killion patted her playfully on her backside then headed out the door. He didn't need to rest. Now, pleased after a night of sex, he had issues to attend to.

****

Gavin began scouring the kitchen, placing different ingredients on the counter as he searched: ketchup, maple syrup, red and blue food coloring, and a measuring cup with the bottom third filled with water. Quickly, he began a careful mix of all the elements.

"What are you doing?" Michael asked, watching it all blend together, the different colors swirling till it became deep red.

"Making blood," Gavin grinned.

Satisfied with the color and consistency, Gavin moved to another part of the kitchen, poured some of the gooey concoction onto the floor, laid down so his head rested in the sticky puddle, and then poured some on to his forehead, tilting his head to the side, allowing gravity to work, a trickle from what looked like an entry wound. Then, Gavin remained perfectly still, his eyes staring off into nothing. Amused, Michael used the phone to take a few pictures, all positioned to create the illusion without revealing too much detail.

"We're good," he grinned, looking at the shots he'd gotten. "This one is perfect!"

Gavin jumped up from the floor and pulled a towel from a hook above the kitchen sink, then looked at the picture, "yeah...looks like he got me."

"I made sure Big Mac will be able to see your tattoos. It'll be a positive ID."

"Send it," Gavin said, smiling as he wiped the mess off his face.

****

Killion parked his Audi across the street from a large gated mansion in Beverly Hills, comparing the address on one of the tall brick columns that flanked the entrance with the numbers Mr. Nelson had provided him. Patiently, he sipped his coffee, waiting for the opportunity to strike.

****

Reverend McNamara lay staring at the ceiling, his eyes already wide open as the alarm on the nightstand announced the arrival of the new day. He hadn't slept. His wife stirred next to him. He reached over, his hand touching her shoulder, but she jerked away, sleepily mumbling what sounded like *not now*.

He sighed, standing, his feet sliding into his slippers. His phone beeped.

"Hallelujah!," McNamara cried as he viewed the message, Gavin's dead body on the screen.

Quickly, he replied, his fingers fumbling in his excitement, *Fantastic! Do you have the key?*

Gavin had just poured a cup of coffee, stirring in his cream, as Rocco's phone chimed. Michael smiled.

No, Gavin typed, continuing the charade, *but I'll have it soon. Gavin didn't speak, but his wife finally broke and told me where it is.*

Fine. Contact me when you have it. Good job, McNamara replied, setting his cell back down on the nightstand and heading for the bathroom, whistling a happy tune as he flipped on the shower.

****

"He said to contact him when we have the key," Gavin explained.

"Then we have our in. We go to Chicago," Michael said, "we get the key, and we send Big Mac an update. As long as he thinks we're his assassin, he'll lead us right to him!"

"To Ashley and your family," Gavin grinned.

"Exactly."

****

"Terry," the voice said over the phone, "I have Ashley Dering, she was delivered last night. Are we still on schedule?"

"Yes, Edward," Killion answered, his eyes scanning the mansion grounds through the rot-iron fencing. "We'll soon know what the Reverend knows and he'll be out of the picture."

"Do you trust our employers?"

"No. These kind of people can never be trusted, but I trust their money."

"We should have come to America sooner," Edward laughed.

"Perhaps, brother…perhaps."

****

"And you're sure of this?" Franklin questioned.

"Of course," McNamara grunted, "I told you last night. I had this under control."

"This Gavin, the hunter, is dead?"

"Yes," McNamara confirmed.

"And the girl?"

"His wife is dead as well."

"What of the key, did your man acquire the key?"

"He has its location."

"But he does not *have* it?"

"The girl told him where it's hidden. He'll deliver it tomorrow. You'll be the first to know when it's in my possession."

"Very good, Reverend, very good."

****

"Something's bothering me," Gavin shrugged.

Michael stared at him, nodding for him to continue.

"If Big Mac wanted Ashley and me dead, then who took her? You said that the same person who has your family is also responsible for Ashley's disappearance. Big Mac wasn't fazed by my message. If he had her, he'd have been surprised by my claim that she's dead."

"Good point."

"If Big Mac is part of The Order, then maybe someone else in the organization took them."

"You're saying the left hand doesn't know what the right is doing?" Michael asked.

"Maybe they work independently?" Gavin reasoned.

"Then we will exploit this fact, starting with Big Mac."

****

Killion watched as the security gate to McNamara's mansion slowly opened. Within moments, a black limousine pulled from the drive and turned left, quickly followed by a young blonde who headed right, the top down on her BMW convertible.

He put his car in gear and followed the woman out of the neighborhood. She wound her way through traffic till finally turning off Santa Monica and onto Rodeo Drive. They passed the shops, taking a left east on Dayton Way, then a quick right down into a parking garage. Killion parked near her, but not close enough that she'd notice. He hurried from his car, pretending to be lost in conversation on his cell phone as he watched the top on her BMW unfold and settle into place. He received a parking voucher from the valet and spotted the elevator leading up to the street, then lingered as she approached, politely holding the door for her before stepping in behind her, his phone still raised, continuing his farce.

"If the contract is in order," he spoke boldly, "then sign. There's too much money at stake and we will not be out negotiated."

He acted as if he ended the call and dropped the phone in his pocket. He'd seen her watching him in the reflection of the elevator's doors.

"My apologies, miss," he smiled as they reached the street, "after you."

She smiled and headed for the boutiques on Rodeo, her heels clicking on the sidewalk. Killion crossed to the other side of the street, staring inconspicuously at the storefronts, browsing the window displays. Carefully, he shadowed her over the next hour, using the stores as camouflage, ducking in and out of shops, browsing.

Finally, it seemed she'd finished shopping, a bag in each hand; a large one from Louis Vuitton, the other a small one from La Perla lingerie.

He followed her as she turned down Brighton, then rounded the corner onto Beverly, crossing to the far side of the street at the intersection. Killion paused as she disappeared into a Starbucks. His eyes tracked her to the bathroom.

Perfect, he smirked.

He swung open the door and stepped in line, ordering a venti triple caramel macchiato, then took a seat where he was sure he'd be seen. She returned from the restroom. He pretended to send a text message, his eyes averted down at the screen of his phone. She slowed as she saw him, then stepped to the counter and ordered.

The barista handed her the non-fat skinny latte she'd requested, then hurried to prepare the next guests drink. The coffee shop was busy, tables were a precious commodity.

"Are you following me?" she teased, approaching the place where Killion sat.

"Pardon me, but do I know you?" he asked, tilting his head in question.

"I saw you earlier, at the elevator," she smiled, "in the parking garage...you held the door for me."

"That's right," he replied, feigning enthusiasm as he stood and pulled a seat out from the table for her. "Please join me."

She placed her coffee on the table, then set her bags down next to the chair, finally sitting and crossing her tan, slender legs, "Thank you so much."

"You're welcome," he grinned boyishly, his left hand outstretched in greeting, "I'm Terrance."

"Barbara," she said, accepting his graciousness.

He took her hand and kissed the back of it gently, his eyes falling on her gleaming diamond wedding band, "That's an *impressive* ring."

"My husband is an *impressive* man."

"I believe he must be, to have tamed a beautiful woman such as you," he winked.

"What makes you think I'm tame?"

"A man doesn't give a woman a ring like that and expect her to be unfaithful. It's a promise of fidelity."

"He gave it to me, but I picked it out. I tamed him."

"To be sure."

They sat for a moment in silence, her looking at him, him staring nowhere in particular. She took a sip of her hot latte.

"So you're British?"

"Yes," he smiled, his gaze returning to her.

"You're accent is charming, Terrance."

"It makes me feel like a tourist, hearing everyone sounding so *different* around me. Perhaps it is not me who has the accent, but you?"

She laughed softly, pulling her hair behind her ear as she blushed, "So you live here then?"

"No, I am a tourist," he admitted with a chuckle.

Their quieting laughter was met by another resounding silence. He looked down at the bags sitting at her feet, pausing to admire her legs on the way back up.

"What's in the little bag?"

"Oh, La Perla," she gushed, "I love that store."

"We have them in the UK."

"Do you shop there for your wife?"

"I would if I had one," he said with a shrug. "That bag is not very big; I don't imagine that's a bathrobe."

"No it's not," she sighed, the rosy blush in her cheeks now extending down her neck."

"Are you embarrassed?" Killion smirked. "There's no need. Beautiful women purchase sexy lingerie and then drink coffee with total strangers every day."

"Really?" she said with an exaggerated look of surprise and interest. "I never realized that happened."

"Oh yes, it happens to me quite often I'm afraid."

Killion's cell phone beeped. He'd received a text message.

Where are you? Franklin.

"Excuse me," he said, "it's my associate."

Killion dialed Franklin and waited for an answer, the phone raised to his ear. It barely rang, the call answered immediately.

"Change in plans," Franklin said gruffly, "McNamara's man came through. He said he'd have the key by tomorrow."

"Lovely," Killion replied, careful with his words, knowing the Reverend's wife was listening from across the table, "wonderful news. Should I continue?"

"Are you with your mark?"

"In a manner of speaking," Killion smiled.

"Don't do anything," Franklin ordered. "How soon can we meet?"

"I'm in Beverly Hills. Where will you be?"

"Meet me at the Santa Monica Pier."

"I'll be there within the hour," Killion agreed, hanging up.

"Work?" she asked.

Killion detected a note of disappointment in her voice, "Indeed. Negotiations were successful, but the deal has changed."

He took a napkin and pulled a Monte Blanc from beneath his suit coat, quickly jotting down numbers. She took it from him without hesitation.

"Call me, Miss Barbara, if ever you're feeling wild," he grinned, standing and heading for the door.

14

"So we get the key and set up the exchange," Gavin planned.

"But, we need to consider, the exchange may go badly," Michael sighed. "We should be ready."

"You think there will be sleepwalkers? If this Big Mac was an associate of Triton's, then he may utilize similar means."

"If not an army of the damned," Michael explained, "an army of hunters, trained assassins, ruthless and elusive."

"Or at least better than Rocco," Gavin laughed. "Regardless, we need to be armed, heavily."

"I agree," Michael said, thinking of his signature Desert Eagles securely strapped beneath his suit coat.

Gavin nodded for Michael to follow as he walked to the other side of the kitchen and pulled open the basement door. He flipped the light on as they descended the stairs.

Michael surveyed the basement as Gavin approached a tall red tool chest, rolled it aside, and leaned against the cinder block wall, revealing a hidden door as it slowly swung open.

Once inside, Michael realized what was hidden so well in Gavin's basement: an arsenal, "This is unexpected."

"I know, right?" Gavin grinned proudly, entering the combination on the safe, then tugging the door open. "I have something of yours."

Michael stared intently as Gavin reached into the safe. The feeling of familiarity rushed through him, a warmth powered by the mask in his pocket.

Gavin unwrapped the sword and held it out to Michael, "I found it, in the debris at the hospital. I couldn't leave it there, it felt...*wrong.*"

Michael closed his eyes as he held the sheath in his left hand, his right grasping the handle. He smiled as he slipped the blade smoothly from its home, the ring of the metal a welcome greeting from an old friend.

But something changed, his smile fading, a thought pounding in his mind like a beating war drum; *Kill him, kill him, kill him.* It went on and on, its pace maddening, the rhythm entrancing, till Michael finally opened his eyes, blinking back to reality.

Gavin was already selecting his weapons. A medium sized, compartmented luggage case was lying open on his work bench. He pulled down his custom-built short-barreled AR15, collapsed the telescoping stock, and quickly removed the takedown pins, separating the upper from the lower and stowing them into the case with a rifle sound suppressor, followed by ten preloaded, thirty round 5.56 magazines. He then took down his suppressed USP 9mm, checking the silencer, and placed it into a custom fit foam insert in the other half of the case. Adding spare magazines and a pair of matching Smith and Wesson M&P 9mm's, he closed the canvas top and zipped the bag securely.

"Anything you want?" Gavin asked.

"I've got what I need," Michael smiled, gripping the sword.

"Fair enough."

Gavin pulled two molle tactical plate carriers, both outfitted with steel armor, down off the wall, checking over the various magazine kangaroo pouches and holsters attached to their fronts, before packing them away as well. Sure he had everything he needed, he grabbed the now quite heavy luggage case by its handle and headed out into the basement. Michael followed, sword sheathed, the secret door closing behind him.

****

Killion could see the famous Santa Monica Ferris wheel in the distance as he parked. He then headed down the boardwalk, making his way to the pier, finding Franklin and Mr. Nelson near the crowded carousel.

"So the Reverend actually came through. Perhaps my services were unnecessary?" Killion smiled as he greeted the men.

"On the contrary," Mr. Nelson said, "you're actually more necessary now than ever."

"As you said earlier," Franklin added, "McNamara may have expressed an interest in keeping it for himself. Our plan to bring the key to us by abducting the families of the two men we suspected to be in possession of the relic was viable, but with the man, Gavin, and his wife dead, our only worry rests in Thirteen. But, McNamara claims his man will have the key tomorrow, that the girl revealed its location before she died."

"Sorry," Killion frowned, "but I think I must have misheard you. You said the hunter and his wife are dead?"

Franklin pulled his cell from his pocket and selected a picture message, "McNamara forwarded this to me this morning. It's him, the hunter, Gavin, dead at the hands of the Reverend's men.

Killion studied the picture, the tattoos, the way the blood spread on the floor: it looked convincing. But there was one inconsistency in the Reverend's story.

"Excuse me for what I'm about to say, but the Reverend is a liar," Killion stated matter-of-factly, "Gavin's wife is not dead. She arrived last night, unconscious, but very much alive. She's here, in Los Angeles."

****

Ashley woke, groggy and disoriented, the sedative used to abduct her wearing off. The room was unfamiliar, the bed not her own. She stood and looked out the window. The street was far below, the smell of salt water was in the air. She gazed into the distance, her vision a little blurry. Was that the ocean on the horizon?

Suddenly, her stomach churned. Ashley scrambled, searching for the bathroom, rushing to the toilet and vomiting.

She wet a rag and wiped her face, tears streamed down her cheeks. But as she stood there, lost and alone, she realized that her tears were not purely from her fear. She knew Gavin was resourceful: he would find her. The room she woke in was luxurious and she deduced that whomever had taken her had little interest in harming her, why the extravagance if she was simply going to end up dead. No, her tears in that moment were tears of joy, for in the darkness, on the verge of succumbing to despair, she had vomited, an unfamiliar twinge in her stomach. She didn't need a pregnancy test to tell her that this was morning sickness, she was sure of it.

****

Gavin returned from upstairs, buttoning up a white collared short-sleeved shirt over a colorful vintage t-shirt. He then picked up his USP 45 from where he'd left it the night before and tucked it into the back of his dark washed jeans, pulling the shirt down to hide the grip of the pistol.

"I loaded your case in the car," Michael said. "We should go."

Gavin nodded, pulling his cell phone and raising it to speak, "Hey, Jamie..."

"Gavin, good to hear from you; Kayla's freaking out, Ashley hasn't answered any of her texts, everything ok?"

"Not really, no. I need your help."

"What happened?"

"Too much to explain now," Gavin sighed. "Will you be around tonight?"

"Of course."

"Ok, I'll see you then, I'm on my way."

"You're coming to Chicago?"

"Yeah."

"Kayla will be so happy to see Ashley," Jamie said relieved.

"That's why I need your help actually," Gavin replied, "Ashley won't be with me; she's gone, someone took her."

****

Ashley tested the knob on the door, but it was locked. She looked around the suite and spotted a phone at a small work desk, picking it up. Just as she'd expected: no dial tone. She searched through the empty, clean drawers at the desk and found a phone book for Los Angeles and the surrounding area.

California? she wondered.

She was startled by a knock at the door. Ashley approached cautiously as a voice called from outside.

"Miss," it said, with a British accent, "I have a fresh change of clothes for you. I'm opening the door."

Ashley scanned the room, looking for something she could use for self defense. She hurried to the kitchenette and searched through drawers till she found what she wanted: a paring knife.

You'll have to do.

The door opened slowly. She held the knife behind her back. A man entered, early thirties and finely dressed, a large shopping bag from Macy's in his hand. He set the bag down on the bed and turned to face her.

"There are toiletries in the washroom, a clean toothbrush, the kitchen is fully stocked. Did you sleep well?" he asked politely.

Ashley readied the knife, then rushed him, the blade raised, ready to strike. She slashed, but missed as he dodged to the left.

"Please, Ashley," he pleaded, "I know you are confused, but let me explain."

"Explain what?" she spat back in frustration.

"Your husband, Gavin, had us bring you here for your protection. He learned of a threat against the two of you and he needed to ensure your safety."

"Why didn't he make sure I was safe himself? He's more than capable. And that's another thing, where is he then!"

"There was no time, we had to improvise. And for that, I apologize. But Gavin is on his way."

"What is this all about, what's this threat?"

"It's the key, Triton's men came for the key."

"What key?" Ashley argued.

"You don't know?" he asked calmly, his hands raised as he tried to earn her trust.

"I have no clue."

"Think back, to New York. Triton had a key, an old key, what happened to it?"

She thought for a moment, trying to recall the chaotic events that took place over the short span of a week five years ago. So much happened so quickly, then she remembered: the old key from the sacrifices. Gavin had found it in that awful hidden room in Triton's office. She'd last seen it with Jamie, just as he slipped it into his pocket before their assault on the hospital.

"My brother-in-law has it, in Chicago," Ashley said, lowering the knife.

"That's good," the man smiled, "at least it's safe. Gavin will be here soon. Please, accept these clothes and the safety of this penthouse. We will protect you."

Ashley watched as the man slipped out the door, the lock clicking as it closed. She set the knife on the counter and emptied the bag out onto the bed with a reluctant sigh. She checked the sizes on a selection of nice shirts, a pair of stylish jeans, and a cute summer dress, then looked over several sets of underwear and some trendy flip flops. Satisfied, but confused, she chose an outfit and headed for the bathroom, turning on the shower and getting undressed.

****

"Either the Reverend is a liar, or his man lied to him," Mr. Nelson grunted.

"Regardless, this lie is concerning," Franklin admitted. "I do not believe McNamara would knowingly lie to me in this instance. He wants so desperately for me to find him of worth and he understands that a lie of this magnitude would have its...*consequences*."

"Perhaps his man is the liar?" Killion reasoned. "But why say she's dead. Obviously he didn't find her there."

"She is not of consequence," Mr. Nelson answered.

"I beg to differ. She is possibly the greatest leverage we have," Killion replied.

They stood there for a long moment, staring at one another in silence. The crowd around them seemed to move in fast forward as they deliberated.

The silence was broken as Killion snapped his fingers, "What if Gavin is not dead, what if Gavin is the one in communication with the Reverend?"

"What makes you say that?" Mr. Nelson asked with furrowed brows.

"Because it's exactly what I would do if put in a similar situation."

Killion's phone rang and he turned away, one hand holding the phone up to speak, the other covering his ear, blocking out the noise around him. Franklin and Mr. Nelson looked on with interest.

"Are you sure, Edward?" Killion asked.

"Yes, quite. She told me the key was safe and in Chicago."

"Good. See that she is well cared for," Killion said, ending the call. "Gentlemen, the girl says the key is in Chicago. What would you like me to do?"

"Wait," Franklin ordered. "The key will find its way to McNamara and it will in turn be brought to me, whether by allegiance or force."

"And if Gavin is not dead and he recovers the key?"

"Then he will still bring the relic to us and exchange it for his wife."

"And Elizabeth, Thirteen's wife?"

"I've seen to it that Thirteen is reminded of where his power comes from. When he arrives, he'll be an incredible asset. I've never met a killer who was his equal."

"Till now, I assure you," Killion said disdainfully.

"What does that matter to you?" Mr. Nelson asked.

"Nothing, as long as I'm paid," Killion grinned. "Now if you don't mind, I want to speak to the hunter's wife, see if there is anymore she might know of the relic and its whereabouts. As for the second part of your plan?"

"Once we have the key," Franklin smirked, "The Order will be of no use to me. You will be free to collect each Elder's *resignation*."

"And the price?" Killion asked, not so much a question as it was a reminder that he had high expectations.

"Five hundred thousand a head," Mr. Nelson confirmed, "a total of eight million USD for the complete extermination of The Order."

Killion nodded his approval and turned, beginning the walk to his car. He slipped his hands into his pants pockets. This was indeed the job he and his brother had been waiting for.

15

Gavin looked down at his watch: he and Michael had been driving for about three hours, leaving most of the morning, and Ohio, behind them as they crossed into Indiana, a large sign on the side of Route 30 West welcoming them to the State. They'd travelled in silence, the black Porsche C4 quickly traversing the miles between them and Chicago. Gavin felt a dark spiritual presence in the car. He couldn't see the demons that were Michael's companions; still, he knew they were there. But his discernment was outweighed by his drive to save Ashley. He accepted this partnership as a means to an end and he prayed that he was right, that this would end well. But the man in the driver's seat, was Thirteen, the greatest evil Gavin had ever faced. Heaven help him.

"How long till we reach Chicago?" Gavin said, shifting in the leather seat.

"Three hours, give or take," Michael replied.

The silence was broken.

"You haven't said much," Gavin mentioned, casually coaxing Michael into conversation.

"All I can think about is my wife and son. I'm sure you

understand."

Gavin nodded, he understood perfectly.

Michael took his eyes off the road for a moment, glancing at Gavin, the tattoos covering his arms, "Actually, I have a question for you, if you don't mind me asking?"

"Sure," Gavin replied.

"Five years ago, in the hospital, just before you detonated the bombs, you said you were ready to die, that death was just the beginning...*was* that true, that you were really ready to die?"

Gavin smiled, "Absolutely. I believe this life is only preparation for the life to come, eternal life, heaven. Death marks the end of life, but only the beginning of the journey."

"So there was nothing that you had to live for, nothing you would have missed?"

"That's just it, anything I have worth living for is also worth dying for, especially now, with Ashley. Life is more than what we have or don't have, it's about love. And what greater love is there than a man laying down his life for his friend, right?"

Michael furrowed his brow, "So if you could save Ashley, but it was a trade, *your* life for *hers*, you would do it?"

"Are you saying that's what will happen? Because I've trusted you so far, as I believe you've trusted me."

"No," Michael answered, "that's not what I'm saying, I just wondered. I feel the same way; I would give my life if it saved Elizabeth."

"Can I ask you something?" Gavin tried.

Michael nodded yes.

"Why kill Triton, what did you really have to gain? And don't say money..."

Michael thought for a moment before answering.

"I wanted his money, yes, for security, for his daughter and his grandchild, my family..."

"Wait," Gavin interrupted, laughing in disbelief, "Triton was your father-in-law? Talk about bad blood in the family!"

"Yes, he was," Michael sighed, "but there's more: I knew that if Triton ever had his way, he would not only destroy everything that you hold dear, but also what I treasure. His evil would have covered over everything, the good and the bad. I didn't want that for my son."

"So you felt like you were saving the world? Evil can't fight evil."

"I know," Michael laughed, recalling scripture from the New Testament, "just like when Jesus was accused of casting out demons in the name of Beelzebub, the book of Luke, chapter eleven."

Gavin turned his gaze out the window, watching the trees blur past, "I guess I shouldn't be surprised...the Bible says that even Satan knows the scriptures."

"I assure you," Michael chuckled, "I'm not the devil..."

"But you use his power. His demons even answer to you."

"I do and it comes at a price, but it's a long story."

"I've got time," Gavin replied, "about three hours."

****

"Leroy, it's McNamara. I need your help."

"Anything, my friend," old Leroy Klebitz replied.

"Delilah. Have her meet my man, Rocco, in Chicago. I need her to assure the safe recovery of the key."

"Why her? Don't you have hunters already in place in Chicago, can't they facilitate your plan?"

McNamara sighed, "Yes, but I do not want to allow any possible mistakes, not to mention hands in the cookie jar. I need the best and Delilah *is* the best!"

"But are you sure?" Leroy asked. "You know that where she is involved, people *will* die."

"I'm counting on it," the Reverend replied.

****

"Where to begin?" Michael thought aloud.

Gavin stared once again out the window, ready to hear Michael's story.

"I was born in Paris. My father is French; my mother, American. She spent the summers visiting family in the Parisian countryside. They met as teenagers, became young lovers and eventually married, buying a flat in Paris. My family also owns an impressive estate near Marseilles, many generations old, passed from heir to heir. My parents still live there, but I haven't spoken to them since I moved to the U.S."

Gavin's story was so different. He couldn't relate to a life of posh luxury. His family had just enough to get by, and sometimes not even that.

"As far as my relation to Triton," Michael continued, "my family has always been associated with him, acting as guardians of The Order. My father before me shared in my particular *powers*, as did my grandfather before him and so on, the same as it's been for centuries."

"By powers, you mean the *occult?*"

"Yes," Michael answered softly.

"So how did your family come into these powers, a pact with the devil?" Gavin chuckled.

"Not quite so cliché," Michael said, pausing as he thought. "It was considered an honor. Triton provided great wealth, long life...and respect. Guardians are feared. Their power is not to be taken lightly."

"But how did you receive your power to control demons?"

"Very simple: Triton was an archdemon, a general in Lucifer's army. He controlled his own minion. As part of our oath to The Order, Triton placed supernatural bonds between us and his hoard. Those of us who possessed a certain propensity could not only call on the demons, but channel their energy, bending it to our will to become..."

"Invincible," Gavin sighed.

"Precisely; how could I say no?"

"Don't you fear for your soul," Gavin asked, "fear eternal damnation?"

Michael sat in silence as he changed lanes, quickly overtaking a lumbering semi, "I've watched my family serve Triton, my father, grandfather, heard the stories of my great grandfather. I was told as a child that this was my birthright, but there has always been a darkness that clouded my thoughts, as much as I believed that I was part of a noble legacy, it came at a price. My grandfather, for all his power, all his wealth, died a self-loathing drunk, his past too haunting to live with. He drank himself to death. I fear the same for my father. When it came my time to serve Triton, I relished it, embraced the power afforded me as a member of the Tri-Six."

"So why kill Triton, the very man your forefathers pledged their allegiance?"

"You questioned whether or not I feared for my soul," Michael replied, "and the answer is yes. But not before I'd met Elizabeth. Before her, I had no other purpose, no other reason to live, except for what I'd been told and readied for my entire life: to serve Triton and The Order."

"So you killed Triton out of love for his daughter?"

"Yes and no. He knew of our relationship, gave it his blessing, made me his son, but to what end? My bond was still in servitude to a monster. As long as Triton lived, my soul, my legacy, was tied to an age-old bloodline. She made me see the truth. I hoped that killing Triton would make amends for the life I lived, the evil I'd done, that perhaps that act would grant my soul freedom from the pact."

"Only one path leads to salvation," Gavin smiled.

"I know," Michael answered. "I've seen the power of God first hand, fought against it, but I wonder, after all I've done, can I ever be truly forgiven?"

"There's only one way to find out," Gavin assured.

"I hope."

"So can I ask you another question?"

Michael nodded.

"If Triton was a centuries-old sleepwalker, how did he father a child?"

"His spirit was demon, but his body was flesh. He lived like a mortal, as his outer shell was just that of a man. He functioned as a man, but twisted and evil, possessed by a maddening archdemon."

"And is your wife, you know...*normal?*"

"She's not a sleepwalker as you call them," Michael grinned, "quite the opposite actually. She knew what her father was and was happy to see his delusions come to an end."

"So what about The Order?"

"I imagine they want me dead, the same as you, hence the reason our families have been taken. I too double-crossed The Order. In killing Triton, I also killed a part of The Order. In their weakened state, a new leader was selected, but there is uneasiness as their focus is unraveling. With Triton gone, their ties to the supernatural are gone as well, now only bureaucrats remain, the last remnants of a forgotten legend. The Order died with Triton. They are now nothing but a myth."

****

"Saba, I haven't heard from you in ages!" she cried excitedly as she answered her cell phone.

"My beautiful Delilah, can you hear me? Where are you, it's so loud!" Leroy said.

She smiled as she hurried across the busy London street, her long black hair flitting in the wind, her olive green eyes concealed behind dark designer sunglasses. A flowing trench coat hid her slender frame as well as the suppressed Sig Sauer 226 she carried holstered close to her ribs. The man she tracked was oblivious to the fact that she was on his tail, glancing over his shoulder as he stepped up to a bus stop, his fingers tightly clasping a fine leather attaché case.

"Sorry, Saba, it is very noisy here, much traffic," Delilah replied, her words accented by her Jewish heritage.

"Are you on a job?" he asked.

"Yes."

"I need your help with something very special, a delicate situation that requires your expertise."

"Where, Saba," she smiled, following her target onto a double-decker bus, watching the man sit, then taking the seat directly behind him as the bus pulled into traffic.

"Chicago, my dear."

"I'll be on the next plane, Saba...love you," Delilah said, hanging up her phone.

She quietly pulled the gun from its holster, placed the end of the suppressor against the vinyl seatback and pulled the trigger. The muffled gunshot sounded like a cough and the man slumped as he took a final labored breath.

The bus slowed and the doors opened as commuters climbed on and off. Quickly, she stood, slickly grabbing the attaché case unnoticed, and exited the bus, disappearing into the mix of tourists and Londoners on the busy sidewalk, Big Ben towering in the distance.

****

Michael pulled the Porsche to a stop: they needed gas. Gavin stepped from the car and headed for the gas station's restroom. Michael removed the nozzle and began filling up with premium.

There was a stillness in the air that made Michael uneasy. For even though his power had been returned, one thing was different: his mindset. He'd spent the last five years trying to forget about the events of New York City, running away from the legacy he'd unwillingly inherited. Michael longed to disappear with his wife and child, and that is just what he thought he'd accomplished. But his past remained, a constant, stinging reminder of the evil he'd done.

****

Gavin stared at his reflection in the restroom mirror. He was angry. But not because Ashley had been stolen away; no, it was the fact that her kidnapping didn't upset him more than it had and that terrified him so. Maybe the last eighteen hours hadn't fully sunk in and maybe when the fact that his wife was gone finally did click, he'd be reduced to a broken, teary victim. But as of yet, it felt like more of an adventure than a tragedy and that is what fueled his rage.

"Is this what you wanted, God, to place me with a killer, is this my *valley of the shadow of death*? I've done nothing but serve *You*, fight for *You*, stand up for *You* when people call me crazy because I pray to a God I can't see. Is this really it? And Ashley? How could *You* let this happen to her?"

Gavin slammed his hand down on the porcelain sink. Tears finally began to flow.

"Just tell me she's alright," he said.

But there was no response. He was alone in the bathroom. Though an unseen dark shadow loomed above the stalls.

"Joseph, I wish you were here. I know you could help me."

Still, he was alone.

And then, from somewhere deep inside, a calm settled over him. He knew exactly what it was. He'd felt it many times before. In his head, he heard the words he needed to hear. Whether it was miraculous, or simply his mind recalling the right words at this exact time, he clung to them.

And surely I am with you always, to the very end of the age.

"Matthew 28:20," he said aloud, his anger subsiding, a smile chasing away his fears.

****

Gavin returned to the car, two bottles of ice-cold water in his hands. Michael finished pumping gas.

"Here," Gavin smiled, "I got one for you, paid for the fill-up too."

"Thanks," Michael replied, twisting off the cap and gulping down half the bottle.

"So I figure we've got about another hour before we reach the city," Gavin said.

"Yeah. Are you sure your brother-in-law can help, that he still has the key?"

"I know Jamie," Gavin explained, "he's sentimental. He'd never have let the key go."

"Right then," Michael nodded, "where's the restroom?"

Gavin pointed toward the convenience store, "It's in the back, next to the slushy machine."

Michael headed for the entrance to the gas station, the automatic sliding doors opening as he approached. The cashier nodded a greeting as he passed. He spotted the slushy machines and awkwardly slipped past a heavyset man who was filling a large, clear, plastic-domed cup to the brim, Michael's nose assaulted by the oddly mixed smell of sour body odor and marijuana.

Some people, he thought, pausing at the restroom door before entering.

The bathroom was filthy. His shoes stuck to the floor as he stepped up to the urinal. The sound of his zipper echoed in the small, stifled room. Michael stared at the dirty grout between the grime covered tiles as he relieved himself. Suddenly, there was laughter coming from the stall to his right, at first quiet, but growing louder into a sickly cackle.

"Are we having second thoughts, Thirteen?" a voice asked.

Michael quickly zipped up and placed his palm flat on the stall door, pausing before slamming it open. Three small demons clambered precariously on the toilet, their taloned fingers clacking on the porcelain.

"No," he stated with conviction.

"Well, it sure looks like it," one said.

"And what's all this talk about forgiveness?" another asked. "You don't need forgiveness when your power will never let you die."

"I was just making conversation," Michael replied. "I need the hunter to trust me. He'll lead me to the key, I'll kill him, and then I'll get my family back."

"A man can only serve one master," the third squealed, "be careful where your mind wanders. You have an agreement, an agreement that has been upheld on our master's end. But you've crossed him once already...this is your second chance. Maybe it's *his* forgiveness you should be worrying about?"

"You know where my loyalty lies," Michael barked, patting the left chest of his suit coat, his mask tucked away just beneath.

"Regardless," the first demon spoke once more, "do not forget. Without us, you'll lose your power, and without your power, you'll never save your family. You *need* us."

"I'm aware of that, thank you," he said.

"By the way," another demon spoke, "you're new friend was in here, balling his eyes out because God had let his innocent little wife be taken away."

"Really?"

"Yeah," the demon laughed. "He's pathetic, blaming God for his troubles. You'll end up just like him if you don't man up and kill somebody soon."

Michael turned and left the restroom, the demons' laughter fading as the door closed behind him. Gavin was already in the car as he pulled his keys from his pocket and opened the driver's door.

"You ok?" Gavin asked. "You look a little pale."

"I'm fine," Michael answered, slipping on his dark sunglasses as he swallowed the lump in his throat.

"Are you ok, Gavin? Do you need to talk about Ashley?"

Gavin thought for a moment, wondering why Michael would ask that question right then and there. After all, it wasn't every day that he yelled at God in a dirty truck stop restroom.

"You know," he said, "I'm good. I just needed a moment alone to sort my thoughts, but I'm good."

"Then let's get going," Michael replied, "we're almost there."

16

Reverend McNamara paced the floor in his tower office high above the Sunrise Chapel. All he could hope is that Rocco would have the key soon. And with the addition of Delilah, he couldn't fail. She would guarantee a successful retrieval.

He stared out over the Los Angeles cityscape. When Triton led The Order, there was peace amongst the members. But Franklin was dictatorial, wanted everything for himself, everything done his way.

When Delilah delivers the key to me, then I'll have all the power. The Order will be mine to bend to my will, he reasoned.

The intercom on the phone at his desk crackled to life, "Your wife is on line three, Reverend."

"Hello, Barbara," he said answering the phone.

"I thought you were taking today off?" she said sweetly, almost pouting.

"What do you want, Barbara? I can tell by your tone you want something."

"Just your company," she replied. "I've been stuck in the house alone all day."

"How much is it?" he barked dryly.

"Fine," she conceded, her sweetness disappearing, daggers in her voice. "Less than last time, only forty-five thousand; but it's a beautiful convertible and I'll let you drive it too."

"Sure, sure," he sighed. "Hey, I won't be home till late."

"As always," Barbara chided before hanging up the phone.

McNamara replaced the handset on the receiver and slumped down in his plush leather executive chair. He remembered a time when she may have actually loved him. If it was ever for more than his money, he was never sure, but she was happy once, respectful. Now, she seemed like a rebellious teenager; and he, the witless father, doing everything to keep her from hating him, never sure if he'd be loved in return. He never believed that their difference in age was a factor, that he was still young enough at heart to keep their relationship exciting, but his hours invested at the church and the mounting pressures of The Order, he too was no longer himself. He'd become angry and controlling, and knew it.

But soon the key will be mine and I'll put an end to Franklin and his nonsense. Yes, soon, he assured himself.

****

Barbara signed the last of the paperwork and handed the finance manager at the dealership a check for her new car. Digging through her purse for her insurance card, she came across the napkin with Killion's number scrawled across it. She bit her lip as her eyes widened, she just spent a lot of her husband's money and she was ready for some fun.

****

"Were you able to reach your granddaughter?" McNamara asked, his phone pressed to his ear.

"Of course," Leroy answered over the line. "She will be in the States by this evening. She's flying straight to Chicago to meet Rocco. She just needs to know when and where."

"Alright," the Reverend grinned. "I'll talk to Rocco and come up with a good place."

"I'll let you know when she lands, my friend."

"Thank you Leroy. Truly, thank you!"

****

Killion's cell phone vibrated in his pocket. He briefly took his eyes off the dancer in front of him just long enough to answer.

"Hello," he said, yelling over the roaring music in the club.

"Is this Terry?"

"Yes it is, who is this?" he said, his eyes fixed on the strippers gyrating hips.

"It's Barbara," she replied happily.

"Barbara...Barbara?" he questioned, playing it cool.

"You know, from the coffee shop the other day, remember?" she explained, disappointment trickling in her words.

He snapped his fingers like it had just come to him, playing the part perfectly, "Barbara! How could I forget someone as pretty as you, how are you?"

"I'm good."

"Sorry, Barbara. I can't hear you, just a moment," he said, standing, swigging down the last of his cocktail, then throwing a fifty at the dancers feet.

Killion smiled as she turned her back to him and slowly bent down to pick it up, one last tease before he left. He grabbed his suit coat and headed out the door, his eyes adjusting as he stepped from the dark club into the bright California sun.

"That's better," he said, the music no longer a hindrance.

"Where are you?" she laughed.

"Business lunch," he replied, "one of those trendy restaurants, where the music is too loud to actually discuss business."

"So you've eaten then?" she wondered.

"Actually no," Killion said. "That was the plan, but I'd much rather enjoy the company of a beautiful young woman than eat lunch with my trite associates. Where shall we meet?"

"Do you know Locanda Veneta?"

"I do," he smiled.

"Great! I can be there in about a half of an hour, sound good?"

"It's a date."

****

Franklin and Mr. Nelson sat in uncomfortable silence. The office was dark, the blinds drawn. A computer's monitor on Franklin's desk webcast a view of another office, a man sitting in front of tall bookcases, a mammoth, hand-carved ivory-mantled fireplace centered behind him. His words were strong, almost harsh, yet controlled, as he spoke. In many ways, the man reminded Franklin of Triton, except for his French accent.

"Gentlemen," he said eloquently, "I trust you have good news for me?"

"Sir," Franklin replied awkwardly, "we are making great progress."

"What of the key?"

"We will have it soon, within the next twenty-four hours, if all goes according to plan."

The man did not respond right away. Mr. Nelson sipped nervously from a glass of water.

Franklin cleared his throat, "I assure you, The Order is doing all it can. I have the asset in place, acquiring the key as we speak. The plan is operating like clockwork."

"Killion's designs are always perfect. That's why I sent him to you. Tell me, does The Order suspect they are coming to an end?"

"No, Sir. They assume the key will be for us, would be ours...if Triton had not been so reckless."

"Don't blame Triton for your incapability. The key is but a means. Triton locked away all the secrets of The Order for too long. Now that he is gone, we will know more than he desired for us. The world will be ours."

"Pardon my asking," Franklin frowned, "but how can I know that upon delivery of the key, you will not simply eliminate me, as you've already asked that I dismantle The Order's eldership? For The Order to achieve what we dream, you will need America in coalition with the other nations who have already pledged their allegiance."

"You Americans, you assume so much, that the world could never operate without your involvement. The world managed to get on for thousands of years before you rebelled against England; surely, we can shape the future of the world without you. The United States is no longer relevant. The world is what is relevant. The old Order must pass away, Triton's Order, to enable the rise of a new Order, a World Order, all nations united under the power that Triton selfishly held for himself."

Franklin swallowed hard. Mr. Nelson was pale as a ghost.

"Get me the key, and I promise, you will have a place in the new Order. Au revior, gentleman."

The screen went blank. Franklin slammed his fist down on the top of his finely crafted desk.

"Call Killion, get a status report. We must speed things up. I want the key now."

****

Killion shook his head in disgust, answering his cell phone as he headed into the Italian restaurant where he'd arranged to meet Barbara. Mr. Nelson was on the other end, speaking quickly, tension obvious in his voice.

"What happens if things don't go according to plan?" he asked.

"As I've explained, everything has been accounted for. McNamara's man will acquire the key and as soon as he arrives in L.A., I will intercept the package and deliver it directly to you. Gavin is dead, which saves me the trouble."

"What about Thirteen?"

"That is exactly why I secured his family. If he were to get the key from McNamara's man before I, he will simply bring it to us and make the trade. They are collateral."

"And you know this will work?"

"Don't worry," Killion said, smiling as he spotted Barbara sitting at a table, "everyone will get what they want."

He hung up the phone as he knelt and greeted her with a kiss on her cheek. She blushed, biting her lip teasingly.

"Business?" she asked, watching him slip his phone into his suit pocket.

"Yes," he said, taking a seat across from her, "investors are afraid our new project is running behind, but I assured them we're still operating within the proposed timeline."

"Wow," Barbara laughed. "And what exactly do you do?"

"Acquisitions," he answered with a wink. "So what's good here?"

Killion opened the menu as he quickly changed the topic. She did the same, scanning over the lunch offerings.

"I like the zucchini risotto, but the pollo mattone is pretty good too."

"Hmmm," he said thoughtfully, "it all sounds good, but I think I'm more interested in something that's not on the menu."

She blushed, feeling his burning gaze as he took her hand in his, "I'm married."

"I know."

"And that doesn't bother you?"

He paused before answering, "You clever girl, such a tease. You flirt, gain my interest, only to act innocent upon receiving my advancements. But you know as well as I why you are here, right now at this table, with me and not your beloved: you're bored. And I for one would love to *entertain* you."

"Why don't we get lunch to go?" she smiled, biting her lip.

"Let's."

****

Ashley stretched in bed, her mouth widening into a yawn. She'd slept for most of the morning. Though trusting that she was in a guarded room at Gavin's request, she still felt like a prisoner. The room was very nice, nicer than any she'd ever stayed in on vacation, but the door was locked and she was confined within these finely decorated walls.

She stood and slipped into her jeans, then headed to the kitchen for a snack. The sun was high in the sky. Bright light shone through the large windows in the suite. She looked out at the ocean in the distance, then realized that the window was really a sliding door which led out to a balcony. The warm breeze caressed her face and she could smell salt in the air. Looking down, she figured she was about twelve stories up, the top floor of whatever building she was in. Ashley decided it was a resort, spotting a luxurious swimming pool below encircled by bikini clad sunbathers.

Suddenly, a sound caught her attention, a whimper from the balcony to her left. She hadn't realized it till just now, but a woman sat on the floor, her back pressed against the railing, her knees tucked to her chest, her face buried in her hands as she cried softly.

"Hey, you OK?" Ashley asked, feeling sorry for the woman.

The woman sighed and dried her eyes. She thought she was alone.

"I'm sorry," she replied, standing and reaching for the handle on the sliding door, "but I can't talk to you."

"Wait, why?" Ashley asked with concern.

"He won't let me. He said he'd kill my son if I talked to anyone."

"Who's…*he?*"

"Edward, his name is Edward."

17

Michael pulled the Porsche to a stop in front of Kayla and Jamie's home in Lincoln Park, a wealthy division north of downtown Chicago. It was late afternoon. The sun's light cast long shadows as the trees that lined the street created a dark canopy above.

"How do you want to handle this?" Gavin asked.

"We tell them what we need and move on."

"No, I mean about your identity, that you're Thirteen. They think you died five years ago in New York."

"Well, we'll let that come out if need be, but for all intent and purpose, I am and always will be Michael Laurent, let's stick to that."

"Alright," Gavin agreed as he stepped from the car, stretched, and then shut the door.

The two men stepped up on the porch, but before Gavin could ring the bell, the front door swung open. Kayla stood wide-eyed, a worried expression accompanying her greeting.

"Thank God you're here," she said, hugging Gavin, "but where's

Ashley, Jamie told me you said she was missing?"

"Yeah, Kay, but I think she's safe," he replied. "And this is Michael: his family is missing too. Where's Jamie?"

"He'll be down in a minute. He just got home from work and was taking a shower. Let's go to the dining room. It's nice to meet you Michael, just wish it was under better circumstances."

Michael shook her outstretched hand and then followed her and Gavin into the house. It was a strange feeling, being welcomed into the home of people who had nearly died at his hands just a few short years ago. He felt as if he shouldn't be there, that it was wrong. And now, he didn't want to bring chaos into their lives.

"Uncle Gavin," a small, shrill voice screamed as little Marley ran up to them, her blonde curls bouncing with each bounding stride.

Gavin caught her as she leapt, raising her up and kissing her on the cheek, "Hey sweetie, look at you!"

"Honey, inside voice," Kayla urged. "Mommy just put Ethan down for a nap."

"Ok, mommy," she laughed, slipping from Gavin's arms and running off to play.

Kayla offered the men seats at the table, then headed for the kitchen and returned with two glasses of ice water. Jamie joined them just as they were settling in. His hair was wet and slicked back from his shower.

"Gavin," he smiled, "good to see you, and..."

"Michael," he said, introducing himself, standing to shake Jamie's outstretched hand, "Michael Laurent."

"Well, Michael Laurent, any friend of Gavin's is a friend of ours."

Michael smiled. For a moment, Jamie paused before sitting. There was something so familiar about this man. Jamie felt like he knew him, his posture, height, frame: he was sure he'd seen him before. But he pushed the feeling aside. One thing he never forgot was a face; it was a cop thing, and he'd definitely never seen Michael before.

"So tell us what's going on? You said Ashley was missing, but you don't seem overly worried?" Jamie prodded.

"Well, I guess it's the circumstances," Gavin answered, trying to think of how to begin. "We believe Ashley, as well as Michael's wife and son, has been taken for a ransom."

"This is about money?" Kayla questioned.

"No," Michael said, shaking his head slightly, "the kidnapper wants something else, valuable yes, but not money."

"Then what?" Jamie frowned.

Gavin looked at Michael before replying. He nodded encouragingly.

"Triton's key."

****

"Don't go," Ashley said in a hushed voice, trying to gain the woman's trust. "At least tell me your name."

"Elizabeth," she replied, disappearing through the door as it smoothly closed.

****

"The old rusted key from the sacrifice," Jamie grunted, "didn't Thirteen tell us it was worthless?"

"Apparently that's not entirely true," Gavin said cautiously, "it just wasn't of worth to him."

"But Triton is dead," Kayla reasoned, "so who would want the key and why would they take Ashley?"

Gavin sighed, *here goes nothing!*

"Five years ago, in New York City, when we first met, I was a demon hunter. I worked and trained with Joseph. We fought Triton and his demonic forces; however, what I didn't know, was that the network of what I thought was comprised of demon hunters, was possibly, in all actuality, a group of contract killers."

151

"Hitmen?" Jamie huffed in disbelief.

"So Joseph misled you into working as an assassin?" Kayla questioned, her sarcasm all but hidden.

"Well, yes and no..."

"It can't be both," Jamie countered.

"The organization who funded Joseph and the other guilds of demon hunters was a partnership of silent investors. I never knew who gave Joseph the orders, but I believe the jobs came down through this partnership. How Joseph determined what jobs he gave to me, I also do not know. But, I also believe that the targets Joseph accepted were truly demonic, in many cases sleepwalkers, just like we encountered in New York. By being selective, Joseph remained in good graces with the investors while also affording him the finances necessary to train and supply me as well as stay close to Triton. Joseph protected me by never accepting targets who were not a supernatural enemy."

"Here's where it gets confusing," Michael continued.

"It gets more confusing than that?" Kayla smirked.

"This partnership of investors calls themselves The Order, but they're not alone. They're members of an international collective, a collective once headed by Triton. So Gavin, though working against Triton, was also working in effect for Triton. I believe this was ironically Triton's way of keeping an eye on Joseph. Triton believed he was invincible, but still secretly feared his greatest adversary."

"So it was all a game? Joseph and Triton both knew what each other was doing, yet allowed each other to continue? It doesn't make sense," Jamie said, looking at Michael, "and how do you know all this?"

"There's something about me you must know," Michael decided, reaching reluctantly into the inner pocket on the chest of his suit coat.

"Michael..." Gavin warned.

"No, they need to know."

Slowly he pulled out a tightly folded black cloth and set it carefully on the table top, an eye slit and several stitches visible. They recognized it instantly: Thirteen's mask. Jamie jumped up from his chair and punched

Michael squarely in the jaw, sending him tumbling backwards, Jamie's fist aching from the force of the strike.

****

Ashley needed to know more. Why would Edward be so kind to her, yet threaten this woman and her son? She hurried back in to the room and raced to the front door, jiggling the handle, but finding it still locked. Her mind was spinning, so may questions.

Gavin wouldn't have done this? Am I really safe? God help me!

She headed back to the balcony and looked across to where she'd seen Elizabeth. She gauged the distance, about six feet from railing to railing. The raised architecture on the building's façade looked like it would be enough to climb on if only she could find a good place to grip and get a foothold.

Carefully, she swung her leg over the railing, followed by the other, and tested the small ledge: it was just wide enough that she could fit her toes. Ashley took a deep breath, then began shimmying her way across the gap. It was such a short span, yet felt a mile long as she managed each terrifying shuffle of a step.

Ashley focused on the railing, inching closer, till finally, it was within reach and she took hold of it, quickly clambering to the safety of the balcony.

You're such an idiot, she told herself, looking down at the ground far below.

She peeked into the room. From the sliding glass door, she could see a young boy sitting on the floor in front of the television, a video game controller in his hands. On the couch behind him sat Elizabeth curled up, her eyes red, teary.

Quietly, she slid open the door and raised her finger to her lips as she saw the woman's startled reaction. The boy hardly looked away from his game.

"What are you doing?" Elizabeth pleaded, "you're going to get us all killed."

"It's ok, my names Ashley," she whispered calmly. "This Edward has me locked in my room as well. What is going on?"

"At first, he was so nice. But something must have happened and he turned on me. He said if I tried to speak to anyone, he'd kill us. I think we're being held ransom. My family is very wealthy. I think the kidnapper is expecting a payout." Elizabeth replied.

"My husband and I are far from wealthy," Ashley reasoned, "we just have enough as it is, so I don't figure that's the case."

"Well what then?"

"Edward asked me about a key, an old key. I told him where it was because he had me convinced my husband had me brought here for my safety as well, he said he was working with my husband."

"Where's your husband now?" Elizabeth asked.

"Searching for me, I'm sure."

"Well, whoever would do this is crazy. They obviously don't know what my husband is capable of. I know he'll find us, I'm just so scared, for my son, more than anything.

"Yeah, my husband is a little over the top, kind of takes everything to the extreme. But if you really care about your son, then we can't hang around here waiting to be rescued like the princess on his video game. We need to get out of here."

"The doors are locked. How are we going to get out of here, and besides, if we managed to get out of here, what would we do? We're all alone, in Los Angeles, no money, no transportation..."

"We can't allow ourselves to be victims," Ashley said clenching her fists with determination. "Does your room phone dial out?"

"I already tried, it goes right to Edward."

"He brought me clean clothes and food, does he do that for you?"

"Yes."

"Then tonight, when it's dark, I'll sneak back over here. You call Edward on the phone and tell him your son is hungry and you're out of food. He'll never expect me to be here. The two of us can take him!"

"No," Elizabeth frowned. "He won't believe that. He only just restocked the kitchen this afternoon."

"Well then tell her Cain is sick, really sick. What do you think?"

"That's better," Elizabeth sighed, "but I don't know that he'll believe me."

"He has to," Ashley replied. "Have faith."

Ashley smiled as she headed back out onto the balcony. She was proud of her plan and the excitement of it all was going to her head. Gavin had really rubbed off on her.

"Are you sure it'll work?" Elizabeth questioned.

"Trust me," Ashley encouraged, "we can do this."

****

As Michael climbed back to his feet, Jamie raced from the room, returning with a 12 gauge shotgun he'd kept hidden on top of the kitchen cupboards. He pumped a round into the chamber as he raised it to his shoulder. Michael stared down the barrel calmly, his eyes fixed on Jamie.

With his hands raised, Michael righted the wooden dining chair and sat back down at the table, "Please, I'm not the same man I was then. Things were so different for me, but I've changed, my mindset, my life."

Kayla stepped behind Jamie and gently took hold of his arms, coaxing him to lower his aim. She could hear it in Michael's voice, he wasn't the same man.

"You have a lot to explain!" Jamie barked.

"Yes," Michael replied, "more than I can amend, and I'm sorry, for your sake, that you have become involved in this situation, my life, I wish you could still think of me as dead, or rather Thirteen as dead, because he is to me. But just as Ashley has been taken, so has my wife, Elizabeth, and my son, Cain. I want them back and I will do anything I must to see them returned to me."

"Would that include lying to us, so that you can gain our trust only to kill us in our sleep? Don't think I've forgotten that dark, rot hole of a holding cell you kept me in, and the things you said...I know I haven't!" Jamie argued.

"I'm armed," Michael replied softly. "And if my intent were to kill you and take the key, you'd be dead already. I am here for your help, nothing more."

Jamie crossed his arms defiantly, leaning back in his chair, the shotgun now sitting on the table, "Why should I help you? Gavin and Ashley are family, *and* they never tried to kill me."

"On the contrary," Michael grinned, "I had every opportunity to kill you, all of you, and never acted on it. I let you all live. I lost a part of myself to the chaos that was Thirteen, but that is history now. I did what I had to do then in order to provide the life I wanted for my family, and I must do it once again to save them."

"So you need Triton's key to trade for Ashley and your family," Kayla asked, quickly changing the subject. "When and where will you be making the exchange?"

"We still don't know for sure who has them," Gavin answered, "but we have managed to convince someone by the name of *Big Mac* that I'm dead. He thinks I'm really one of his lackeys. All I have to do is tell him that I have the key and he'll tell us where to meet him. We continue the charade, get to Big Mac, and he'll lead us right to Ashley and Michael's family. So, Jamie...all we need is the key."

Jamie looked at Kayla, then eyed Michael reluctantly before standing and heading for his study. The room was neatly organized, everything in its place. He passed his desk and stopped, staring up at an ornately carved wooden cross that hung centered on the wall, tall windows on each side. He vividly remembered pulling it down off the crumbling plaster walls of Joseph's study, the remains of what was once a beautiful monastery hidden deep in upstate New York woodland. He smirked with fondness as he carefully raised it off the nail that held it and flipped the cross over. And there it was, Triton's key, resting in a hollow on the back of the weather-worn relic. Jamie took it gripping it tight, then hung the cross back on the wall.

As he returned, silence fell over them as they sat at the dining room table. Gavin looked on nervously: never had something so inconsequential meant so much to him.

"May I?" Michael asked, his hand outstretched.

Jamie hesitated, then laid the key in Michael's palm. Michael closed his eyes, a forgotten energy surging through him, his limbs suddenly warm, tingly, electrified.

A voice whispered in his head, "You have it, kill them…"

Michael ignored the voice, picturing his wife and son safe in his arms.

"Again it spoke, raspy, enraged, "Kill them now, before they kill you, Thirteen!"

As he opened his eyes, they fell on Kayla. Little Marley had reentered the room and hopped up on her mother's lap. He thought again of Elizabeth and Cain, the pain nearly unbearable.

"Here," he said, passing the key to Gavin, "you hold on to it. It burdens me too much to touch it."

Gavin took it, examined the old Latin etchings on its side, and then slipped it into his pocket. Jamie couldn't believe it: Michael had kept his word, at least for the moment. He half expected a fight once Michael had the key. Maybe he had changed, maybe Thirteen did die in New York and Michael lived on, reborn from the ashes.

18

Delilah watched Chicago pass below the plane, looking out the oval window on the port side of the red, white and blue tailed Boeing 777 as it circled into its final approach at O'Hare International.

Within minutes, the jumbo jet landed, its wheels screeching as they made contact with the tarmac. The plane slowly taxied around the airport, finally docking at Terminal 5. Exiting the craft was in itself as much a grueling venture as was an unplanned flight stateside, her last minute first-class ticket out of Heathrow a *£5400* expense as she rushed in haste to traverse the Atlantic.

She worked her way through the stifling congestion of immigrations much faster than the other foreigners seeking admittance to America, smiling as she handed security her Israeli passport, the man focusing more on her ruby lips than the important document in his hand, not even bothering to ask a single question before adding his stamp to the pages. Next, Delilah navigated the impetuous flow of sluggish passengers lugging their carry-ons, waiting for their checked baggage to appear. Her ears perked at every voice she overheard, a lingual buffet where Cantonese and German, Spanish, French, and just about any other globe-spanning dialect imaginable mashed and mingled into a chaotic, panic-inducing anthem. She watched as a wife greeted her husband with a kiss, apparently returning home from an extended overseas business trip. A group of Asian tourists snapped pictures to mark their first time in the U.S., some holding camera phones at arm's length, straining to catch a self portrait at the bustling airport, quickly uploading the photos to mobile media sites for all their friends to see. She quickly found her luggage at the baggage claim, a single large suitcase, rich brown leather with gold stitching.

Customs, like immigration, was also no problem. Again, the security seemed more interested in her alluring smile and silky olive skin than anything she may have packed in her bag from London. The man skimmed her declaration form and passed her through.

From there, officially accepted into the United States, Delilah sought out the ladies' room, her single bag in tow, taking the escalator up to the second level concourse. A sign led her to the nearest restroom and upon entering; she peered beneath the stall doors, searching for feet. Surprisingly, she was alone.

Perfect, she thought.

She quickly chose the stall furthest from the entrance and let the suitcase rest on top of the toilet's tank, then turned to lock the stall door before unzipping her luggage.

Inside the expensive case was an aluminum lined, padded wooden box reminiscent of a humidor, as well as some designer clothes, her makeup bag, and a set of hair curlers. The weight inside the box shifted to one end as it was handled. Delilah removed the lid, dumping the contents on top of her neatly folded clothing, then picked up the hair curlers, flipped over the container and removed the bottom panel, revealing a secret compartment. Hidden amongst the wiring for the heating element was the frame of her Sig Sauer 226.

Delilah retrieved the grip and set it down next to the slide, sound suppressor and loaded magazine which all had been stowed in the box. She checked the barrel, guide rod and recoil spring and then slid it onto the frame of the pistol, finally twisting the suppressor onto the threaded barrel. Lastly, she picked up the 9mm magazine and fed it into the grip. Pulling back on the slide, Delilah chambered a round, then slipped the fully assembled gun into a custom fabricated holster worn tight against her body, hidden beneath a chic cashmere poncho.

She made her way to the monorail, garnering attention from every man she passed, her red-soled heels clicking with each step, their eyes drawn to her long legs wrapped in breathtakingly tight skinny jeans.

"Saba, I have arrived in Chicago," Delilah said, her cell phone raised to her ear as she rode the airport monorail, or *ATS* as it was noted on the signs, to the main terminal. "I'm ready to contact McNamara's man."

"I have his phone number right here," Leroy replied, "his name is Rocco, are you ready?"

The ATS stopped in front of the Hilton Hotel which towered over the metro station, the hotel itself part of O'Hare.

"Yes, Saba," she replied as she stepped off the train, pausing to look up at the luxury hotel, then following the signs directing her to the Blue Line Metro.

He gave her the information and she thanked him, then hung up. Fortunately for her, she'd just caught the next train to Chicago. She took a seat and felt the car lurch as it started and then listened to the clacking of the wheels as they moved along the rails. Her phone was still in her hand, her fingers tapping away, dialing the number her grandfather had provided. She wanted to get right to business.

****

Gavin was startled by the unfamiliar ring of the phone in his pocket. He pulled it out and looked at the screen.

"Is it *Big Mac*?" Michael asked.

"No, a new number...hold on. Yeah?" he said as he answered, trying to imitate Rocco's Bostonian diction.

"Is this Rocco?" a woman's voice asked from the other end.

"Yeah," Gavin shrugged.

"McNamara has brought me in to avoid any complications and ensure a quick retrieval of the package."

"*McNamara*, huh? And who are you?"

"Delilah," she replied. "We need to meet and come up with a plan.

160

Do you know the location of the package?"

"Yeah," Gavin answered, thinking quickly, trying to match her serious demeanor, "it's in Chicago."

"I know," she replied, irritated by his unprofessionalism, "I just landed at O'Hare."

"You're here, in the city?"

"Yes, I'm on the Blue Line now. What is your status, you haven't made contact yet have you?"

"I've been...uh...staking out the *location* and have observed the *targets*. We definitely need to discuss the *operation*," Gavin said, holding back a laugh.

"Where should we meet?"

"Um..." Gavin hesitated, watching the unapproving faces looking at him from around the table, "someplace public and inconspicuous, how about Wrigley Field, by the Harry Caray statue?"

"*Harry Caray?*"

"Yeah, he's a legendary baseball commentator, you know, *Hey,*" Gavin said, awkwardly impersonating Caray's uniquely unmistakable voice, "*how about that!*"

There was a moment of dead silence. He wasn't sure that she hadn't hung up on him.

"Alright, I'll see you tonight. Give me two hours," she agreed, obviously irritated.

"How will I know who you are? Should we have some kind of pass phrase, or a verification code, or....*something?*"

"Are you serious?" Delilah laughed. "You must watch too many spy movies. Trust me, you'll *know* me when you see me."

She hung up. Gavin shook his head foolishly.

"I think she bought it; she thinks I'm Rocco."

"And you plan to do what when you meet her?" Kayla asked.

"Easy," Gavin grinned, confident they'd caught a break. "We're going to trap her and find out what she knows. She'll lead us right to McNamara and The Order."

"You know there's a Cubs game tonight right? Wrigley Field will be a zoo!" Jamie pointed out.

"Exactly," Gavin explained. "You and Michael will be able to blend into the crowd, but still be able to keep an eye on me. Once I meet up with her, I'll suggest we go somewhere quieter and then we'll take her wherever we want."

"We need someplace secure we can hold her," Michael suggested, "and far from witnesses."

"What do you think, Mr. Policeman," Gavin joked, nodding at Jamie, "know where to take her?"

"Well, we're not making an arrest, so we don't dare take her to the station..."

"And you can't bring her here," Kayla stated.

"What about the park just east of the stadium?" Jamie wondered. "It's dense and no one would be there at night. When we're done, we can leave her there, it'll take forever for her to find her way out alone. We can jump on Lake Shore Drive and be gone before she could ever catch up."

"That's it then," Gavin decided. That's the plan."

****

Delilah studied the city transit map that hung on the interior wall of the metro car, committing the station names to memory. At the same time, she viewed various maps of Chicago on her phone, locating Wrigley Field and determining her route. She decided to ride the Blue Line into downtown, switching over to the Red Line at Jackson St and then getting off at Addison. She'd be right there at the stadium.

Now, she thought, *what's my exit in case it's a trap?*

She searched the map, looking for a place she could take Rocco. This wasn't the first time she'd planned a meet under similar circumstances and truth be told, there was always the chance of a trap, a double-cross.

There, she smiled to herself as she found what she wanted, *Graceland Cemetery. If you have a tail, we'll use the L train to lose it and we'll use the cemetery as our cover.*

****

Killion and Barbara burst through the exquisite front door of the McNamara mansion in Beverly Hills. Their lips met kiss after kiss, their bodies colliding as they embraced.

"Do you want to do it in the pool?" she asked, kicking off her heels as he began unbuttoning her blouse.

"Tempting," he grinned. "How long before we can expect your husband?"

"About an hour, maybe two."

"Then I say you lead me right to your bed, I don't want to waste a single minute."

Killion chased her up the stairs and into the master suite. She stripped down to her underwear and slinked onto the bed, rolling onto her back.

"Do you like them?" she asked, teasing him with her body as she tugged at the lacy waste of her panties. "They're the ones I bought the day we first met."

"I do," he smirked, removing his suit coat, careful to keep his shoulder holster concealed as he slipped it off with his jacket.

He pulled his feet from his shoes and took off his shirt and tie, followed by his trousers, and laid them over a chair that sat in a sitting area within the spacious bedroom. Lastly, he slipped off his socks and underwear and joined her on the bed, resting gently on top of her.

****

Ashley had scoured the hotel room, searching for anything that could be used as a weapon. But the paring knife she'd found earlier was the only sharp object she could find. She decided she'd take her chances and carry it along. Otherwise, there was a solid brass table lamp, very heavy. She'd remembered seeing an identical one in Elizabeth's room. That just might work.

Though she had a plan, her nerves were beginning to get the best of her. On top of that, she was hungry, but at the same time, her stomach was still bothering her. She paced the room, her mind kept returning to the untaken pregnancy test sitting in her bathroom drawer at home. A knock at the door stopped her where she stood.

"Yes," she asked.

"It's Edward. I'm coming in."

Hearing the lock turn, she quickly moved to the couch and sat down, picking a magazine up from the coffee table and casually flipping through the pages. The door opened and he entered, a foam food container in his hand.

"I brought you a Greek salad for dinner, one of the chef's signature dishes. I hope it's alright."

"Thank you," she smiled, watching as he walked past her to set the container on the kitchen counter.

As he passed, she noticed a peculiar shape protruding beneath his suit coat, just above his waste at the small of his back. She knew exactly what it was: a gun. Gavin carried a pistol many times and in the exact same way. A holster hidden there could be very inconspicuous if worn with the proper outfit. To almost anyone else, it would probably have been overlooked.

"Have you heard from my husband?"

Edward turned and smiled, a lie resting on the tip of his tongue, "Yes. I spoke with him not but an hour ago. He was checking on you, wanted to let me know that the danger was almost past and that he'd be coming for you."

"That's good,' Ashley replied with a forced smile.

"Do you need anything then?"

"No," she said, "but thank you for looking after me so well. I feel so helpless without my husband. It's a dangerous world out there for a girl."

"Then I'll be leaving. I'll check on you in the morning. Goodnight, Mrs. Dering."

"Goodnight," she replied, hoping he'd bought her feigned distress.

Are you in for a surprise, she thought, watching the door close, the lock clicking into place.

****

Barbara rolled off of Killion, her face and neck flushed, her skin glistening. He smiled coyly, raising himself up to rest on his elbows.

"I didn't want to stop," she smiled. "I wish we could have kept going all night!"

"But your husband will be home soon. I'd hate for him to find us together."

"I don't care," she said, biting her lip.

"You say that now..." he grinned.

Killion watched as she stood and headed for the on-suite bathroom. He heard the shower kick on.

"Want to join me?" she called from around the corner.

"I'm afraid I wouldn't be able to keep my hands off you," he answered, standing and quickly dressing.

He checked the time on his watch as he leaned against the footboard. From this spot, Killion faced the bedroom door. McNamara would be home any minute.

The water stopped. Barbara returned to the bedroom wearing nothing but a short silk robe, left open in the front, her skin still wet from the shower, her hair stringy, damp.

"Dressed already?" she asked in a disappointed, pouty voice, taking his hand and holding it to her breast.

"Sweetheart," he urged, "your husband could be home at any moment."

"I know, isn't it exciting?"

"Barbara..."

"Shhh, Terry...I know what'll make you stay," she teased, dropping to her knees and unzipping his pants.

Killion smiled, trying to keep his mind on his task, but she was doing a good job distracting him. One minute, maybe two passed; when suddenly, the door to the bedroom swung open: it was McNamara.

"Barbara, what in the..."

"Hello, Reverend," Killion said, whipping his pistol from beneath his jacket.

The suppressor stifled the sound of the shot. McNamara dropped to the floor. Panicked, Barbara sprang up and stared at the dead body of her husband. Another shot sent her flopping lifelessly to the bed.

Killion holstered his gun and zipped up his pants, then headed straight for McNamara. He rifled through his pockets, searching for his cellphone. Upon finding it, he double checked the room, making sure he had all his belongings, then bent and picked up the two spent bullet casings and made his way out of the mansion.

The sun was beginning to set, only a few hours of daylight remained. Yet there was still so much left to do.

Killion slid into the driver's seat of his Audi and opened McNamara's text message folder, scrolling through, searching for any information or updates pertaining to the key. There were two unread messages. The first from Rocco, saying that he'd reached Chicago, the second was from Leroy Klebitz. Killion looked dumbfounded as he read the text. Delilah was also in Chicago. How did she get mixed up in all this?

19

Kayla, Jamie, Gavin, and Michael still sat at the dining room table. If they were going to pull this off, then they needed to get moving. An hour had already passed and they couldn't afford to be late to the meeting place and miss this opportunity.

"So we know what we're doing?" Gavin asked, seeking confirmation.

"You approach Delilah and we watch from the crowd," Jamie stated.

"Then you'll suggest going someplace quieter and we'll follow you to the park," Michael continued.

"And once she's dropped her guard, you guys swoop in and we make her tell us everything," Gavin grinned. "Let's go!"

"And remember," Jamie said, "it's a straight walk east from the stadium. We'll be behind you the whole way."

****

Mr. Nelson answered the phone in Franklin's office as it rang. He listened to the voice on the other end and then smiled.

"That's wonderful news, I'll inform Franklin at once. And yes, I'll tell him you'll call when you're ready to make final arrangements. Thank you."

"Was that Killion?" Franklin asked, puffing on a cigar as he watched Nelson hang up the phone.

"Yes, and he said it's done: McNamara is dead."

"Excellent," Franklin mused. "And the rest of The Order?"

"He said he'll call when he's ready."

"Good."

****

Leroy looked down at his beeping cell phone. He hated technology. It was bad enough that he was expected to carry this device so that he could be reached at any time, but what made it worse was that more often than not, he received text messages rather than calls, which left him irritated, trying to type responses on a small keypad.

"*From: Reverend McNamara,*" he read aloud. "*What is Delilah's phone number? I must speak to her at once.*"

Slowly he input the numbers, searching for each digit as he typed, and then hit send. His phone buzzed almost immediately with another message.

"*Thank you,*" Leroy said, reading the response aloud.

****

Killion forwarded the picture of Gavin lying dead on the floor from McNamara's phone to his own. Then, he punched in Delilah's number and forwarded it to her with the message, *beware.*"

****

168

Delilah stood on the Red Line platform at Addison St. If ever there was an opportunity for a double-cross, this was it: the sidewalks were packed with an ever pulsing flow of fans on their way to the stadium. Strategically, the crowd would allow for an easy approach and an even easier escape if need be, but it also meant that it would be more difficult to discover a tail and she knew that. She followed the stairs down to the street, her suitcase at her side, and disappeared into the flow of people. Once near Wrigley Field, Delilah spotted the statue of Harry Caray, but as she approached the legendary icon, she intentionally passed the monument, moving in the opposite direction. She found a place where she could safely watch for Rocco, yet slip away without his knowledge if their meet was compromised.

Her phone buzzed in her pocket. She set her suitcase down beside her and checked the message It was from an unfamiliar number. However she recognized it as a London extension. The message said *beware* and the picture was of a man, apparently dead on the floor, lying in a puddle of blood. The image was small and a little dark, so it was difficult to make out his features, but tattoos covered his arms.

Who are you? she typed in reply.

She waited a moment for a response, but there wasn't one.

****

Jamie pulled his white BMW X5 to a stop beneath where the L train crossed Addison. A procession of train cars rattled loudly as it passed overhead. From here, they could see the Caray statue.

"It's a quarter to eight," Michael said, looking down at his watch.

Gavin chambered a round in his 9mm USP compact and clicked back the hammer, then made sure the safety was on before returning it to his holster, "That's fine. Just keep me covered."

"No problem," Jamie assured, as Gavin climbed out of the SUV. "We'll see you in the park."

Gavin covered his holster with his t-shirt and zipped up his hoody. It was a cool summer night. He maneuvered through the crowd of people, the smell of beer and hotdogs lingering in the air. The stadium lights at Wrigley Field were already glowing brightly, illuminating the diamond, outfield, and famed ivy walls, as the sun slowly sank into the west.

He finally arrived at the statue and paused, briefly looking away from the crowd and gawking at Harry Caray's enormous glasses. He shook his head, imagining the voice of Caray exclaiming, *Holy cow!* Gavin turned from the statue and scanned the crowd. How would he know Delilah?

Before he could give it anymore thought, a woman caught his eye as she glided through the sea of people. She was beautiful, ridiculously beautiful, the kind of beautiful that can't be real, afforded only under the knife of the most expert of surgeons or on the heavily airbrushed pages of a magazine. But she was real and the crowd seemed to part for her as she approached.

"Rocco?" she asked.

Gavin was momentarily speechless, before finally speaking, "Uh, yeah...*Rocco*."

"So you know where the key is?"

"Yeah," he grinned. "But it will be difficult to get."

The crowd grew louder as the game was beginning to start, people pushing their way through the gates of the stadium.

"Sorry," she said, nearing a shout, "but I can't hear you."

"Why don't we go someplace a little more private so we can talk."

"Here, I can get that for you," Gavin volunteered, taking her luggage case.

As he did, the cuff of his sweatshirt pulled back, revealing the tattoos around his wrist. She spotted the ink instantly and thought of the picture in the text message.

"So, *Rocco*," she asked as they began walking, "you have lots of tattoos?"

"Oh, yeah."

"Can I see them? Tattoos are such a turn-on; I think they're so *attractive*."

"Um, alright," he answered, using his free hand to pull up on his sleeve, revealing more of his left arm.

"Fascinating," Delilah smirked, mentally matching his arm against the one of the dead man in the picture.

She knew he wasn't Rocco, but if he could lead her to the key, it was worth playing along. Gavin was none the wiser.

"So the information which led you to Chicago and provided the whereabouts of the key, how did you obtain it?"

Gavin thought quick, "I paid a visit to one of the last people to see the key. He cooperated for the most part, but once I extracted the information I needed, I killed him. Couldn't have him sending a warning now could I?"

"And you're sure he's dead?" she questioned.

"Yeah."

"Ok. So where are we headed?"

"There's a park east of here, about twenty minutes walk, quiet, secluded; a perfect place to talk, figure things out.

"Perfect," Delilah smiled, the wheels in her head turning.

Gavin was uncomfortable in the fact that, suitcase aside, they looked like tourists, and that they, the proverbial *sore thumb*, suspiciously stood out as they walked away from the crowded Wrigley Field. Though, no one seemed to notice him: they were all too busy gawking at Delilah. Even so, Gavin was never this nervous. Maybe it was the fact that it had been years since he last found himself doing the things he'd done in just the last forty-eight hours or maybe it was that he was with this beautiful women, this unnordinarily stunning, seductive woman, but regardless, he found his hands uncharacteristically sweaty. They were now a block away from the ballpark, closing on the Addison St station.

Now was the time. Delilah unexpectedly reached beneath her poncho and slipped her pistol from the holster, pressing the tip of the suppressor into Gavin's ribs as she used her other hand to firmly take hold of his arm, pulling him tightly against her.

"What's this?" Gavin exclaimed.

"Change of plans," she said. "Keep hold of my suitcase; place both hands on the handle. If you let go, I shoot. If you run, I shoot. If you are who you say you are, then you'll cooperate. Now, turn here and take the stairs up to the platform. We're getting on the train."

****

"I lost them!" Jamie groaned. "I could see them in the rearview mirror as they approached, but then there was a crowd beneath the L and they just vanished."

"Impossible," Michael argued.

He exited the vehicle and stepped off the sidewalk, disappearing between two houses. While doing so, Michael pulled the mask from his pocket and quickly slipped it over his face.

"What are you doing?" Jamie pleaded from within the SUV, but Michael was gone. "Great, *just* great."

Thirteen leapt into the air, landing gracefully on the rooftop of one of the houses. From there he could see the length of the street, Wrigley, and the train platform. And that's all he needed: he caught a glimpse of Gavin as he stepped into the train car, Delilah close to his side.

He dropped back down to street level, landing on the passenger side of Jamie's BMW, speaking through the open window, "They're taking the train. She must have figured things out."

"How?"

"I don't care," Thirteen growled, "but if we don't move, we could lose Gavin."

Jamie nodded.

"I'll go on foot, you follow the tracks. When they stop, we'll be ready."

Thirteen took to the sky again, landing on the tracks and sprinting behind the train as it began northward. He easily caught up and bound to the train's roof, now riding along, glancing over the side of the tracks to see if Jamie was able to follow. He was there, caught in slow traffic, a half of a block behind, but there. What was Delilah's plan?

172

****

"Brother," Killion asked, stepping into the hotel room across the hall from Ashley's and Elizabeth's rooms, "how are our guests?"

Edward smiled, "Good. The Dering girl believes I am a friend of her husband and that she's here for her own safety at his request. She is however a tough one, she came at me with a knife, but I calmed her down."

"Interesting, a little fighter...and Mrs. Laurent?"

"She is living under the fear that if she were to misbehave, she'd be risking her son's life."

"It's all about motivation isn't it," Killion sighed. "Did you get me what I asked for?"

"It's in the briefcase on the counter."

"Was it difficult to make?"

"Not for me," Edward grinned.

Killion patted his younger brother on the shoulder and headed into the kitchen space. Carefully, he flipped open the clasps on the case and raised the lid. A stainless steel box sat inside, metal tubing connected a row of compression chambers to the box. On top of the unit was a red push button protected by a flip-up plastic cover. Below that was a square vent with what looked like a cooling fan one would see in a PC. Beside the contraption was a full-face gas mask, rubberized, with sealed eye protection and built-in air filtration.

"How does it arm?"

Edward approached and showed him a small toggle on the left side, "Flip that and you're armed. Push the button and it's the point of no return. Make sure you have the mask on!"

"And this will kill them quickly?" Killion asked.

"Yes, very. How are you planning on getting everyone in a small enough space for the chemical to deliver maximum effect?"

Killion smiled coyly, obviously proud of his plotting, "I've arranged for Franklin to call a meeting in McNamara's heavily secured office at the top of his church tower. Franklin will activate the device and kill his own people."

"And what about Franklin?"

"I have something special planned for him," Killion said, once again patting his brother on the shoulder before disappearing out the door.

****

Gavin and Delilah headed north on the L. She made him sit, both hands still holding the suitcase, as she stood over him, the gun secretly aimed at his chest. The train slowed as it neared Sheridan, the platform just ahead.

"This is us," Delilah said, motioning for Gavin to get up and follow her to the door.

The train stopped and they stepped out into the evening air. It was cooler than he'd expected and Gavin was now thankful for the extra layer he'd chosen in his hooded sweatshirt, that and it hid the shape of his gun.

Thirteen crouched on the roof, trying to keep his profile low, his black suit and mask camouflaging him as the sun set. He was nothing more than a misplaced shadow, no reason for alarm. Gavin and Delilah headed down the metal stairway and out of his line of sight. He left the top of the train and maneuvered across the rooftops of buildings that sat on the corner of Sheridan and Irving Park. Where was Jamie?

****

Delilah led Gavin beneath the elevated tracks, behind a row of houses, before merging on the sidewalk of a small street, called N Seminary, which separated the residents on its east side from Graceland cemetery to the west. They quickly traversed the freshly cut grass, hurrying away from the lights and prying eyes of the homes behind them.

****

Thirteen finally spotted Jamie's white BMW, approaching from the east on Irving, not from the south as expected. Voices beyond his control echoed in his ears, demonic shouts and laughter telling him that Gavin had been primed for slaughter, taken to a cemetery to die, told to *let him die*. He dropped down from the rooftops and hurried, still masked, to Jamie's vehicle as it idled at a red light.

"Hurry," he said as he pulled the door shut behind him, realizing how he'd startled Jamie but having no time to address it, "She's taken him into the cemetery. She's going to kill him."

****

"Here is good enough," Delilah said, as they stood amongst an outcropping of tombstones, partially hidden from view, a dense grove of trees on one side, a Victorian mausoleum cut into a hill on their right. Frogs splashed in a nearby pond.

She kicked Gavin in the back of his knees, then forced him to the ground, the suitcase tumbling from his grip and landing several feet away, her suppressed pistol no longer hidden, now openly aimed at his head. Gavin remained silent, his back pressing against cold marble, the shadow of the tall grave marker looming over him like death itself.

"Who are you?" she demanded, her finger poised on the trigger.

"I'm Rocco."

"Shut up and tell me the truth!"

He weighed his options, which were few, before he answered, "Gavin, my name is Gavin. Rocco is dead."

"Then you are the man who possesses the key?" she asked, his revelation not surprising, but perplexing.

****

Jamie slammed on the brakes and the two men quickly exited the SUV. They'd wound along the narrow paved roads and stopped on a loop that they figured was near the center of the cemetery, but where to look?

****

"Answer me!" Delilah ordered, adjusting her aim slightly to the right and firing over his shoulder, the sound of the bullet slamming into the tombstone louder than the actual shot.

"Sorry," Gavin pleaded, "but this is a little inconvenient for me, I mean, I don't even have a plot here, so where will they burry me?"

She fired again, this time between his legs, narrowly missing his crotch, "How about now?"

****

"Did you hear that?" Jamie said, raising a hand to slow their pace.

"Yeah," Thirteen replied, peering into the darkness, "sounded like a suppressed gunshot."

"But from where?"

"That's the point of a suppressor," Thirteen reasoned, "not to fully silence a weapon, but to confuse someone who would hear the discharge, to dislocate the sound."

"Then they've got it all wrong in the movies, huh?" Jamie chided.

The men stood in silence, scanning in all directions. Something finally caught Thirteen's eye. There, not one hundred yards away, a Louis Vuitton suitcase lay basking in the moonlight.

****

"Seriously?" Gavin shouted, glaring at the broken dirt between his legs. "What's wrong with you?"

She smiled. He was right where she wanted him.

"Tell me where the key is and I'll end your life quickly. Don't make this take longer than it must," Delilah said, "I'm not dressed for proper interrogation, for...*torture.*"

You guys need to hurry up, he thought. *If you don't get here soon, I'm a dead man!*

"I don't have it with me," he answered, trying to stall, "but I can make arrangements, can get it for you."

"That won't be necessary," she said, readying to take another shot, this time aiming at his stomach. "Now you'll die slow, each bullet placed will create pain, but ultimately not death, at least not immediately. For every response you give that doesn't answer my question, I will shoot. You will decide how long you suffer. And know this, now that I have your name, *Gavin*, even with you dead, it would not be difficult for me to track down your loved ones and kill them one by one till I have what I want. So I say again: where is the key?"

****

Killion pulled his Audi to a sharp stop, the front passenger side tire kissing the curb. Quickly, he stepped from the car, the case carrying the chemical weapon in hand, and headed for the Cadillac that was parked in front of him, opening the door to the backseat then pulling it closed behind him.

"Is that the device?" Franklin asked.

Franklin sat on the other side of the backseat. Mr. Nelson was behind the wheel. Killion set the case down in the space between them and flipped it open, showing Franklin the gas mask and giving him a quick rundown of the procedures.

"And this will take care of all of them?"

"Yes," Killion smiled, "every last one."

Franklin pulled out his cell phone and tapped a message outlining a command for The Order to meet immediately at McNamara's office. Within seconds of him pressing send, affirmative responses beeped back at him.

"They'll all be there," Franklin grinned, "tonight at midnight."

****

A twig snapped from somewhere in the darkness, interrupting her as she pressed Gavin. She peered into the trees, then cocked her head to the side, not sure if she was seeing what she was seeing. She couldn't make out a shape, just what appeared to be two white slits spotted amongst the low hanging, dark branches, now racing towards her. She focused and realized they were eyes, and then, everything went black.

****

"Will you be tagging along, Terrence?" Mr. Nelson asked from the front seat.

"No," Killion answered, taking hold of the door handle, "I have something else to attend to this evening, a loose end you could say. Oh, and one more thing, Franklin. I almost forgot. Take this pistol. Use it to protect yourself...you can never be too careful. Incidentally, that is the same gun that solved your little McNamara problem earlier today, consider it a memento."

"Thank you," Franklin said, watching as the assassin stepped from the car. "I'll call you the moment it's done."

"Indeed," Killion replied, his back to the car as he strutted away.

****

Gavin dumped the contents of her luggage onto the ground and examined them with a flashlight as Jamie pulled her arms behind her back and fastened the zip-tie cuffs around her wrists, then checked the swollen lump forming on her brow. Michael stood over her, his mask pulled down over his face.

"Was that really necessary?" Jamie asked, looking up at Thirteen.

"Sorry," he shrugged, "old habits."

"Well, she came more prepared than I anticipated," Gavin said, holding up her Sig Sauer pistol, a silencer attached to the barrel.

Jamie picked up her passport. Michael paced.

"Is she going to be ok?" Gavin asked, stuffing her belongings back into her suitcase.

"Yeah," Jamie nodded, his eyes fixed on the passport, "as long as our friend here doesn't feel the need to prove his manliness by beating up on her anymore."

Michael sighed. The mask was feeding his ego, imbuing him with unimaginable confidence and power.

"In the last six months, she's been through London, Italy, Russia, even China," Jamie mused.

"Where's she from?" Gavin asked, watching as she regained consciousness.

"Israel," she said, her eyes piercing as she stared the men down, her mind quickly assessing the situation and plotting a course of action, realizing that she now sat exactly where Gavin had been.

Jamie helped her sit up, double checking the cuffs as he did. She was secure.

"I should have killed you," she stated, her eyes settling on Gavin.

"Too late now," Gavin smirked.

"Perhaps," she continued, "but I must say that I was impressed. Very clever, how you faked your death and posed for that picture."

"So you knew the whole time that I wasn't Rocco?"

"True. And I knew you were bating a trap. I first had doubts as to your authenticity when we first spoke on the phone, but the moment I saw your arm, just that brief glimpse of your tattoos, it confirmed my suspicion: you weren't Rocco, therefore you must be my target, ergo, you needed to be eliminated."

"Then why did you agree to meet, if you knew it was a trap?"

"…Hence my reverse trap. I am not afraid of you and I figured you either had the key on you or it would be close. So I would kill you and take it, or you would give me the information I needed and I would then kill the next person in line and so on."

"I believe you," Gavin nodded.

"I have killed many men, a lot more than you, I'm sure. I will only warn you once," she said, her voice militant, cold, "even now, do not underestimate me."

"Like I said before, I don't have the key with me, but I'm willing to make a trade," Gavin explained.

"Let's hear it then."

"I'll give you the key if you let my wife and his family go free."

"I don't know what you're talking about," she answered calmly. "I know nothing of hostages. My mission was to acquire the key."

"Where are they?" Thirteen demanded angrily, tired of the posing and banter, grabbing her by the arm and lifting her to her feet.

"I will not repeat myself," she replied.

Thirteen pulled his arm back to strike her across the face, but as he swung forward, Jamie grabbed his wrist, jerking it to a halt. Gavin took his eyes off Delilah for only a moment, but that was all she needed. With the men distracted, she slipped free from the cuffs, and in a blur, swung her body in a flurry of kicks, dropping the men to the ground. Before they could react, she once again had her pistol and it was trained on them.

"Give me the key," she said.

"I'm telling you, we *don't* have it here," Jamie answered.

She looked at Gavin, "You, keep the *dead man's* phone on you. I'll call you tomorrow, in the morning. We will arrange an exchange."

"You'll bring me Ashley?" Gavin questioned. "You said you knew nothing about hostages?"

"That's still true," she smiled, backing away slowly into the foliage till all they could see was a faint glint of moonlight on the tip of the silencer. "The exchange is for your own lives. If you do not do as I ask and give me the key, I *will* kill you."

20

Franklin marched through the Sunrise Chapel facility, his left hand carrying the case, his right shaking hands with the many armed guards he passed. He was a familiar sight at the church and was known to be McNamara's business partner.

He paused at the elevator to the Reverend's tower, adjusting his tie as he stared into the mirrored doors. They opened and he began his ascent. The elevator stopped at the top. Two guards stood at the office door.

"Gentlemen," Franklin said jovially, "there will be a meeting tonight, many important members of the church will be here, please go down to the lobby and make sure they find their way here and also, the Reverend wanted me to tell you that your presence will not be required this evening."

"Yes, sir; thank you, sir," they said, stepping into the elevator.

Franklin walked to the end of the board table and placed the case down at his seat: the head seat. He pulled the gun that Killion had given him from beneath his suit coat and chambered a round, ensured the safety was set, and returned it to his waist, satisfied, then stepped to the window and looked out over Los Angeles. The sun was setting over the Pacific, the last light would soon be but a shimmer on the horizon. The moon was already glowing white, full.

Soon, very soon, he thought.

****

"Well I wasn't expecting that," Jamie sighed as the men climbed into his BMW.

Gavin shrugged from the backseat. Michael pulled off his mask and tucked it away in his suit coat, immediately feeling more human, less like Thirteen.

"So what do we do now?" Jamie asked, merging into traffic and beginning the drive home.

"I guess we wait for her call in the morning," Gavin answered.

"We need to be more prepared this time," Michael added.

"For now, let's get some rest," Jamie replied, "I have a feeling we'll need it."

They wound their way from the stadium neighborhood back to Jamie's house in Lincoln Park. Unnoticed, a taxi followed cautiously several cars behind, slowly passing as Jamie pulled the SUV into his driveway. From inside the cab, Delilah raised her cell phone and snapped a picture of the Branson Home, then ordered the driver to take her to the Sheraton on Water Street.

"How'd it go?" Kayla asked, sipping on a mug of freshly brewed hot tea.

The kids were in bed, she'd stayed up, awaiting any news from the men. There was no way she could sleep.

"We had her..." Jamie began to explain.

"But she sort of got a way," Gavin said, cringing at the words.

"What do you mean, *got a way*?" she frowned.

"She overpowered us," Jamie mused.

"More like outsmarted us," Michael corrected. "She is clearly a professional, highly trained, extremely dangerous and not at all pathetic like Rocco. She reversed our trap and Gavin nearly paid with his life. We underestimated her, that's for sure. But it won't happen again."

"So what's the plan then?" Kayla asked, shaking her head.

"She's going to call us in the morning, on Rocco's phone. She wants the key in exchange for our lives," Jamie said, placing it on the kitchen counter.

"What about Ashley, and Michael's family?" she questioned, her hands thrown up in frustration.

"The woman claimed to know nothing about them," Michael replied. "I believe her. If she is working for this Big Mac, then there must be someone else in the picture, a puppet master so to speak, someone else pulling the strings. Big Mac is just a rung on the ladder, we need to get to the top."

"So let's say we give her the key," Gavin said, "then how do we get our families back?"

"If she doesn't know where they are, then there's no point giving away our only piece of leverage," Jamie reasoned.

"I say we arrange the meet," Michael said, "and kill her, then go after Big Mac. He can't be that hard to find."

"But she's a mercenary, not a hunter," Gavin argued. "Maybe we can come to some sort of agreement? We give her the key in exchange for information: the whereabouts of Big Mac."

"She's ruthless," Jamie said reluctantly, "she'll never go for that. She'll kill us as soon as she has the key. I hate to say it, but I agree with Michael. She needs to be taken out of the picture."

"Jamie!" Kayla scolded, her voice softening as she remembered the sleeping kids upstairs. "I can't believe you would say that!"

"No, he's right," Gavin admitted. "They're right. She's too dangerous to let live and, in the end, I know she can't be trusted."

Rocco's phone beeped. Gavin picked it up.

"It's a picture message, no name, just a number," Gavin said, opening the inbox on the phone, an image loading on the screen.

"That's our house!" Jamie said, looking over Gavin's shoulder.

"She followed us," Michael grunted.

"Then here's what we do," Jamie decided, fear and anger driving his thoughts. "When she calls, we tell her to meet us at a public location; someplace she'll know we can't openly fight her. We'll be ready this time. I say Michael uses Thirteen's power to kill her...somehow. Then we find this Big Mac and get your families back."

"Won't she be expecting another setup?" Kayla reasoned. "That was your plan: have her meet you someplace public, then lead her to a secluded area and strike."

"But this time, she's in control; she has all the leverage," Jamie replied. "We need to take that control back. Thirteen can do things that Gavin and I, and Michael for that matter, cannot."

While they'd been talking Gavin had been pacing the kitchen, not sure if they should be considering willingly unleashing Thirteen's wrath. He'd stopped to look at some framed family photos that Kayla had hung on the wall above a letter desk: the Branson kids, Ethan and Marley, on Christmas morning, greedily tearing into festively wrapped presents, a picture of Kayla and Ashley in full costume, trick-or-treating when they were young girls, Kayla a pink detailed princess and Ashley a cute baby girl complete with oversized bottle. The last picture was from Jamie and Kayla's wedding. The word *family* hung on the wall above the frames. Then beneath the pictures was an organizer made of aged, painted wood, adorned with antique glass doorknobs and decorated with old rusty skeleton keys. Hooks along the bottom held their miscellaneous key rings: a set for each of their cars, the shed out back, and extra master keys for the house.

Gavin spun around excitedly, "Jamie, let me see the key!"

As soon as it was in his hand, he turned back to the organizer and compared the key to the others on display. They were all similar; it would be difficult for anyone to tell the difference, especially if they'd never seen the real key. Though they weren't as old, they would be a good enough decoy.

"Look," Gavin grinned, "we give her a fake, the real key never leaves the house. Maybe then we won't have to kill her. She'll take it to McNamara and we follow her!"

"McNamara?" Jamie asked, confused by the name.

"Oh yeah," Gavin nodded, "that's what she called him, Big Mac, I mean. His name is McNamara."

"Well, it might work," Michael laughed, returning their attention to the key.

"Yeah," Jamie agreed, "it just might."

****

Delilah set her bag down on the bed in her hotel room and pulled her phone from her jacket, dialing Leroy and raising it to her ear. It rang.

"My beautiful grandchild," Leroy answered, "did you get it, do you have the key?"

"No, Saba, not yet. Rocco is dead. The man I met is an imposter," she explained, staring down from her window at the lights glittering off the rippling surface of the Chicago River. "It's Gavin, one of McNamara's hunters, another man I do not know but I believe to be a police officer, and one of Triton's men, I recognized his mask."

"A Tri-Six lives?" he said, his voice mixed with fear and astonishment. "They have great power, Delilah. You cannot kill this man."

"I have yet to find a man I can't kill, Saba."

"There's more though, Delilah. I fear something has happened to McNamara. I have called him several times today and he has not answered, or returned any of my calls. Franklin called a meeting of The Order for tonight; I must be there within the hour. Something is not right."

"Give me McNamara's number," she said, "I will speak directly to him, tell him I will have the key tomorrow. I will fly it to Los Angeles as soon as it is in my possession."

Leroy gave her the number. She leaned against the glass.

"Saba, how do I kill a Tri-Six?"

"It cannot be done, but if anyone would know, it's the Reverend. He never trusted Triton, no more than I trust Franklin now. That is why he had his hunters, a private army in case Triton ever double-crossed him. The head of The Order holds many secrets, information to which we are not privy, and McNamara has studied such things. Triton's Tri-Six were half-man, half-devil. I suppose if you could separate one from the other, then you could kill the mortal, but only the mortal. Man's weapons can only injure flesh, not spirit."

She thought for a moment, processing his words. The glow of a lighthouse drew her attention beyond the city's harbor.

"Can I ask you something, and be honest."

"Anything, Delilah, anything!"

"Is The Order good or evil? The Reverend, he is a man of God, no? Even so, he worked side by side with a man who was obsessed in the Occult, a man who empowered his soldiers with demonic energy?"

"I have heard rumors amongst the members, whispers that Triton was not even human, but a demon himself. I do not know what to believe, but I do know that The Order is not what it was when I joined. They have become greedy, starved for power. What I once thought was a solution to the evils of the world, a hope for peace and unity, has become another wave of oppressors. It's Poland all over again, Delilah, but now I am too old to resist."

"And what is so special about this key?"

"All I know is that it was once Triton's and when he lost it, he was destroyed. Franklin wants the key now, believing it will give him the power Triton once held. But what the key is actually for, I do not know."

"Alright, Saba. I'm going to call McNamara. Promise me you'll be careful."

"Yes, my girl, yes. Now I must go."

"Goodnight, Saba," she said, hanging up her phone.

Quickly, Delilah dialed the number her grandfather had given her. The call went right to voicemail.

"Reverend," she said, "this is Delilah. I wanted to speak directly to you. Your man Rocco is dead: Gavin killed him. I made contact with Rocco, but discovered that Gavin is masquerading as the dead man.

Tomorrow, the key will be in my possession. There's just one thing, Gavin is working with one of Triton's Tri-Six. He wears a black mask, the mouth stitched shut, and his eyes glow with a power like I have never seen. Please advise."

Delilah dropped the phone into her bag and undressed, pulling back the covers and slipping into bed. She flipped off the lamp that sat on the nightstand and tucked her Sig Saur under her pillow. Her head raced with questions, her grandfather's words making her doubt the mission, whether she wanted to turn a key assumed to have so much power over to an already powerful man. Her grandfather had been through Hell at the hands of the Nazis during the Second World War and his instincts had always proven right. If he no longer trusted The Order, then why should she? Slowly, she drifted into sleep, her thoughts colliding as she slipped into darkness.

21

Killion listened to the voice message that Delilah had left on McNamara's phone. He smiled at how perfectly his plan had taken shape. Everything was going as he'd hoped, each trap set, only waiting to be tripped, ensnaring his victims one by one.

He returned to his hotel room and toasted his success with a mini-bottle of whiskey taken from the small refrigerator under the galley counter. Shooting the bottle, he dropped it in the trash and checked his watch: almost midnight. Killion postponed any more celebration and returned his focus to the plan. He flipped open his laptop and opened Google Earth, typed *Sunrise Chapel, Los Angeles, Ca* into the search bar and watched as the onscreen globe rotated, then zoomed down over the West Coast before settling directly over the massive church complex. Carefully, he double checked the layout. He'd previously selected a rooftop several blocks away from the church, far enough that he'd never be seen, but close enough that he would only need one shot. The height was right, nothing blocked the view. The path of the bullet would be unobstructed, just as he'd planned.

He picked his HK sniper rifle up from the coffee table and ejected the steel magazine: five rounds of brass jacketed .308 greeted him. Killion returned it to the receiver and pulled a suppressor from his suitcase. He twisted off a knurled thread-protector from the quick-detach designed flash hider and put the flat back can in its place on the end of the barrel, a ratcheting sound ensuring a secure fit. This was followed by a quick onceover on the gun. He applied a thin layer of oil to the cocking tube, inspected the bipod for proper functionality, switched the selector from safe to fire and back, and then shouldered the weapon, testing the cheek weld and scope sighting.

Satisfied, Killion slung the long, black gun over his shoulder, concealed the weapon by draping his trench coat over its frame, and exited the suite.

****

Franklin stood at the end of the table, his chair pulled out, but he chose not to sit. The members of The Order stared up at him from their places, Reverend McNamara's seat glaringly empty. Leroy eyed the case on the table curiously.

"Thank you all for joining me this evening. We have something to discuss which requires our immediate attention," Franklin began.

"Where's Harlow?" Leroy questioned, speaking out of turn as Franklin had only just opened the meeting.

"The Reverend will not be joining us this evening...or *ever again*. He was disloyal to The Order and was made an *example* of."

"What did he do?" Leroy pushed.

"He was...*disloyal.*"

The members shifted uncomfortably in their seats, casting glances around the table. Leroy stood.

"Well then, I am resigning as a member of this council. I no longer wish to be involved with you," he said, his old crooked finger pointing at Franklin.

"Very well," Franklin said, pulling Killion's pistol from beneath his coat and firing a quick shot into Leroy's chest, "resignation accepted."

Leroy's body hit the edge of the table as he collapsed before finally settling on the floor, short gasps lessening till he took his final breath.

"Now then," Franklin said matter-of-factly as he set the gun down on the table, "shall we continue?"

The room sat silent, their ears ringing from the blast. No one dared speak out now.

****

"Whoa," Mr. Nelson cried out, startled by the sudden opening of the Cadillac's rear door. "I wasn't expecting to see you here."

Killion smiled from the back seat, then looked up at the tower standing tall above the rest of the church facility, "Did he do it yet?"

"The last of The Order arrived moments ago. They should begin soon. Franklin is pleased with the job you've done. And though the original agreement was for you to dispatch with the members, he is excited to be the one to pull the trigger, metaphorically speaking."

"I understand," Killion said, "just glad I could facilitate. Now, is my money ready?"

"Eight million in cash, as agreed, all non-sequential and untraceable: the briefcase is in the trunk. Franklin will settle with you when he returns."

"I'm sure he will," Killion replied, pulling a switch blade from his pocket and ejecting the blade.

Before Mr. Nelson could react, Killion slit the man's throat sending blood spurting in pulsing arcs, splattering abstractly on the car's windows. Quickly, he wiped the blade and pocketed the knife and then reached up between the front seats and pressed the trunk release on the key fob that dangled from the steering column. Killion stepped from the car and collected the briefcase from the trunk, flipping open the clasps to ensure the money was all accounted for. Tightly wrapped bundles of one thousand dollar bills were neatly packed inside the case.

He casually walked to his Audi parked just outside the lot of the mega-church and placed the briefcase in the backseat, then jumped in the driver's seat and pulled away from the curb.

****

"We all remember what The Order was like under Triton's leadership, but he is gone, for several years now in fact. I have led you the best I could in his stead, but now, the time has come to make some changes, and frankly, I couldn't be more excited. You see, you were all *his* followers, true to *his* Order. But there is a larger head to this beast, one who is even greater than Triton and it is to him I owe my allegiance. Simply put, you are no longer necessary to our greater plans."

With those words, he opened the case. The men and women sitting around the table gasped as he removed the gas mask and slipped it down over his face. He then armed the device, and triggered the chemicals. At first nothing happened; but then, a soft hiss. Soon, the whole room was filled with noxious gas, the ill-fated members choking on the reeking odor, writhing in the awfulness of Killion's contraption. Members of The Order began dying left and right, succumbing to the toxic fumes. Franklin smiled beneath the mask, a fitting end he believed, an end to the charade Triton had began so many years earlier: absolute loyalty demanded with nothing in return.

The last of the gas dispensed: the device deactivated. Franklin holstered the pistol beneath his suit coat and headed for the elevator, leaving Leroy and the rest of The Order behind.

****

Ashley listened at the door to her room, her ear pressed against the finely painted steel door. From what she could tell, the hallway was empty. She turned and headed for the balcony, sliding the glass door open, the warm ocean breeze calming, though she was on the edge of panic: the time had come.

The moon glowed down on the building's façade, giving plenty of light for Ashley to swing her legs over the railing and ready herself for the leap across to the next room. She steadied herself, took a few long, deep breaths, and jumped.

Her hands tightened around the railing, but her shoes slipped off the edge, leaving her dangling, the ground fatally far beneath her feet. Ashley struggled and her muscles burned, but she had to climb up, finally managing to catch the ledge with the toe of her right foot, then finding the leverage to raise up and over to safety. Ashley looked up into the night sky, the stars twinkling like a sea of diamonds, and whispered *thank you*.

The lights in the room were on. Ashley peeked through the glass, making sure Elizabeth and Cain were alone. The boy slept on the couch, curled up beneath his mother's arm. She sat deathly still, staring at the clock on the wall. Edward was nowhere to be seen.

Ashley slid open the door and greeted Elizabeth in a hushed voice, "You ok?"

Elizabeth nodded a yes, but didn't speak.

"We're getting out of here. What I need you to do is pick up the phone and try to dial out."

"What number, who should I call?" Elizabeth asked.

"Any number, it doesn't matter. Edward will get the call. If your room is like mine, he's monitoring the line."

Again, Elizabeth nodded.

"Tell Edward that your son is very sick, a fever, and that he needs immediate medical attention or he'll die. As long as we're alive, we're leverage and he won't want any of us dead. I'll hide in the closet over by the door. When he enters, I hit him over the head with the lamp, grab his keys and gun, and we get out of here before he comes to."

"You think it'll work?" Elizabeth worried.

"It has to."

****

Killion pulled down a service drive that led behind a tall building several blocks from the Sunrise Chapel. Mr. Nelson had been taken care of, now Franklin was alone. He parked, pulled his rifle from beneath his trench coat in the backseat, and hurried up the building's fire escape, his shoes clanking softly on the metal steps as he climbed.

He carefully scanned the roof. The church's tower could be seen in the distance. Killion headed for the roof's edge and knelt down, hidden by the low wall that lined the rooftop. He flipped down the bipod that was mounted on the gun's hand-guard and stood it on the ledge, resting his cheek on the stock and searching through the scope. He spotted Franklin's car in the parking lot, then progressed to the church's front door, up the building's façade and finally settling on the tower itself. The windows were dark, no movement as far as he could tell.

Killion began to lower the gun when he spotted the elevator slowly descending. Franklin was on his way down.

✳✳✳✳✳✳✳✳✳✳✳✳

Elizabeth picked up the phone and prepared to dial, "Ready?"

"As much as I can be," Ashley said, with a feigned smile, grabbing the lamp and pulling its cord free from the outlet before slipping into the dark closet. "Let's do this!"

Cain had been instructed to *play* sick and pretend to be asleep on the sofa. He was doing a great job. Elizabeth dialed a random number and waited. Within moments, Edward had picked up.

"It's late," he yawned, "who were you trying to call?"

"A...um...a *doctor*," she said, no need to pretend she was afraid, her heart pounding. "It's my son, he's very ill. He's burning up with a fever and he's been vomiting everywhere."

Nice touch, Ashley thought.

"Alright, I'll be in to check the boy. If he requires more attention, it can be arranged. I'll be just a minute."

Ashley watched as Elizabeth hung up the phone. Edward was on his way.

✳✳✳✳✳✳✳✳✳✳✳✳

The elevator disappeared beneath the sloped roof of the church. Killion's phone rang.

"Franklin," he smiled as he answered, speaking into a Bluetooth earpiece, "how'd everything go?"

"Perfectly, my friend. Everything went exactly as planned."

"I'm glad to hear it. Tell me, did you have need of the pistol I gave you?"

"I couldn't believe it, but yes, in fact," Franklin chuckled, smiling as if the whole ordeal was a punch line to a joke. "Old Leroy Klebitz mouthed off, offered his resignation. He was useful once, but now he was too old and narrow minded to contribute anyway. I shot him in the chest, right in front of them. And let me tell you, that put everyone in their place really quick."

"Good. I'm glad everything worked out for you. And where are you now?"

"I'm still at the church, but I'm on my way out," Franklin grinned. "Where would you like to meet? I want to settle our debt and make preparations for the final stage of our plan: the acquisition of the key."

"Well, I have new information actually. The key will be on its way to California. All I have to do is make a call."

"Very good," Franklin replied.

Through the scope, Killion watched the church doors open as Franklin emerged confidently. He followed him through the parking lot, the crosshairs centered on Franklin's chest.

"There is one more thing," Killion said. "I have a message for you from Paris."

Franklin stopped dead in his tracks, the smile disappearing from his face, "What do you know of Paris?"

"It would appear that your partner, the Frenchman, has *other* plans. He thanks you for the part you've played, that you single handedly destroyed the last of Triton's legacy and have now left him free to lead The Order as he sees fit. As a typical, arrogant American, you proved, though cooperative, unwilling to bow completely to his power, so you, like the others, need removing."

Franklin scanned the parking lot nervously, searching for Killion, ready for a fight. He reached into his suit coat and pulled the gun, aiming it into the darkness.

"I wouldn't do that if I were you..." Killion scolded.

Slowly, Franklin headed towards the car; his phone still held to his ear, the gun raised, "Why would you do this? I paid you very well."

"Yes," Killion agreed, "you did. But you see, two jobs pay better than one."

Franklin was now close enough to the Cadillac to spot the blood, the splatters drying into red steaks on the glass. He realized Mr. Nelson was dead.

"My God!" he exclaimed.

"*Exactly*," Killion said, holding his breath, steadying as he held the wooden grip and pulling the hair trigger on the PSG-1.

The suppressor masked the sound. Killion watched as Franklin dropped to the ground, the bullet striking him, knocking him backwards.

"Goodbye," Killion whispered.

****

The women heard the sound of a key card swiping through the lock, then the handle depressed and the door swung open. Edward entered the room.

"Over here," Elizabeth called out in the dark. "The lights were hurting his eyes, so I turned them off. He's so sick, please help him!"

Edward hurried to the sofa, his eyes slowly adjusting to the darkness. Cain lay beside his mother, a blanket wrapped tightly around his body, just his hair visible at the top. He reached to pull the blanket back, but didn't get any further. Ashley rushed him from her hiding place, bludgeoning him in the back of the head with the lamp. He was staggered, but didn't go down.

She swung again as he stumbled around, clearly in pain. Just as the lamp was about to strike, he blocked it with his forearm, taking hold of it and twisting it from her hands. She began punching him in the face as hard as she could till he toppled to the floor, her on top of him, pounding away till he stopped moving.

Her hands ached as she reached into his pocket and grabbed the keys. Ashley knew they had to move quickly. She rolled him to one side and pulled his pistol from the holster tucked in his waist.

"Is he dead?" Elizabeth asked, standing from the couch and taking Cain's hand.

"No," Ashley answered, watching his chest move with each subtle breath, "just unconscious."

Lastly, Ashley grabbed his wallet and stood. She quickly unlocked the door and peered into the bright hallway.

All clear.

Together, they raced to the elevator and selected the parking garage, then began the painfully slow descent. Ashley tucked the gun into the back of her jeans and handed the wallet to Elizabeth. Cain yawned, still wrapped in the blanket, his eyes red, tired. Ashley looked down at her knuckles, swollen, covered in blood.

"I think I broke his nose," Ashley winced, slowly opening and closing her fist, feeling the tenderness in her fingers.

Elizabeth was in a daze. She clenched Cain's hand, Edward's wallet in the other.

Finally, the elevator doors opened. They stepped into the quiet garage cautiously, aware of their vulnerability. Ashley pressed the panic button on Edward's keyless entry. They could see the lights flash as the horn drew their attention to a Mercedes SUV two aisles to their left and three cars down.

"Turn off the alarm before someone hears!" Elizabeth warned as they hurried toward the vehicle.

Ashley unlocked the doors as Elizabeth helped Cain into the backseat, laying him down to sleep and covering him with the blanket, then rounding the SUV and climbing into the passenger seat. The engine revved to life and Ashley backed out, then whipped the Mercedes around and headed for the exit.

"Where are we going to go?" Elizabeth asked as Ashley turned onto the street and sped away from the hotel.

"Use the GPS," Ashley said, pointing at the dash as they slowed and stopped at a red light. "It looks like we're in Los Angeles. Edward said Gavin was in Chicago, but I don't know for sure. We need to get out of L.A., somewhere that Edward won't find us."

"Las Vegas is close, but also far enough away," Elizabeth suggested, "and it's heading east, towards Chicago, if that's where we need to go."

"Ok," Ashley agreed, typing in *Las Vegas* on the menu and mapping the route.

"Why'd you take his wallet?" Elizabeth wondered, flipping it open and searching through its contents.

"I was looking for his cell phone, but settled for that. I figured it would slow him down even if it didn't necessarily help us," she replied, accelerating when the light blinked to green.

Elizabeth counted out five hundred dollars in cash, "It does help; this should cover gas."

"Is there any change that we can use at a pay phone?"

"No, nothing."

"I need to call Gavin. We should have enough gas to get to Vegas. Once there, we need to eat and find a phone. Sleep if you can: it's going to be a long night."

22

Michael sat alone in the living room, his suit coat lying next to him on the couch, his tie loosened, collar unbuttoned, and his sleeves rolled up. He looked tired, worn.

With Kayla's help, he'd convinced Gavin and Jamie to rest, that he would stay up and keep watch, just in case Delilah chose to strike in the middle of the night. He held a pistol in his right hand, his left was outstretched, palm up, the key resting in his hand.

"What are you waiting for?" a voice hissed from the shadows.

"You have the key," another voice joined in, "now kill them."

"Kill them all!"

"Kill them."

"Kill them."

"KILL THEM!"

"Shut up," Michael growled, gritting his teeth, aware of the half-dozen red eyes blinking at him in the darkness.

"I thought all you needed was your power back?" a demon taunted, slinking into view. "All you needed was your mask and we got you that."

"Yes, we got you that," one whispered from over his shoulder, "so kill them, Thirteen."

"You will call me Master," he replied softly.

"We will only call you master when you act like our *master*. You aren't him, you're nobody."

"Then leave," Michael urged. "I don't need you. You can't help me anymore."

"If we leave, then so does your power."

"Not so long as I have the mask. It's the source of my power, not you. You simply bow to that power."

"You can't control us, Thirteen. We control you."

"No, I am my *own* master. Leave me."

"You'll be sorry."

"Leave!"

One by one, the demons faded away, their eyes no longer visible. Michael sighed in relief. The more time he spent with Gavin, the more he felt he didn't need the demons, that he could handle things with his own power. He reached over to his jacket and grabbed his mask from an inner pocket, pulling it down over his face.

His body surged with energy and he was no longer tired. The power was still there, unstoppable, unrelenting. A noise startled him and he turned, looking towards the kitchen. Had Delilah slipped into the house unnoticed? Had he been distracted by the demons?

Michael stood and slipped the key into his pocket, the gun at his side, but ready. He crept through the dining room and into the kitchen. What had he heard?

The room was empty. A light on the underside of the microwave illuminated the stovetop. Another under-cabinet light glowed above the sink. He turned to head back to the living room and froze. Little Marley stood staring up at him, a tall glass of water in her hands. She sipped at it, studying his masked face curiously.

"I'm thirsty," she said softly.

Michael tucked the gun in the back of his pants and knelt down, his evil face drawing close to her innocent eyes, "Aren't you scared of me?"

She thought for a moment, then shook her head no, sending her pigtails swinging. Michael cocked his head to the side in confusion. Here was this tiny little girl, young, innocent...and fearless.

"You should go back to bed," he said, the father in him speaking from behind the hideous grin of the mask.

Marley smiled and ran off towards the stairs, the water nearly spilling from the glass with each bounding step. He couldn't believe it. Why wasn't she scared?

Michael sat back down on the couch and pulled the mask off, feeling it tingle like static as it slipped off his face. He stretched it out in front of him and thought of what it meant, what evil he'd done while hiding behind the stitching, and then something inside him broke.

He sobbed into the mask, wadding it up and burying his face in it. Michael wasn't completely sure why he was crying. He knew for certain that he missed his wife, his son, and perhaps seeing Marley reminded him of his family. But he felt like it was more than that deep down inside, a word came to him, a word he'd never understood till that moment, a moment that he felt would somehow come to define the rest of his life: *regret*.

****

Killion stood at the entrance to a posh club, a velvet rope to his right, three dozen people waiting to enter, irritated that he'd bypassed the queue. The doorman raised an arm, welcoming him through the door. Music thumped from inside. He pulled his phone from his pocket and typed a message to Edward as he entered.

Mission accomplished. We must now acquire the key. Tomorrow, we begin phase 2.

****

Gavin woke in a panic. He sat up in the bed, his eyes darting about Jamie and Kayla's guestroom. He thought he'd heard voices, the kind that make the hair on your neck stand on end. Maybe it was just a dream? He tried to think of the last time he'd heard a demon's whisper, but couldn't remember. Still, once it's heard, it can't really be forgotten.

He stretched, scratching the back of his head as he yawned. It must have been a dream. Soon, he was back to sleep, praying that tomorrow, things would go better.

****

Ashley cruised along Interstate 15. They'd been on the road for about two hours. Los Angeles was behind them; now, desert, as far as the eye could see. The fact that they'd successfully escaped was still amusing to her and she smiled as she drove, wondering what Gavin would say when he heard the whole story. She was sure he'd be proud; after all, it was only because of him that she would have ever managed to do something like that.

She glanced in the rearview mirror. Cain was fast asleep, stretched across the back seat. Suddenly, as she watched the boy sleep, all other thoughts left her mind. All she could think about was her possible pregnancy. She'd pushed it from her head, a distraction as she'd planned their escape, but now, on the road, with Elizabeth asleep and no one to keep her company, it was driving her crazy. She remembered the pregnancy test that she'd tried to take only days earlier, but that seemed a lifetime ago.

In the distance, she spotted lights glowing in the vast nothingness of the Nevada desert. Getting closer, she recognized the large red and yellow Shell Oil logo: it was a twenty-four hour service station.

Ashley pulled the SUV off the interstate and parked in front of the store. Elizabeth was still asleep.

This'll only take a minute, she thought, shifting into park and climbing out of the Mercedes.

****

The elevator stopped, the doors sliding open. Killion stepped from within, a beautiful girl on each arm, as he headed for his hotel room. He unlocked the door and led them into the suite.

"Make yourselves at home ladies," he smiled, picking up the phone and dialing room service, ordering several bottles of champagne.

They sat on the couch, already a little drunk, their eyes glassy.

"Come here, Terry," one girl said, twisting her blonde hair with her finger, "we want to help you celebrate."

"Yeah," the other said seductively, "you work so hard."

"Just a moment ladies," Killion said, I'll be right back.

He slipped out of the room and knocked on the door of the next suite over. Killion checked his phone, his brother had never replied to his text.

"Edward?" he urged, knocking again. "I brought entertainment."

There was no response. He placed his ear close to the door, but heard nothing.

More for me, he thought, *see you in the morning, chum.*

Killion returned to his room. The girls had undressed, their risqué club-wear tossed on the floor.

"More for me, indeed," he whispered, closing the door behind him.

****

Ashley stood in an aisle at the road-side service station, staring at the only pregnancy test on the shelf. It was a brand she'd never heard of, so she was trying to decide if it was worth trying. She picked it up and read the directions, debating whether or not it would be accurate. Finally, she decided it was better than nothing. She then picked up a bottle of water and a small snack-size bag of trail mix as she headed to the register.

The man behind the counter yawned as he rang the items through and took her money. He handed her the change and then sat down on a stool behind the counter.

"Can I use the phone? I really need to make a call."

"The store phone is for *store* use only," he replied in a monotone voice. "There's a payphone next to the restroom."

"And where's the restroom?" Ashley asked.

He mustered the strength to point to the rear of the store, another yawn erupting on his face. She nodded and turned, the small bag of items in her hand.

She found the phone next to a door with a sign designating it as a unisex restroom. She reached for the receiver, but realized there was none, the metal-wrapped chord dangling from the unit, wires protruding from the cut end. She rolled her eyes. At least she could use the restroom.

Ashley's nose scrunched as she opened the door. The stench of urine hung in the air and the fluorescent bulb flickered above her as she closed the door, locking it behind her. She set the bag down in the sink and stared at herself in the dirty mirror. Decidedly, she pulled the test from the bag and ripped into the box, then removed the little white stick from its cellophane sleeve.

She glanced at the toilet, knowing what she had to do. It, like the mirror, the walls, and the floor, needed a good cleaning. There was no way she was going to sit on that seat. Ashley pulled down her pants and awkwardly squatted just inches above the filthy toilet, the pregnancy test held beneath her.

At first, her bladder refused to cooperate. All she could think about was the gross state of things. And on top of that, it seemed comical, even ironic, that she would be in this situation: miles away from her husband, abducted, on a road trip to Vegas with a stranger, and now hovering over a toilet while she attempted to pee onto a stick that may or may not prove what she had come to suspect.

She closed her eyes and focused, breathing through her mouth so as not to smell the foulness around her, imagining herself in the comfort of her own bathroom. Finally, she relaxed and went. She couldn't help but smile.

As soon as she finished, she put the cap back on the stick and pulled up her pants. She placed the pregnancy test on the edge of the sink and waited, staring at the small window that would announce the results: a smiley face for positive, a frowning face for negative.

The anticipation was almost too great. She stared and stared, waiting for a little smiling glimmer of hope amidst the chaos. Two eyes appeared on the stick.

"Come on, come on," she chanted, cheering along the little face as it took shape.

There was a knock on the door.

"Almost done," Ashley called out.

They knocked again.

"I'll be right out," she said, growing annoyed.

This time, the knock was a little stronger.

"Occupied!" she yelled.

The knocking stopped.

Ashley stood, rocking from foot to foot, her tennis shoes sticking to the grimy floor as she shifted back and forth. Finally, the mouth began to take shape: it looked a little like a smile.

"Yes!" she shouted, raising her hands triumphantly.

As she celebrated, she bumped the sink, sending the pregnancy test skittering down the basin. Ashley quickly snatched it up and flipped it over.

"No!" she whined, the window which only seconds ago looked to be smiling was now a blob of color.

She'd missed it. She was sure it was a smile, but it was faint and hadn't completely taken shape.

Dejected, she picked her bag up from the sink and dropped the pregnancy test in the trash. Ashley opened the door: a heavy-set woman dressed in a flowered muumuu stood beside the door, sweaty, snorting heaving breaths. Apparently the desert wasn't agreeing with her.

"It's about time," she huffed.

Ashley pushed past her and headed for the SUV. Elizabeth was awake.

"Bathroom break?" she asked as Ashley climbed back into the driver's seat and started the engine.

"Something like that," she said, backing up, then swinging around to continue east on I-15.

****

Edward rose slowly from where he lay on the floor. The room was dark and he was disoriented. His head was throbbing, his face tender. Edward touched the back of his head, his hair matted with blood from where Ashley had bludgeoned him.

He managed to stumble to the door, grasping for the handle in the dark. It was locked. Edward searched his pockets for his keys, but they were gone, as was his gun.

"You've got to be kidding me?" he mumbled.

****

Killion lay awake in bed, staring at the ceiling, a girl nestled up on each side of him. But oddly enough, he couldn't stop thinking about his brother. Why hadn't Edward answered the door?

"Excuse me, love," he whispered, climbing over one of the girls.

He pulled the sheets back over her and watched as, in his absence, they cuddled up together. Amused, he quickly dressed and checked his phone, hoping he'd simply missed Edward's call or text, but there were no new messages. He tucked a pistol into the waist of his pants and grabbed his keys, then headed into the hallway.

Killion stopped at his brother's room and knocked, "Edward, you there?"

He could have sworn he heard a muffled reply, but it sounded like it came from another room. Killion called him again. This time, the response came as pounding on the door behind him: the secure room where they'd kept Elizabeth and her son.

Killion turned, his head cocked in suspicion, "Ed, that you?"

Edward shouted from behind the locked door. Killion quickly sorted through the keycards in his pocket. His brother scowled at him as the door swung open.

"They got away," he grunted, his eyes adjusting to the bright light that flooded in from the hall. "Elizabeth and the boy, and the girl from the bloody other room, they got away. Somehow, Ashley must have found her way into their room and they tricked me, saying the boy was sick. Before I could react, she was beating me with a lamp."

Killion was furious. His jaw flinched, the veins in his forehead pulsed.

"You let them get away? We don't yet have the key. They were our leverage!"

"Look at my face," Edward argued, "you think I didn't put up a fight? She jumped me from the bloody shadows!"

"You got beat up by a little girl," Killion grunted. "She should have been no match for you."

"Well it happened."

Killion grabbed his brother by the arm and led him back to his suite, slamming the door behind them. Startled, the girls woke.

"Clean yourself up," Killion ordered his brother, before turning to the girls, "and you two, get out now!"

They clambered out of bed in a frenzy, gathering their clothes as quickly as they could before finding themselves ushered hastily into the hallway, naked and confused.

"I see you were celebrating," Edward sighed, washing the blood from his face and hair. "I take it everything went according to plan?"

Killion didn't answer: he was still fuming. He stood over the disheveled bed, quickly packing his clothes, gathering up all his things from the room.

"Not everything," he finally said. "The Order is dead and we have the money. I also provided Franklin with a gun, the same gun I used to kill the police officer, the stewardess, *and* McNamara, so that further conceals our presence in Los Angeles."

"And the .308 rounds?"

"The custom made, hand loaded rounds you specialize in, no prints, no trace; one spent shell, here in my pocket," Killion answered. "Everything was perfect, except that you let our only leverage escape."

Edward stepped from the bathroom and glared at his brother. His face was bruised, but he looked much better with the blood washed away.

"There was no way Ashley could have made it out of her locked room and into another locked room. There was no reason to assume there was a threat."

"Well it happened," Killion barked back. "Now gather your things, the equipment, everything. Get the *heli* loaded."

"And where are we going?" Edward asked.

"Chicago."

23

A young man, not yet twenty, hid behind a stack of round wooden barrels in an alleyway just off the dark, moonlit cobblestone street. To his right, a butcher shop, on the left, a clockmaker. He wore dirty trousers and a torn woolen jacket. A 1930's-esque driving cap sat crooked atop his curly-haired head. A white band wrapped around the sleeve of his jacket, a blue Star of David stitched onto it. A man across the street spoke in Polish, pointing at the clockmaker's house. The young man held his breath as two armed guards saluted the informant, then spun quickly on their heels and marched up to the home, pounding loudly on the door.

"Nazis," the young man muttered disdainfully under his breath.

"Leroy," a boy, several years younger, whispered from the shadows deeper in the alley, "what are we going to do?"

"We wait. When they enter, we follow."

"And then?"

"We strike," Leroy said, brandishing a razor sharp knife he'd lifted from the butcher's.

The boys listened intently as the door creaked open, the sound followed by commands in German. *Jude* was all they understood.

"Are you ready?" Leroy asked.

"No," the younger boy answered.

"It's too late for that," he replied. "Let's go."

Quickly, they crept from their hiding place in the alley and snuck in through the open front door. There stood the clockmaker, a hunched, old Jew, wire framed glasses perched upon his nose, a tattered apron tied around his waist. His wife stood cowering behind him. A fireplace illuminated the room with orange flickers that danced in the drafty stone row-house.

Leroy moved without hesitation. The two Nazis stood between him and the old couple, their backs to the door. He leapt forward, knife in hand, taking hold of the first guard and slashing his throat. The second man spun quickly, a Luger raised and ready. He fired, the shot ringing loud in the silent Polish village. Leroy lunged, grabbing the German by his uniform and butting him in the head before thrusting the blade into the man's belly, twisting the knife, blood spilling out from beneath the soldier's jacket. Leroy watched as the life in the man's eyes fled, till finally, he let the body slump to the floor.

There he stood, covered in German blood, breathing hard, the adrenaline flowing through his young veins driving him with the ferociousness of a lion. And then it hit him, a burning in his side. He looked down, a hole in his shirt marked where the bullet had entered. There was so much blood; hard to distinguish what was his and what was that of his victims.

The room began to spin and the burning began to fade as utter cold consumed him. He felt as if he fell right through the floor, plummeting into an infinite chasm of darkness, spinning, tumbling, churning, on and on. The pain was gone, all memory retreated as time became meaningless. All that was left was despair.

Delilah woke in a cold sweat, throwing off the covers and sitting up in bed. She looked at the clock: *5:00 AM*.

"It was just a dream," she sighed in relief, knowing that her grandfather had survived the German occupation of Poland.

She stood and stretched, looking out over the city, the sun glowing on the eastern horizon. Delilah filled a glass with water from the bathroom sink and gulped it down, then set the glass on the counter and stared at herself in the mirror. Her hair fell across her shoulders and she wore a white, ribbed tank-top with lacy black underwear. Though to the world she was the perfect image of beauty, what she saw in her reflection both excited and disgusted her. Glaring back was a killer, cold and calculating, her eyes piercing. And she had the body of a lover, exotic and tempting. But her heart was soft, broken. Orphaned and raised by her grandfather, she had followed only one path in life: *his*. He trained her to kill, forged her into a lethal weapon from a young age, taught her how to strike from the shadows and use fear as an ally. She was excellent, a master of death and seduction, but had never known love. True, her grandfather, Leroy, loved her very much, but it never replaced the emptiness in her heart.

Delilah pushed aside her insecurities, once again embracing the killer within, and headed back to the bed, pulling a pair of designer slacks from her small suitcase and sliding into them. She removed her top and put on a bra, followed by a tailored blouse and finally a pair of heels.

She picked up her phone and dialed her grandfather. It was early in the morning but he always answered whenever she rang. The call finally went to voicemail.

"Saba," she said, "I had a terrible dream. I saw you during the war and you killed two Nazis who were threatening an old Jewish couple, but one of the men managed to shoot you. You fell into darkness, Saba. It was so real. Please call me back: I must hear your voice!"

Delilah felt better having simply spoken the words. She scanned through her previous calls and found McNamara's phone number, she wanted to inform him that today she would have his key.

The phone rang and she heard the other end pick up, "Reverend, it is Delilah. I have excellent news: today, I will have your key!"

Killion hesitated before answering. He stood on the roof of the hotel, at the edge of a helipad, his brother loading the last of their gear and equipment aboard their specially outfitted Blackhawk helicopter.

"My, that is good news," he said coyly.

Delilah was speechless. She hadn't heard his voice in years.

"Terry?" she managed.

"Yes, love."

"Are you working for the Reverend as well? Are you on this job?"

"I've missed you, Delilah," he toyed.

"Answer my question, Terry."

"No," Killion admitted. "The Reverend *was* my job, as was his partner, Franklin."

"Is McNamara dead?" she prodded, a knot growing in her stomach.

She knew that death followed Killion wherever he went. He was an equally sufficient killer; and, once upon a time, her first and only love.

"He is; Franklin too," he explained triumphantly, knowing that what he was about to say would crush her. "The Order has been taken care of as well."

"What?!"

"Yes, love; all of them."

Delilah felt faint as she quickly sat down on the bed, tears welling in her dark brown eyes, "What about my grandfather, does he live?"

"I'm sorry to say, *no*, Delilah."

"How dare you," she growled.

"My contract required it. Surely you understand. Nothing personal, he was just a mark. Now you said you'll have the key today?"

"Don't change the subject," Delilah scolded.

"This is now the subject. You're grandfather, much like us, is now history. We can still work together: we're both professionals."

Delilah sat in silence.

"I'm truly sorry for your loss."

She still refused to react.

"You know I still think about you," Killion said wistfully. "No woman has ever satisfied me like you. I'll call you upon landing and when I arrive in Chicago, and you deliver the key, perhaps we can...*celebrate*, for old time's sake?"

She'd had enough. Delilah hung up the phone and wept.

****

Ashley spotted the warm glow of the Vegas Strip a few miles ahead on the interstate. They would soon be one step closer to safety, Los Angeles now four hours behind them. Elizabeth stared out the side window. Ashley had been silent since they'd left the road-side service station.

"What's the plan then?" Elizabeth asked as they neared the Strip.

Ashley thought for a moment and then replied, "We need to find a twenty-four hour diner, someplace low-key where we can eat and use a telephone. I have to call Gavin, let him know I'm alright."

"I can call Michael as well," Elizabeth smiled.

****

Gavin woke to the smell of coffee. Stumbling down the stairs groggily, he found Jamie and Kayla already in the kitchen. Michael stood at the front door, still keeping watch.

"Morning," Gavin said, coming off the last step.

Michael turned and nodded. Jamie poured Gavin a hot cup of coffee.

"Did she call yet?" Gavin asked.

"Nothing yet," Kayla said as she buttered some toast.

"It's still early," Michael added from the other room. "She thinks she's in control, so everything will be done on her schedule."

The three men gathered around the dining room table, the key and Rocco's phone resting in the very middle. They sipped anxiously on their coffees, staring at the phone, willing it to ring. No one dared say a word, but they all knew the anticipation was almost too great. If all went according to plan, Delilah would soon be of no threat and they could focus on getting their families back.

****

Ashley and Elizabeth were now in the heart of Vegas. Everywhere they looked, brilliant signs battled for their attention, each one flashing with allure and promise.

"Whoa," Cain said sleepily, awoken by the lights. "Are we in Disneyland?

"Disneyland for adults, baby," Elizabeth answered drolly.

Ashley smiled at her new friend as they continued on down the Strip. Finally finding a place to eat, they pulled into the parking lot. Ashley took the first spot they came to and they quickly climbed out of the SUV.

"Mommy," Cain said, tugging on Elizabeth's hand, "I really have to pee bad!"

"Alright, sweetie," she replied.

Ashley offered to get a table while the two of them headed for the restroom. She looked around anxiously for a phone as the greeter led her to a small booth in the back corner of the diner.

"Is there a payphone around?" Ashley asked as she slid into one side of the table.

"Right out front, by the street, Hun," the waitress said between chomps on the gum she chewed like a cow with cud as she pointed in the direction of the parking lot. "Now can I get you a coffee or some soda?"

"Decaf?" Ashley said.

"Sure thing. And you've got two more coming?"

"Yeah."

"Back in a flash."

Ashley looked around the restaurant nervously. She'd tucked Edward's gun in the rear waist of her jeans, hopefully no one had seen it. Elizabeth led Cain to the table, helping him into the booth across from Ashley, then sliding in next to him just as the waitress returned with Ashley's coffee.

"What are you drinking, Hun?"

"Um, coffee as well, black," Elizabeth answered the waitress, "and milk for the little guy."

"Right away. I'll be back in a minute to take your order."

The waitress returned as promised and they ordered a huge plate of *The World's Largest Pancakes*, or so the menu claimed. Ashley stirred cream into her coffee. Elizabeth yawned as Cain began coloring on the placemat with some crayons he found tucked away by the salt and pepper shakers on the table.

"I can't wait any longer," Ashley finally blurted. "There's a phone outside. I'm going to go call Gavin."

Ashley hurried from the table and left the restaurant, passing a group of obviously drunk men on the last leg of their bachelor party. She did her best to steer clear of them.

"Hey, baby," one of them said as best he could, slurring disgracefully, "what'll an hour cost me?"

Thank God I've got a gun, she thought, ignoring his distasteful advance.

She dropped the change into the slot on the payphone and dialed Gavin's cell phone.

****

Nearly forty-five minutes had passed as Gavin, Jamie and Michael sat in silence. Jamie stood and headed for the coffee pot, ready for a refill.

"Anybody want more?" he called from the kitchen.

Neither of them answered. A cell phone's ringtone screamed in the stillness of the morning. Jamie raced back to the dining room, nearly spilling his hot coffee as he did.

"Is it Delilah?" he asked.

"No," Michael frowned. "It's not Rocco's phone."

"It's mine," Gavin explained, reaching into the pocket of his jeans.

"Who is it?" Jamie wondered.

"I don't recognize the number...area code *702*?"

"Well answer it," Michael urged.

"Hello?" he said, raising the phone to his ear.

"Gavin!" Ashley cried excitedly.

24

The rotors on the Blackhawk beat against the cool night air. Edward and Terrance Killion sat in the cockpit, Edward piloting, both wearing headsets so they could communicate.

"What's our status," Terrance asked.

"We're now in Nevada airspace. We'll need to land and refuel when we reach Colorado, but then we'll make it to Chicago with our auxiliary tanks full. We have a little over a thousand mile range."

"Where will you refuel?"

"Kit Carson County Airport," Edward explained, "it's a public strip where there will be no questions. Back in the air, at a steady one hundred and fifty knots, we'll reach the next airfield in a around six and one half hours. There, we'll have a place to hangar and rest for the night."

"Rest?" Terrance questioned angrily. "We're this close to obtaining the key!"

"Hey," Edward laughed, "I'm flying for nearly twelve straight hours. We'll be in the Chicago area around 8PM. The key can wait till morning."

"Wasn't your nap on the floor in the hotel room enough for you?"

"Very funny," Edward scowled.

Killion glared out the side of the cockpit, but knew his brother was right. By the time they land in Chicago, he'd be pushing thirty-eight hours without sleep. He needed to be sharp. What would one more night hurt?

****

"Ashley!" Gavin exclaimed, leaping to his feet, nearly toppling the chair in which he sat. "Thank God! Are you ok? Are you hurt? Where are you? Come on, Ash, talk to me!"

Jamie listened intently. Hope grew in Michael as he considered that if Ashley was alive, his family most likely was as well.

"Gavin, slow down," she said, "I'm alright, I'm in Las Vegas."

"How'd you get to Vegas?"

"We escaped from a hotel in Los Angeles where a man named Edward was holding us hostage."

"Wait, *we?*" Gavin asked.

"Uh huh. There was a woman named Elizabeth. She and her son were being held in the room next door to mine. We helped each other escape."

"Elizabeth is with you, her son as well, and they're both ok?" Gavin asked.

Michael listened curiously when he heard his wife's name. Jamie perked up as well. This was unexpected news.

Ashley was confused, "Yes, they're fine."

"She says they're alright!" Gavin said, turning to Michael.

"Who are you talking to?" Ashley wondered.

"Elizabeth's husband, Michael Laurent."

217

Ashley wasn't making sense of the situation. Was she to believe that by some inane chance the husband of the woman she'd randomly been kidnapped with, then helped escape, was somehow connected to Gavin? How could this be?

"Her husband is with you now?"

"Yes, since two nights ago. We were working together to find all of you," Gavin explained.

"How did you two end up helping each other?"

"It's a long story, Ash. And I promise I'll tell you everything. But for now, you guys need to keep safe and work together."

"We have a long drive ahead of us and I can't wait that long, these questions driving me mad. I need your explanation."

Gavin took a deep breath, he knew what he was about to share would possibly send Ashley into a panic. He needed her strong, focused for the journey home.

"Ash," he said, pausing briefly, "We know Michael. We met him in New York City, five years ago."

Ashley stared as a metro bus rumbled down the street, slowing to pick up the drunken bachelors, "I don't remember a Michael?"

"Ashley, what has Elizabeth told you about herself?"

"Um, not much really, we haven't had time to talk. Things have been rushed. Why?"

"Well," Gavin replied, "she, Elizabeth, is the daughter of Dr. Maurice Triton…"

Ashley stood in silence.

"…as in Tri-Corp Triton…"

She did not respond as she processed the information.

"Ash, you ok? Did you get what I said?" Gavin asked.

She thought for another moment, then spoke, "Yeah, I get it. But that doesn't explain her husband…we never met her husband."

"We did actually," Gavin sighed, ready to lower the boom, "but we never knew him as Michael, we knew him by another name: *Thirteen.*"

****

Delilah still sat on the edge of her bed as she watched the sun rise over Lake Michigan. Her face was red, streaked with tears. Desperate and alone, she reached beneath her pillow and took hold of her pistol. She raised it to her head, the barrel pressed uncomfortably against her temple. Slowly, she clicked back the hammer and then switched the safety to fire. Delilah closed her eyes and took a deep breath as she readied to pull the trigger.

"I'm sorry, Saba," she whispered, his face flashing before her eyes.

She exhaled, then took another deep breath: it was now or never. Delilah softly prayed in Hebrew, asking God to forgive her for the many deaths she'd been responsible for and for what she was about to do.

"Accept my blood as atonement for all my sins," she said tearfully as she began to put pressure on the trigger.

Her finger flinched: there was a knock on the door. Delilah turned and looked at the entrance to the room.

"No thank you," she answered, thinking it may be room service.

She closed her eyes and raised the gun once again. Another knock echoed in the room, this one stronger, more demanding of her attention.

Delilah stood and approached the door, her gun hidden behind her back as she peered through the peep hole. No one was there. She opened the door and cautiously peeked out from behind the frame. The hallway was empty.

Confused, she stepped back into her room and closed the door. She tossed her gun onto the bed and wiped the tears from her eyes, then leaned against the window, her face glowing in the warmth of the rising sun.

The shadows in the room gave way to light as the sun's rays illuminated every corner, washing away the darkness.

Again, Delilah began to cry; but now, tears of joy. Outside on the window ledge, down by her feet, sat a white dove, its head bobbing as it looked up at her. She knelt down, her heart full of hope. The dove flew away, disappearing into the glare of the sun.

"A peace offering," she mused softly.

Only moments ago, she was ready to take her own life. But this was a sign, she was sure of it. God had spoken to her and she knew exactly what needed to be done.

****

"Gavin, that's not funny," Ashley blurted, "Thirteen is dead. He died in the blast at the hospital, remember? There's no way he survived. The fact that you escaped with no more than a broken arm was nothing short of miraculous."

"I can't explain it any simpler," Gavin admitted, "he did survive and he's here with us now."

"So where are *you* then?" Ashley asked, changing the subject as she wiped a tear from her cheek.

"We're in Chicago, at your sister's," Gavin answered.

"And Thirteen is there? Is everyone alright?"

"Yes, we're all fine, better than, knowing that you are free."

"And you trust Michael?"

"Yeah," Gavin smiled, "as I said, he's working with me. We've been trying to figure out how to rescue you and Elizabeth. You were being ransomed for Triton's old key. But it sounds like you've done alright on your own."

Ashley was so unsure, nearly in shock, from what she'd learned, "We've managed, I'm sure you'd have been proud."

"I am! Now tell me how you escaped."

"Well," Ashley said, pausing to straighten out the facts, "I was being held in a room neighboring Elizabeth, in a hotel of some sort. I managed to traverse from my balcony to hers and we came up with a plan. We tricked Edward into thinking her son was severely ill. When he came to check on him, I attacked Edward, took his keys, wallet, and gun, and then we stole his SUV and used the GPS to get to Las Vegas. I figured we would blend in if there were more people, easier to hide in case Edward came after us."

"So this *Edward*, was he acting alone?" Gavin wondered.

"No. He had a partner, someone I never saw, but Edward mentioned that he was negotiating our safe return, that this other man was a friend of yours and that you were on your way to meet me in LA. Elizabeth did mention meeting another man, Killion, I think she said."

"Well, I had no idea you were in Los Angeles," Gavin admitted, "in fact, we were grasping at straws trying to figure out where you guys were being held. How'd you end up in LA in the first place?"

"I was at work and strange things started happening, displaced voices, creepy feelings, just like New York. I was wandering the museum during my lunch break when suddenly everything went dark. I woke up in that hotel room. I could smell salt water and see the ocean from my room; and when I watched the sunset over the water, I knew I was on the west coast, but I didn't know it was Los Angeles for sure."

"The city of angels," Gavin said sarcastically, "seems fitting after all we've been through."

"So how did Thirteen end up working with you?" Ashley asked, skeptically returning to the unlikely partnership.

"Well, long story short," Gavin laughed, "I don't think I have a job at the toy store anymore. From what I could gather, Rocco, a hunter who worked out of Boston, not my favorite guy, severe Napoleon complex...anyway, he must have sent a unit to capture me at the store while he planned to find you at the house."

"So what happened at work?"

"An assault team raided the building and shot it up, but I managed to escape."

"Uh huh, go on," Ashley said.

"When I got home, I found Rocco dead on the kitchen floor and you gone. That's when I ran into Michael. That first night was uneasy, but I've grown to trust him. He has as much at stake in this as I do. He explained that his wife and son were being held, same as you, and that the only way to get our families back was in exchange for the key, so here we are in Chicago."

"Well, we're no longer captives," Ashley said, "and you still have the key. We can just tell them no, right?"

"I wish we could," Gavin sighed. "But even with you free, whoever is after this key will keep coming after it. And now that they know it's in Chicago, they won't stop until they have it."

"Well we can't let that happen then. What's the plan?"

Gavin thought for a moment before he replied, "You've got a long way to go before you reach Chicago. You have cash?"

"Yeah," Ashley answered, "it was in the wallet."

"Good. Go to a convenience store or gas station, someplace low key that sells prepaid cell phones. Pick one up and hit the road. Call me as soon as you're out of Vegas. That way I'll have your number. And it's good you took his gun, smart thinking! Hopefully you won't need it, but if necessary, you're ready."

"What are you going to do?" she asked.

"We're waiting on a call from a contact, the person with whom we're supposed to make the exchange. We'll make sure she's taken care of and then we'll work our way up the chain till we can finish this once and for all. Tell me, Ash, did Edward ever mention the names Delilah or Big Mac?"

"Not in front of me, no."

"Well, hopefully we'll get more information when we meet with her today. She's expecting to receive the key, but that's not going to happen."

"Be careful," Ashley warned.

"I will. Now get moving: the sooner you can get a cell phone and get on the road, the better! I love you, Ash."

"Love you too, Gavin, love you too."

****

Gavin had only just hung up the phone when Michael spoke, "So your wife managed an escape?"

"Yeah," Gavin said, shaking his head in amazement, "and your family is with her. They're in Las Vegas. Apparently they were being held in LA, but they managed to get away."

"And now we have the upper hand," Michael smiled.

"Let's not get ahead of ourselves, guys," Jamie reasoned. "They've got a long road ahead of them; and when we meet with Delilah, things could still go wrong. If she manages to get the key, then who knows what could happen when it's in the hands of whoever is after it."

"Is there anything more you can tell us about the key, Michael, anything that would explain why it's so valuable?" Kayla wondered picking it up off the table.

"It's just a trinket. Triton was obsessed with it, thinking it unlocked some secrets to the occult. But it's just a key."

"And you're sure of this?" Jamie questioned.

"Well, no," Michael replied. "But I've held it, sensed its energy. There's nothing special about this key,."

"What if you're wrong?" Gavin prodded.

Michael stood, the chair legs squeaking against the hardwood floor as he did. His countenance grew stern and his brow furrowed as he thought. What if he was wrong? What if this key was not just a scrap of rusty old metal, but a key that could unlock the beginning of the end, a key that could open the gates of hell, the great abyss? What if he was wrong and this key unleashed the power of Satan on this earth and marked the arrival of the apocalypse? But how could it; after all it was just a key?

"You had better pray I'm right."

****

Outside, crows gathered on the power lines, their shrill caws looming hauntingly in the briskness of the morning. Sunlight broke over the peaks of the rooftops, chasing away the last remnants of night. An angel stood watch on the porch of the Branson home. Beautifully detailed armor graced his chiseled frame and his white feathered wings glowed in the morning sun. At his side was his sword, his hand resting on the hilt as he paced.

Though the skies were clear, a storm was coming; the end of a peace that had lasted for five years. Triton tried to unleash the wrath of hell but, in the end, failed. Now, a force, darker and more evil, threatened to break that peace. Even so, the angel stood guard, watching as the crows chattered amongst themselves, sharing their findings with the demons that lurked in the shadows.

"It's here," they said, over and over, cawing and pecking at one another in a frenzy, "it's here."

25

Delilah checked her watch: it was time to contact Gavin. She'd formulated her plan and decided her course of action. Dialing the number for Rocco's cell, she waited for someone to answer.

Killion would regret what he'd done. Her grandfather's death would be avenged.

****

"It's her!" Gavin said, grabbing the phone up off the table as he prepared to answer. "Hello?"

"There's a change of plans," Delilah said.

"You've got that right," Gavin replied. "You're leverage escaped last night. With my wife free, you have nothing to trade."

"No," she answered, her voice soft, fragile, "please listen."

Gavin was confused. This was not the same woman who had overpowered them in the park the night before.

"I am no longer concerned with the key. I have cancelled my contract and I ask for your help," Delilah explained.

Gavin listened intently. Michael paced as Jamie stared on, his brow furrowed.

"I must speak to you in person. The man who took your families, the man responsible for all of this, crossed a line and I must have revenge."

"So you're telling me you don't want the key now," Gavin recapped sarcastically, "and that you want my help in exacting revenge? Sounds like some reverse psychology *BS* to me; definitely a trap."

"Of the two of us, you are the one who set a trap for me, a rather poor one at that," she said, "but, I speak the truth. I will let you choose our place of meeting. Please, help me."

"Just a second," Gavin said, muting the cell phone and turning to face Michael. "She says she needs our help."

"I don't trust her," he replied.

"Yeah," Jamie added, "it doesn't make any sense. She's trying to trick us."

Gavin nodded and un-muted the phone, "Fine: you want to talk, we'll talk. Union Station, two hours."

He hung up the phone without waiting for her response. Kayla looked on anxiously as Gavin set the phone back down on the table and crossed his arms.

"So what are we going to do?" Jamie asked.

"We go on as planned," Gavin said. "We'll take the decoy key and give it to her, then we follow it like bread crumbs to the so-called *man responsible* and we finish this."

"Suppose she's telling the truth," Kayla reasoned. "What if she has had a change of heart."

"She's a killer," Jamie answered, "and killers don't change."

Michael shifted uneasily as Jamie's words slapped him across the face, "Do you really believe that?"

"Sorry," Jamie apologized, realizing what he'd just said.

"Regardless," Gavin jumped in, bringing their attention back to the real issue, "we can't just pretend that now that Ashley and Elizabeth are free, our problems are solved. This Delilah is a big problem. We'll meet and talk, give her the fake, and see where it leads. Got it?"

The group nodded their confirmation. They believed they had the upper hand; but still, Kayla felt a knot twisting up inside her. Something wasn't right, but what?

****

Ashley returned to the table, praying that the distrust she felt for Elizabeth wasn't showing on her face. Elizabeth smiled as Ashley sat and they quickly ate their food in silence, anxious to get back on the road.

Upon finishing their hasty, yet much needed meals, they retreated quickly to the stolen SUV and used the GPS to find the nearest convenience store. The drive was short and they found themselves roaming the food aisles, gathering snacks and drinks for the road.

"How about cheese and peanut butter crackers?" Elizabeth asked Cain, placing the package into the shopping basket which he tried to carry with some degree of difficulty.

He smiled, "Yes, please."

Ashley watched the two interact, imagining herself in the same position. If she really was pregnant, which would she want: boy or girl? She hadn't even thought of that yet, but the topic of gender suddenly seemed overwhelming. A girl would be so cute, pink and bows, like playing dress-up every day; but a boy, she smiled at the thought, a little daredevil.

"I'll be right back," Ashley said.

She read the aisle signage, searching for health and beauty. It was the last row of gondolas, but she finally found it. Ashley studied the multitude of pregnancy tests, each one claiming to be the best, most doctor recommended. Some used plus or minus signs, others answered *yes* or *no*, but which one to trust?

Elizabeth turned the corner just as Ashley picked up a box. Cain followed behind, softly humming a melody.

"You're kidding?" she asked, hurrying to Ashley's side. "Are you really?"

"That's what I'm hoping to find out," she sighed. "And so far, things haven't been easy, so I need the most accurate, most precise test that will tell me whether or not I am, God forbid any more...*interruptions*."

"Here," Elizabeth offered, taking the box from Ashley's hands and replacing it with another brand. "This is what I've use whenever I thought I might be. So far, it's never been wrong."

Ashley scanned the marketing on the package, "99% accurate, obstetrician recommended, easy to understand response: sounds like all the others, but I'll keep my fingers crossed. Thanks!"

They headed towards the front of the store. Prepaid cell phones were displayed behind the register, hanging on pegs, dangling above shelves filled with cartons of cigarettes. Elizabeth took the full basket from Cain and rested it on the checkout. Ashley asked the clerk to ring up a phone as well, selecting the one that came with the most minutes. She also purchased a car charger. He handed her the change and they made their way out to the SUV.

"So when are you going to take the pregnancy test?" Elizabeth asked as they settled into the vehicle and fastened their safety belts.

"In a while, the next time we stop for food. I just want to get back on the road," Ashley replied.

Elizabeth removed the phone from its packaging and plugged in the charger: a little green light lit up on the front of the phone. Ashley set Chicago as their destination in the GPS. Soon, Las Vegas would be behind them, one step closer to home.

****

Gavin left the others to their discussion at the dining room table and stepped out onto the front porch, the warm morning greeting him. He was immediately aware of the angel's presence, but neglected to turn and face him.

"What are you doing here?" Gavin asked, his voice aloof.

The angel grinned, "You, of all people, need not be reminded that you are never alone."

"Well; recently, it doesn't seem like you guys have been around much when I've needed you."

"Reality, perception does not make, my friend."

"Yeah thanks, Yoda," Gavin quipped.

They stood in silence, the angel watching the crows, Gavin staring at nothing in particular.

"So why are you here then," Gavin finally asked, "have you come to help?"

The angel thought before answering, "I am not here for what is, but what is to come."

"Seriously," Gavin chided, "cut the Jedi gibberish."

"What happened to you, Gavin?" the angel asked. "Are you not still the warrior God created you to be?"

"Well God and I haven't been speaking much. Or at least I talk to Him, but it seems He never has anything to say. I figured God was telling me I'm on my own on this one."

"He's answering, I assure you. But maybe you're not listening, maybe He's not saying what you want to hear?" the angel reasoned. "Either way: this is just the beginning, and you know it."

Gavin turned his gaze to the darkly stained wooden planks of the porch. He knew the angel was right.

"So how has the church hunt been going, found one you like?"

Gavin laughed, "What does that have to do with anything?"

"It is everything. Without fellowship, the spirit inside grows weak. Iron sharpens iron and you're getting dull, my friend."

"Well the whole *Ashley-getting-kidnapped* thing kind of threw a wrench in those plans and besides that, it just seems like the churches around us have nothing to offer and..."

"And?" the angel asked.

"I'm just making excuses," Gavin admitted. "No church is perfect, no church ever will be. We need to find a place and settle in."

"Church, like anything else, only gives what you put into it. As much as a church serves its people, the people must also serve the church."

Gavin smiled at the angel. It was as if something woke inside him, something that had been sleeping for years. The fire that he'd last felt in New York City was rekindled and he realized that life was just as exciting now, only different.

"Thanks," Gavin said, feeling the angel's comforting grip as he placed his strong hand firmly on Gavin's shoulder.

"One more thing," the angel said, stepping from the porch and stretching his wings, "Joseph sends his regards."

With those words, he leapt into the air and disappeared into the sun. Gavin leaned on the porch railing, thinking about what the angel had said. The cawing of the crows drew his attention to the power lines and the angel's words rang in his ears: *I am not here for what is, but what is to come.*

****

"It's time to go," Jamie said, picking up the decoy key from the table. "Where's Gavin?"

"On the porch, I think?" Kayla replied.

They stepped out the front door and stared curiously at Gavin. He seemed mesmerized by something, his gaze fixed upward, his head tilted back.

"You ok?" Jamie asked.

Gavin didn't respond.

"Hey, buddy..." Jamie urged, reaching out and tapping his brother-in-law.

"The birds," Gavin finally said, his eyes unblinking, "more and more keep landing on the power line; look!"

Gavin was right. They watched as a mass of black birds teetered on the wire high above the street, cawing and pecking.

"What's the deal?" Kayla wondered. "I've never seen so many, not like this."

Michael shook his head, "Watchers, that's what they are. They're here to intimidate, something I would have done in my previous life to invoke fear in my prey. But they're harmless. I prefer hell hounds personally."

"Who sent them?" Kayla asked.

"Don't know; maybe Delilah?" Michael reasoned.

Jamie turned to Kayla, his hand outstretched, "Here's the key. I want you to hold on to it while we're gone."

She nodded, taking it from him, her fingers wrapping around it tightly.

"If you don't hear from us in the next hour, I want you to take the kids and go straight to the police station. Take the key. Go there and wait for me."

"I will."

****

Delilah watched as the cab she'd waived down slowed to a stop. She entered and dirccted the driver to take her to Union Station.

She stared blankly at the city as they navigated the traffic. Her mind was racing. She was well aware of Gavin's distrust, but she had to reason with him, make him understand.

Her purse sat next to her. Delilah reached in and took hold of her Sig Sauer pistol, feeling the safety and checking the hammer: safe, but cocked. She prayed she wouldn't need to use it: killing valuable allies wouldn't help her cause.

The car stopped at Union Station. She paid and stepped from the cab. Soon, she would find out whether she could gain Gavin's trust; and then, she would have revenge.

26

"This is it," Jamie said, pulling the BMW to the curb. "You guys ready?"

Gavin chambered a round in his pistol. Michael nodded calmly. The men stepped from the SUV and headed for the bustling main hall. They chose a bench which provided a good view of the station.

"I don't like this," Jamie frowned. "There are too many people here."

"What do you mean?" Michael asked.

"Think about it," Jamie explained. "She knows what we look like, but she could have any number of assassins planted in this crowd and we'd never recognize any of them. We don't know who she's working with?"

"Then let's keep our eyes open," Gavin agreed.

Minutes passed with no sign of Delilah. Their confidence waned as they expected a trap to spring at any moment.

Jamie perked up, his eyes darting to their right. He heard the distinct sound of high-heels clicking against the stone floor. They watched as Delilah emerged from a group of people.

"Hello, Gavin," she said, approaching the bench.

"Are you armed?" he asked.

She turned around slowly, raising her arms slightly, her purse slung over her shoulder. Her clothing was too tight to conceal a weapon.

"My gun is in my bag," she admitted, "but I'm not planning on needing it."

"Sit," Gavin offered, his hand gesturing at the space next to him.

"Thank you for agreeing to meet," Delilah said, crossing her legs and resting her hands delicately on her knee. I confess that I would not trust myself in this same situation, and with just cause."

"Before we go any further, we brought the key," Gavin offered.

"I do not care," she replied earnestly. "I want only your help. My Saba, Hebrew for *grandfather*, was murdered by the man who is behind all of this."

"And who is that?" Jamie questioned.

"A hired killer, a mercenary like me; in fact," she hesitated, "he was once my lover. His name is Killion, Terrance Killion. He's former British intelligence and very good at what he does."

"That's a lot of information," Gavin smirked, "maybe too much, enough to conveniently peak our interest while leading us down a false trail. How do we know you're telling the truth?"

"Killion was hired by a secret society which refers to itself as *The Order*. My grandfather was a member of this group."

"The Order is gone," Michael said matter-of-factly. "Triton founded the society and it died with him. She's lying."

"No I'm not," Delilah refuted. "I do not recognize the name Triton, but my Saba, he spoke of a man named Franklin. He must have continued The Order in Triton's stead."

Gavin hung his head. He recognized the name Franklin: it was on every check he'd received during his time as a demon hunter. How could Joseph have allowed him to be used like that?

"I know the name Franklin," Gavin said reluctantly. "It would appear that he's my employer, or at least was during my time in New York City. I was a demon hunter, but I recently came to learn that I was only a pawn in someone else's game."

"Well, Franklin is dead. Killion eliminated him as well as the rest of The Order. My grandfather raised me, cared for me, taught me how to live, how to kill...and now he's gone. I will not be satisfied till Killion pays in blood for what he's taken from me."

"Then answer this for me," Gavin said, "if this is true, and all Killion wants is the stupid key, why kill the people he works for?"

"But that's just it," she smiled. "Killion is like me, a hired gun. His allegiance follows the money."

"So The Order wasn't who he was working for," Jamie said, snapping his fingers in revelation. "The Order was just another job. There's someone who's using him to acquire the key and that's who we need to find."

"Exactly," Delilah confirmed.

"So..." Gavin sighed, "any idea who this mysterious benefactor is?

"Yes, a man I've done several jobs for."

"What's his name?" Michael asked.

"I'll tell you when Killion is dead."

They sat in silence. Gavin actually believed her. Jamie remained somewhat skeptical. Michael seemed indifferent.

"So what do you think, do we have a deal?" she wondered.

"I don't think we have much choice," Gavin said reaching out to shake her hand in agreement.

****

Kayla had kept careful track of the time, noting to the minute how long it had been since the men left, nervously awaiting a phone call saying that everything was alright. The kids were up and playing in the living room.

She set the key down on the dining room table, her palm sweaty from holding on to it so tightly for so long.

When she wasn't watching the clock, she'd been peeking out the front windows at the black cloud of birds looming ominously overhead like storm clouds. And, she was still haunted by the feeling that something was most definitely going to go wrong.

Marley climbed up on the couch and leaned on the back cushions, peering outside, wondering what had her mother's attention. Kayla looked down at her and smiled.

"Look, mommy," she said, "a birdie."

"Yes, baby, lots of birdies," Kayla said before realizing that her daughter wasn't looking up, but rather focusing on a black bird that had landed on the porch railing.

She watched as another touched down next to it, then another, till a dozen or so had glided onto the porch. They sat perched on the railing, screeching wildly. Their commotion was soon accompanied by the sudden tapping of beaks on glass, which before long turned to a sharp cracking.

In utter horror, Kayla grabbed her kids and pulled them close, hiding them beneath her on the living room floor as the front windows shattered, black birds rushing through the bare frames, their wings beating in a frenzy. She felt them rush past her, heard them banging into the walls, clawing and pecking at her arms and neck, crying out in shrill, angry caws.

And just as quickly as the chaos began, the birds were gone, exiting through the same windows, leaving behind a mess of feathers and overturned odds and ends. Kayla stood up, inspecting her kids for injuries, but they were fine, just confused and scared.

It was then that Kayla realized what had really happened. She stared at the dining room table: the key was gone. The birds had taken it away.

✳✳✳✳✳✳✳✳✳✳✳✳

Jamie's cell phone rang. He reached in his pocket and checked the caller ID.

"Hey, Kay," he said as he answered. "We're OK."

"Well, I'm not," she replied, her voice wavering as she spoke. "It's gone, Jamie: the key. The birds attacked and took it, Jamie, it's...gone"

****

"What time is it?" Elizabeth asked, yawning as she woke from a light sleep.

"A little after 10am," Ashley answered. "We're nearly half way to Denver. We'll stop for gas and food in Green River, then put the rest of Utah behind us and then it's on to Colorado."

"Ok," Elizabeth said, looking over her shoulder at Cain in the back seat, sleeping soundly beneath the blanket. "Wake me when we're at Green River."

"Sure," Ashley smiled, focusing on the road ahead.

****

"This is crazy," Gavin huffed as the four of them jumped into Jamie's SUV.

"Michael, I thought you said the birds were just for intimidation?" Jamie questioned.

"Well, that's what I thought. I didn't expect this to happen," Michael replied.

"I'm confused," Delilah said, "what birds would ever break into a house and steal a key."

"They're not just birds," Michael said, "they're supernatural, a distortion of nature, like the hellhound. Think of them as tools for demonic reconnaissance."

"That's ridiculous, like something from a movie," Delilah scoffed.

"Kind of," Gavin replied, "but crows or ravens have been seen as spiritually significant creatures through most of recorded history. Poe glorified the raven in his gothic writing and it was believed that witches used crows as familiars for their eyesight and speed."

"How do you know this?" she laughed.

"Well, I *was* a demon hunter, which required a certain amount of knowledge pertaining to the occult."

"And you actually believe in that nonsense, demons and witches? Next you'll be telling me that vampires are real."

"Well actually," Michael sighed.

"Regardless," Jamie interrupted, "the key is gone. Delilah, could Killion have sent the black birds?"

"Absolutely not," she said, "and he'd have laughed at all of you for your superstition. But the man who I believe Killion is actually working for is a different story. Franklin was also superstitious. These old men are all the same: praying to the shadows, whispering in strange tongues."

"Just like Triton," Michael said. "I've seen firsthand the power granted through dark rituals, through service to Satan; and if Franklin is indeed dead, then The Order in the United States is leaderless. Franklin inherited his position when Triton died. Delilah, who does Killion work for?"

She paused for a moment, debating whether to share anymore of what she knew, "He's a Frenchman and that's all I'll say."

Michael grew pale. Things were worse than he could have imagined. He suddenly feared for all their lives, knowing that if he was right, they were now in more danger than ever.

****

Edward set the Blackhawk helicopter down at the Kit Carson County Airport in Colorado and readied to refuel. Killion checked his watch and smiled: they were making good time. He reviewed the plan in his head. They would arrive in Chicago and meet with Delilah. She would deliver the key and he would kill her. Then all that was left to do was give the key to the Frenchman. Things couldn't be easier.

"Alright," Edward said, returning to the cockpit and putting on his headset. "I'll do a quick flight check and we'll be on our way."

Killion nodded as he watched his brother flip switches and check dials. Everything looked good.

"So once in Chicago, you'll contact Delilah and arrange the meet?" Edward asked.

"Yes," Killion answered. "She'll give us the key and..."

"And," Edward interrupted, "you'll be able to follow through?"

"Killing her won't be a problem. In fact I'm rather looking forward to it."

"I thought you loved her?" Edward smirked.

"I did, once. But she was incapable of reciprocating. As far as I'm concerned, she died the day she walked out on me."

"That's harsh, brother."

"It's the truth," Killion replied solemnly. "Now let's go."

The rotor was already whirring overhead, chopping the air. Edward throttled up and the helicopter lifted off the ground.

"Are you sure you want to do this?" Edward asked, heading east.

"I don't have a choice," Killion reasoned. "I owe the Frenchman my life and he's not the type of man you say no to. No, I have no choice. It's destiny."

27

A strange figure stood at the entrance to Oz Park, not far from the Branson house in Lincoln Park. He wore a long black trench coat, the bottom hem skimming the ground, and his face was hidden beneath a hood. Joggers and stroller-pushing mothers avoided him as he looked curiously at the red ruby-slippered statue of Dorothy and her little dog Toto. It wasn't that they were afraid, nor was it that he seemed especially threatening, just out of place. In fact the way he studied the famous statue carried a certain air of innocence that seemed an unexpected contrast to his appearance.

A shadow cast by low-flying birds drew his attention away from the statue and he looked up just in time to see the black cloud of beating wings disappear into the leafy foliage of a nearby tree. The man moved on, past the playground and towards the cover of the trees.

He approached the birds with an outstretched arm and one glided down gracefully, landing on him like he was a branch, then dropped the key from its beak into the man's gloved palm. Immediately, his cell phone rang, scaring off the skittish raven.

"Allô? Sebastian à l'appareil," he answered in French.

"Avez-vous la clé?" the voice asked.

"Oui," he answered. "The key is in my possession. I will return to Paris."

****

Gavin stood on the porch, inspecting the broken windows, shards of glass hanging precariously from the frames. Black feathers lay fallen on the sill.

"But you're ok?" he heard Jamie say from inside, Kayla holding a whimpering Marley in her arms as Ethan played on the floor at her feet.

Michael leaned against the door frame, his arms crossed. He seemed frustrated. Delilah hung back, yet to set foot on the porch. She was drinking in the scene; unsure of in what she had now become involved.

"Yeah, Jamie, we're fine," Kayla replied as she wiped tears from her daughter's cheeks, "just a little shaken. It happened so fast and all I could think of was the kids."

"That's all that matters," Michael interjected.

"But the key is gone," Kayla sighed.

"They would have acquired the key whether you tried to stop them or not," Gavin reasoned. "And how would you have fought off dozens of ravens? We'll get the key back."

"Yes," Michael said, "your children are safe, that was your only real option."

Delilah crept up to the porch and peered into the living room. She saw the baby, then the little girl in Kayla's arms. The floor had been cleaned of broken glass, but the shattered windows and claw-scratched table still displayed the chaos this family had experienced. She thought back to herself, as a child, orphaned, in the arms of her grandfather. She almost cried.

"May I enter?" she asked, looking at Kayla.

Kayla nodded cautiously.

"I'm Delilah. I'm so sorry this has happened and for what part I have played in all of this."

Kayla stared her down, distrust in her heart. Ethan crawled up to Delilah and took hold of her leg, using her as support and pulling himself up to stand.

"May I?" Delilah wondered, reaching down to pick up the little boy.

She raised him to her chest, held him close as he giggled. Kayla watched curiously. In front of her was a cold hearted assassin, a temptress, a woman who preyed on men, using their lust as a weapon against them, now lovingly holding her child? Kayla's gaze fell on Michael. She shuddered for just a moment, remembering the trail of death that followed Thirteen only five years earlier in New York. Two of the most violent, remorseless killers she'd ever encountered were standing in her living room. She swallowed her pride, pushed off her doubt, fighting to believe that people can change, that God can do anything, even with the ones that some would believe He could not.

"Welcome to the team," Kayla smiled forcedly.

"I know you want nothing more than for all this to be over, everything to be back to normal," Delilah said, "and I want to do everything I can to remove Killion from your lives. Yes, it will all be over soon."

Kayla wasn't sure how to feel about this woman, beautiful, possibly more so than any other woman she'd ever seen, and ruthless: Kayla could see it in her eyes. But there was fragileness just beneath the surface and sincerity in her voice. Kayla chose to trust her.

"Well," Jamie said, sensing the tension, "everyone's alright and I'm starving. Anyone else hungry? I think we've got some beef patties in the freezer and some hotdogs, I can fire up the grill."

Gavin chuckled: in the midst of everything, all the pain and hurt and loss, Jamie had suggested a cook-out. And somehow, knowing that Ashley was safely on her way back to him, even though the key was gone, the simplicity, the normalcy of a summer tradition, seemed absolutely perfect, even if nothing else was.

"We should eat," Michael agreed. "I'm sure we'll hear from Killion soon."

"Alright," Jamie smiled, "let's eat."

****

Ashley nudged Elizabeth after pulling the Mercedes SUV to a stop in the parking lot of a McDonald's in Green River. Cain had been awake for the last hour, staring blankly out the window, but smiling as soon as the golden arches were in view.

"We need to eat," Ashley urged.

Elizabeth nodded and called back to Cain, "Let's get some food, baby."

As they exited the vehicle, Elizabeth reached in the plastic bag that had been sitting at her feet and tore into the pregnancy test box, removing one, and slipping it in her pocket. She wanted Ashley to know for sure, no more wondering.

They ordered and carried their trays to a booth near the play area. Elizabeth knew her son would want to stretch his legs: they'd been driving for almost seven hours and he'd done better than she could have imagined any other six-year-old doing.

Cain hurried through his chicken nuggets, his eyes full of hopeful longing, his gaze unwavering as the slide outside beckoned him. Ashley and Elizabeth ate in silence.

"Mommy," Cain said, jumping up from his seat, his tennis shoes squeaking on the tile floor, "can I go outside...'puh-lease'?!"

Elizabeth smiled and nodded, then they watched as he sprinted for the door and b-lined toward the jungle gym, his charge accompanied by a spirited, "*WOO HOO!*"

"He's so funny," Ashley said, nibbling on a golden French fry.

"I could never imagine life without him now," Elizabeth said. "When I first found out I was pregnant, I cried and cried."

"Awe," Ashley grinned, "because you were so happy?"

Elizabeth laughed, "No. I cried because I thought my life was over. I wasn't yet thirty and I felt like I still had so much to do."

"Really?"

"Yeah. But truth is, it wasn't till Cain that I fully understood purpose," Elizabeth explained. "I loved Michael, with all my heart, but this is such a different love. He made me realize just how wrong I was: my life wasn't ending, it was finally beginning!"

Ashley ate another fry, contemplating what Elizabeth had said.

"Of course there were times during the pregnancy that I wasn't sure I could do it, you know...make it for nine months, not to mention the actual birthing. But I did."

"And it looks like things have turned out fine," Ashley admired, watching as Cain rode the slide and then climbed back up to do it again.

Elizabeth shifted in the booth, slipping the pregnancy test from her pocket and setting it down on the table in front of Ashley, "You need to know for sure."

Ashley stared at the test. The moment of truth had come at last.

"Here goes," she said picking up the pregnancy test and heading for the restroom.

****

"When Killion calls, we need to have a plan ready," Gavin said. "We need a place to meet where no one can get hurt, someplace secluded."

"We could use the cemetery where Delilah led Gavin," Michael considered aloud. "The trees offered plenty of cover."

"Too much cover," Delilah replied. "I had over a dozen paths for escape, not to mention that Killion will most definitely be accompanied by his brother. They're partners of sorts. The trees only give him a place to hide."

"So something secluded, but wide open?" Kayla questioned.

"Highly visible, but not easily accessible," Delilah reiterated.

The group stood in silence, the moment passing briefly before Kayla spoke excitedly, "What about the lighthouse?"

"The one way out in the harbor?" Jamie smiled. "That just might work."

"A lighthouse?" Michael asked.

"Yeah," Jamie explained. "It can practically only be reached by boat and there's no place to hide; plus, being so far out of the way, no innocents would have the potential to wander into the meet. It's perfect."

"Do we have a boat?" Gavin wondered.

"My brother does," Kayla answered, "he uses it for fishing. It's small, a single outboard motor, but it'll do the trick."

"The lighthouse it is," Gavin said sternly. "But we have to be careful. If something were to go wrong, so far away from shore..."

"I'm with you, Gavin," Jamie nodded. "It could be disastrous..."

"...life and death," Michael frowned.

****

The restroom door closed behind Ashley. She peered down the row of stalls: it appeared she was alone. Stepping up to the counter, she was pleased to find the sink clean. Maybe this was a sign that all would go better than her last attempt. She quickly opened the wrapping and headed for the stall nearest her, locking the door, then pulling down her pants and sitting on the cold toilet seat.

Ashley had no trouble this time. She placed the protective cap on the end of the test and stood without incident, buttoning and zipping her jeans. Now all she had to do was wait.

****

"It's all set up," Kayla said as she ended the call on her cellular. "Jake said his boat is already loaded on a trailer and parked alongside his garage. Pick it up and you'll be set."

"So we'll use your brother's boat and be done with this once and for all," Jamie confirmed. "What are we doing about weapons? The hit-man will most definitely be armed."

"I brought my .50 cals," Michael replied.

Gavin smiled as he answered, "I have my suppressed USP and a half a dozen magazines."

"I can't use my service Beretta, this is not a police matter," Jamie reasoned. "The only other gun I have is a 12 gauge Remington pump."

"That'll do," Gavin grinned. "I also brought a Smith & Wesson 9mm you can carry as backup."

"I have my Sig Sauer," Delilah said, reservedly, almost child-like, "if you'll allow me?"

Gavin and Jamie shared a gaze, silently communicating their questioned trust in this newest addition to their fight. Could she be allowed a weapon?

Michael answered before the other men could, "As far as I'm concerned, every bullet is another breath, another chance to live. If you are coming with us, then you must be armed as well."

****

Ashley grew faint, the blood rushing from her head as the restroom began to swirl, her vision obscured by tears and disorientation. She grabbed the counter top and steadied herself. Gazing into the mirror, she froze in panic: a horrid shadowy creature loomed just behind her, its eyes glowing fiery red, its lips sneered into a sickening grin, exposing the razor-like teeth within.

"Vos portare vitae," it spoke in hissing Latin, "vita fert multo mortem."

"What?" she asked, tears streaking her face, no clue what tongue he used or what was said.

"Benedictionem et maledictionem," it whispered, its voice like the wind that precedes a terrible storm.

"Please leave," she cried.

"Benedictionem et maledictionem," it said louder, the whisper now a threatening wail, "benedictionem et maledictionem... benedictionem et maledictionem..."

"Please stop, I don't understand you!"

The creature rushed forward, pressing into her, forcing her against the sink, its grotesque jaws inches from her quivering mouth, her tear-streaked face. Ashley closed her eyes as she felt its hot sulfurous breath against her skin.

"BENEDICTIONEM ET MALEDICTIONEM!" it shrieked, before twisting and contorting into a black mass of smoky wisps and shadow, then vanishing before her very eyes.

Alone and confused, Ashley quickly turned and grabbed the pregnancy test from the counter, clutching it to her breast as she dropped to the floor. She sobbed, taking heaving, erratic breaths as she purged the panic from her shaking body.

Calmness returned and she wiped the tears from her blurry, burning eyes. Slowly she softened her grip on the pregnancy test, opening her hand, revealing the test in her open palm. She studied it for a moment, trying to come to terms with what had just happened while also trying to understand the message the test relayed. She stared at the grouping of letters displayed in the small oval window on the face of the test, letters that made a word, one word; the word she so longed and hoped for, yet now, for some reason, after the demonic manifestation, a word that brought fear.

Pregnant.

28

Ashley slid into the seat across from Elizabeth, her face pale, lips agape, "We need to go...now!"

Elizabeth looked into her new friends eyes and didn't need to question. She recognized that fear, the horror that was only known by someone who had shared similar visions; the same visions she herself had seen when she'd first learned of Michael's power and her father's true nature.

"I'll get Cain," she replied. "Are you ok to drive?"

Ashley nodded as she quickly tidied up the table, gathering their trash onto the tray so it could be easily thrown away, "Yes, just hurry."

Cain fought leaving the playground at first, this being his first time to escape their circumstances and act like a real little boy in days, but Elizabeth would not have it, taking him by the hand and leading him, his face tear-streaked, out to the car. They needed to get back out on the road.

Elizabeth helped Cain fasten his seatbelt and then jumped into the front seat, watching as Ashley checked the Glock pistol they'd stolen from Edward, verifying the round in the chamber before returning it to the glove box. Ashley started the SUV and slammed it into reverse, backed out, then shifted into drive and fled the parking lot, leaving McDonald's and, hopefully, the demon behind.

"Are you ok?" Elizabeth asked, motherly concern in her soft voice.

"Yeah..." Ashley hesitated, "just something, I don't know...I must have imagined it."

"Really? And I'm supposed to believe that? Your husband was a demon hunter, you told me of your experiences in New York, Thirteen, the abomination that was my father, but this, whatever you saw, you imagined? Lie to yourself, not to me."

Ashley sighed. Elizabeth was right.

"I saw something I haven't seen in a long time," Ashley explained, "something out of a nightmare; the eyes, its teeth...a demon. And it said something."

"What did the demon say?" Elizabeth asked.

Ashley paused, the words etched into her memory, "*Vos portare vitae, vita fert multo mortem, benedictionem et maledictionem.* What does it mean?"

"*Vita, vita...*" Elizabeth whispered, thinking aloud. "*Vita* means life in Latin. And you said *mortem*, which means death, but that's as far as my understanding goes. I speak French, and the lingual roots are in Latin, but I don't recognize the words exactly. *Vous* is you, maybe the same as *vos*? *Portare* may be the same as *porter* in French, to carry, and *benedictionem* is probably *benediction*, or blessing. *Et* is and, but the last word, I' don't know."

"So," Ashley said, piecing the words together, "*You carry life, life –* something, something – *death, blessing and...*"

"*Maledictionem,*" Ashley said, "it kind of reminds me of the word *malady.*"

"Sickness, disease?"

"*Mal* is Spanish for evil," Ashley shivered.

"French too."

"Maybe *maledictionem* means evil, or *maldito*: cursed."

"Blessing and a curse," Elizabeth said. "You carry life, life-death, blessing and curse."

"What does it mean?" Ashley said, teary-eyed.

"So you are pregnant?"

"Yes."

"Then it means we pray," Elizabeth frowned.

****

"So that's it?" Gavin asked, staring out over the churning waters of Lake Michigan, high-powered binoculars raised to his eyes.

Jamie nodded, "We'll dock the boat on the eastern side of the breakwater. We can climb up, unseen from the Chicago side. The only way out there is by water, so we'll see them coming."

"It is quite a ways out, isn't it, just in case of an emergency?" Michael said, noting the distance from where they stood on the Navy Pier.

"We'll have vests on," Gavin grinned.

"Yeah, and you've got your hocus pocus to protect you," Jamie smirked, pointing at the inner pocket of Michael's suit coat, a reference to Thirteen's mask.

"Touché," he replied with a smile, a smile that hid the wince of resentment in his eyes. "But I'm not that man anymore. I am only using the power of Thirteen till I regain my family; then, and only then, will I perhaps be free of my curse."

Jamie patted Michael firmly on his shoulder, his expression one of unspoken apology. Michael clearly understood, and though not a word was spoken, trust was shared.

****

Kayla sat on the couch, Marley curled up against her, sleeping safely beneath the reassuring comfort of her mother's arm. Delilah sat in a wingback chair that graced the front corner of the room, diagonally placed from the sofa, watching as Kayla's thin fingers played with a curl of her daughter's hair. Ethan was upstairs, napping in his crib, worn out by the frantic events of that morning.

"I'm so sorry for what happened here today," Delilah spoke," her voice calm, understanding, but an interruption to the welcomed silence none the less.

Kayla blinked as if waking, though her eyes were open. She'd been lost in a stare.

"Thank you," she replied softly.

"You do not seem as shaken as I would expect," Delilah stated.

"There was a time when I would have been in a panic, when I would have never believed that the unbelievable could ever happen, but..."

Delilah listened curiously, "But, what?"

"That all changed for me five years ago. Do you believe in the supernatural?"

"I am a Jew, my friend," Delilah smiled. "My peoples' history is nothing but tales of the supernatural: Moses, Abraham, the prophets. Though my lifestyle may contradict at times, I know the words of the Torah."

"And what of the devil, of demons?" Kayla asked matter-of-factly.

"They are figurative, are they not? Lessons and teachings: words passed down by old men to warn young men of the dangers of the world."

Kayla allowed the silence to return as she thought. Delilah was intrigued.

"I noticed that the man named Michael, he is not close to you. He lingers; in range to listen and speak, but not intimately. He is not family?"

"Jamie is my husband."

"The police officer."

"Correct. And Gavin is married to my sister: my sister who was recently abducted, along with Michael's wife and young son. So no, he is not in the family."

"But there's history?" Delilah reasoned.

"How so?"

"Obviously, two unrelated men's families are not taken by the same party if they are not in some way truly related, if not by blood, then perhaps tragedy?"

"It's complicated," Kayla sighed.

"Aren't all great stories?"

Kayla stared up at the wall as she began to speak, as if the fireplace mantle and the painting hanging above it faded away into a vision of her past, home movies playing before her eyes. "Six years ago, only a short time after I finished college and the academy, I was requested by a police captain named Patrick O'Donnell. He had me transferred from Pittsburgh and promoted me to detective in his homicide department. Cheesy, *I know*...like one of those over-the-top, overly dramatic cop movies where there's no way the detective has enough experience to be in their position, but you just go with it for the sake of plot."

"Yes," Delilah smiled, "I have seen many American movies: the beautiful, young, yet aptly capable hero rising to the sometimes unenviable occasion, usually in times of crisis."

"Right, well that was me," Kayla sighed. "Anyway, on my first day, Jamie was introduced to me. O'Donnell told me I was his new partner. I fell for him instantly, but he was slow to come around. Over that first year as partners, we began seeing each other secretly, hiding our relationship from everyone, doing our best to separate our private and work lives. Things moved quickly and we were in a great place in our relationship. And that's when things turned....*strange*."

"Please, tell me more," Delilah urged.

"My younger sister had recently transferred to Colombia University as a fine arts student. I'd helped her get setup in the city, a reasonably safe and affordable studio apartment. Sorry, that's not really important...um, back to the story...Jamie and I were put on a case, a possible mass ritualistic homicide, thirteen bodies in the basement of an old apartment complex. The next morning, an unexplainable...*force*...ripped through a section of the city near Times Square. It was absolute chaos. And even though we were on the murders, O'Donnell wanted us on the scene of the blast. We checked it out, but nothing made sense. The only evidence or clue we found was a set of footprints seemingly burned into the cement of the sidewalk. At the apartment, in the basement with all those bodies, we found two things that stood out: first, a spot of wood was visible in the shape of an old skeleton key on a wax covered table; and second, roman numerals had been literally etched in the walls encompassing the entire room. The number thirteen was circled in blood."

"How bizarre," Delilah grinned, taking it all in, "and the missing key from the table?"

"I'll get to that in a moment," Kayla continued. "In the meantime, as we were knee deep in questions, my sister was having nightmares, visions of the actual murders, the ritual slayings. She also saw whatever *power* tore up Times Square. There's more to the story, but I won't get into too much unnecessary detail. Ultimately, our investigation led us to Dr. Maurice Triton. He seemed harmless, but in the end, he was hiding his sinister actions behind the upstanding face of his company, Tri-Corp. We discovered that he'd been at this for years. In fact, my own brother, an NYPD cop, was killed because he'd come too close to uncovering the truth."

"So where did Gavin come into the story?"

"I was directed, by something....*supernatural*...to an old priest named Joseph. He had his own incredible story."

"Which was?" Delilah asked curiously.

"He claimed to have been chasing Triton since the time of the crusades," Kayla said with a smirk, as if, even after having borne witness to the actual events in New York City, everything still seemed unimaginable. "He claimed that Triton was demonic and sought absolute power and control over the entire world."

"The Order..." Delilah whispered in revelation.

"Exactly, or at least now I understand. This conspiracy was tied to the past and similarly, all speculation would reason, the future. But Joseph led us to Gavin, which is really how we've gotten to where we are now. You see, Triton had his own army: a horde of eighteen men, all dressed in black suits and ties, wickedly stitched masks hiding their faces. The leader of this group and apparent heir to Triton was a man simply known as Thirteen. He was behind the chaos; and in the end, he had plans of his own. We thought

Triton's plot died in New York, at Triton's office suite on the uppermost floor of the Tri-Corp building, when Thirteen killed his master. And had I not seen what happened next, I would never have believed it myself. As Triton's body fell, Thirteen summoned an enormous demonic entity from within the dead man."

Kayla paused briefly to laugh at the absurdity of what she was saying, watching the apprehension grow in Delilah's eyes. She continued.

"At that same moment, Joseph revealed himself to be an angel, not the feeble old man he'd portrayed. The two of them fought to the death, Joseph finally landing a victorious blow."

"So," Delilah smirked, "Triton was a demon and Joseph was an angel...and you *saw* them battle, before your very eyes?"

"That's what I'm saying," Kayla admitted reluctantly, sheepish even.

Delilah thought for a moment, processing what she'd just heard. Kayla sighed.

"My people have seen such things; I have seen such things," Delilah finally replied.

Kayla was now the curious one.

"The prophets of old spoke of these demons. Angels carried God's own words to Israel," Delilah explained. Jacob wrestled with an angel, Moses, after receiving the Ten Commandments, was led by an angel, angels adorned the Ark of the Covenant. Isaac was spared from death at the hand of his father Abraham by an angel. Elijah declared God the *God of Hosts*. And then there's Isaiah, Ezekiel, and Daniel...need I continue?"

Kayla smiled, remembering the feeling of sitting in Sunday school, recalling the stories, "I understand."

"Yes," Delilah said firmly, the holy and unholy are always at war; and they use us for our part. Tell me, the leader of Triton's army, Thirteen, what exactly did his mask look like?"

"It was black, tight-fitting. The eyes glowed white and the mouth was stitched into a horrid smile, ear to freakish ear."

"I have seen this as well. The man, Michael," Delilah said, "he wore this mask on the night I was supposed to meet McNamara's contact but was instead misled by Gavin and your husband."

"Michael is Thirteen, or was. I'm not sure anymore," Kayla admitted, "but something inside tells me he's genuine, something in my gut."

"And what then of the key?"

"The key was nothing more than a trinket to Thirteen, a ploy used to leverage Triton against himself. Thirteen hid the key from his master, all the while pretending to search for it, which nearly killed us all. Thirteen left the key with us: he had no use for it after Triton died."

"So the key belonged to The Order and not Triton," Delilah deduced. "Triton was led to believe that Gavin had the key and must have communicated that to the other members in some way. But they would have known of Thirteen's treachery and understood that the key was used as a tool against his fallen master. With Triton gone, they wanted the key, wanted to reclaim whatever power it must hold and so devised a plot to retrieve the key. McNamara knew of Gavin as a hunter, but also knew of Thirteen. They were logically the last two men to have access to the key and therefore the prime targets. Their loved ones were taken to ransom and now we are here. But something went wrong."

"Did it?" Kayla asked, following Delilah's thoughts as she worked through the events.

"Well, The Order is dead, destroyed by Killion."

"The man who kidnapped Ashley?"

"Yes. Franklin, the one who inherited The Order upon the death of Triton, he employed Killion as his insurance policy."

"That was dumb," Kayla smirked.

"In hindsight, yes."

"And is this Killion as dangerous as you say?"

"Even more so."

29

Ashley smiled: she'd been watching for miles as the Colorado Rocky Mountains grew on the horizon and now, they were nearly on the other side, Denver their next stop. They'd been traveling on I-70 for hours and she was ready for some sleep. Denver marked the approximate halfway point from Los Angeles, which meant Elizabeth would be taking over and Ashley could get some rest.

In Des Moines, their plan was to switch once more, with Ashley taking the wheel for the last part of the journey. She glanced at the time glowing on the console: *4:27pm*. Hopefully, only fifteen more hours of road separated her from her beloved Gavin. And then, if all went well, she could share her news, her wonderful, joyous, terrifying news.

****

Gavin hung up his phone and stared blankly at the screen, his head hung low in obvious disappointment. Michael sat next to him on the bench. Jamie paced up and down the pier, thinking and rethinking their approach.

"I haven't heard from her all day," Gavin sighed. "And she's not answering now. Do you think they're ok?"

"I believe they are safe. There's a lot of country between us and California, too much for the kidnappers to search," Michael said, assuring himself as much as his friend. "And if Delilah is right, and this Killion is coming to Chicago as we've planned, then our families are no longer of consequence to him."

"I just want to hear her voice, you know?"

"Of course," Michael replied. "I nearly cry when I think of Elizabeth's soft voice, my mind playing tricks, hearing her whisper my name, and to hear Cain laugh..."

"You know I've never been away from her this long? Since we met, I've been with her every day."

"Last summer," Michael said, turning to face Gavin, "we had planned a trip to France, a chance to make things right with my estranged father. He'd yet to meet his grandson and I wanted an opportunity to bury certain ghosts from our past. But Cain came down with chicken pox and couldn't travel. I chose to leave them and left for Paris: she understood. On my first day at my father's chateau, Elizabeth sent me pictures of Cain's itchy red sores and I felt so awful for leaving, like I'd abandoned them. That week was torture. Since then, I hadn't gone a day without them."

"I never pictured you to be such a softy," Gavin smiled, "a real teddy bear of a man."

"That is who I am, I'm afraid," he answered with a laugh. "And when this is all over, I'll throw my mask into the water of this lake and never look back."

****

Terrance Killion looked down at the ground far below, watching as the land passed by beneath the helicopter. The terrain hadn't changed much since they'd stopped to refuel, nothing but farms and rolling plains as they travelled across the Midwest.

"What's our ETA?" he asked his brother, speaking into the flight headset.

"Twenty hundred hours...so 8pm or approximately two hours from now. Will you call her as soon as we land or can we spare a little time to rest?"

"I'll call," Killion grinned. "We're so close; rest can wait a few more hours. She'll play right into our hands. We'll receive the key and tie off all the loose ends."

"Loose ends?" Edward asked.

"Ashley and Elizabeth are most likely heading to Chicago to meet their husbands. We'll still have our opportunity to kill them, especially after what they did to you, brother. In a way, they're coming to us."

"Are you sure you're not just a bit overconfident? Delilah is dangerous on her own, but you read the files. What Thirteen did in New York is really shocking. His power is unimaginable. If everything we heard is true, you will never faze him with bullets, even rockets. He's unstoppable."

"Don't be such a superstitious twit," Killion grinned. "If what the Frenchman told me is true, then Thirteen's power is meaningless. He is more vulnerable than he knows."

****

It started small, a light breeze from the northwest; cool, comforting on such a hot summer day. But the wind carried with it a threat. In the great distance, far beyond sight, dark clouds loomed, slowly moving towards the city. The storm marched forward like soldiers, thunder claps their boot tromps, shaking the earth below. Lightning flashed like muzzles of guns at war. It leveled everything in its path. And soon, it would be upon them.

****

"When you speak of Killion, you grow cautious," Kayla said, "but it also sounds like you respect him greatly."

Delilah nodded her agreement, "It's true. I hate him, hate him more than words can explain. But I also love him. So much has changed in the last ten years. We were young, foolish, but very much in love."

"What happened," Kayla asked, "if you don't mind me prying?"

"No, it is only fair. You told me your story. Now you are entitled to mine. It was not long after the attacks of the eleventh of September. A year had passed since the terrorists had flown planes into the towers, but the world was still on high alert. My Saba, grandfather, was highly regarded by my government. He was able to have me placed in the military, his training of me carrying more merit than the army's basic boot ever could. I became a member of a task force, Israeli Special Forces. America had only just gone to war in Iraq and our Prime Minister feared that the mounting tensions in the Middle East would mean imminent attack on my peoples' soil. We worked in secret, striking from the shadows, eliminating threats before the world would even know they were in danger. The U.N. would deny that any joint operations ever took place, but while America chased Saddam, my small team, as well as a squad of American SEALs and British MI6, continued our secret war. This is how I met Terrance Killion."

"Wow," Kayla said.

Delilah continued, "After several months of black ops, our governments pulled the plug. We had gained intel on the whereabouts of bin Laden, which meant politics would then take precedent over actions. I returned to Jerusalem, but I missed the life I had become accustomed to. One day, there was a knock on the door of my apartment: it was Terrance. We went to lunch, then dinner. A week passed, our affair more lust than love, but life was exciting once more. We made love everywhere we could, anywhere we could, sometimes simply on impulse, with the risk of being caught. There was this time, in the small unisex restroom of a restaurant overlooking the Mediterranean, an overweight woman walked in on us. We laughed through our embarrassment as she yelled at us, her fists waiving emphatically above her head. We dressed and ran from the restaurant like two children caught in their mischief. Soon lust turned to love, real love. If my Saba knew of my promiscuity, he would have given me the lecture of all lectures, that my body was a temple, a holy place, and that it was trained as a weapon, lethal and quick, that it should not be wasted on such youthful endeavors. But I was in love.

Terrance and I lived together for the next several months, travelling the Mediterranean: one week exploring Greece, the next spent lying on the beach in Cyprus. During that time, he would fly away for a day or two, sometimes at odd hours, in a hurry, but never rushed. He explained it was for business, but he always returned.

This continued and one day, for what reason I do not know, I realized I had been blinded by my love. I had never questioned the money we spent on our travels, the yacht we sailed through the blue waters of the Mediterranean, the origin of his seemingly endless funds

When I asked him, he said he'd tell me if I really wanted to know. I begged him to share. It was then he revealed that he'd defected from MI6 and had found a way to use his talents to make money, more money than the British government could have ever paid. He admitted he was a killer for hire, working for a man, a Parisian, who would one day shape all of Europe, possibly even the world. I was shocked at first, but also intrigued. By my Saba's design, I was made for one thing: death. I wanted in. I could feel the thrill of the hunt already returning to me and I told him I wanted to meet this man.

Terrance took me to the Frenchman who gave me a simple test. I was given a target in the city. My objective was to slip into Paris, eliminate the man, and return, leaving nothing but death behind me. I was not told why this man was the target, why he needed to die, simply that he did. He was nothing more than a figure in an equation. Needless to say, I passed the test and Terrance and I worked as a team.

But something happened. Terrance began to change. After four more years together, when we were our closest, we grew the furthest apart. He had begun hinting at marriage, of family: retiring from the life I so loved and settling down, disappearing into the English countryside. I tried, but couldn't. That life was a part of me. When he proposed, I refused, without reluctance. I left him and continued on. I quit the Frenchman and began to freelance. I was able to do things that governments, trapped by bureaucrats and red tape, could not. Terrance was devastated and grew brazen in his heartbreak. I hate to say it, but I'm somewhat responsible for making him the killer he is today."

Kayla sat in silent awe. That was a story.

"And yes, I do still love him. He was and will be my only *true* love. I have been with other men since Terrance, but only as my job has required. I use my body like any other tool, often times getting closer to my target simply because I am a woman, because he *or she* desires me. Yes, I've loved with my body, but never my heart."

The two women sat in silence, Delilah's story complete. Marley still slept, cuddled against her mother's side.

Kayla finally spoke, "Do you have any regrets?"

It was a long moment before Delilah replied. She was thinking, deciding. Perhaps it was the first time she'd actually really thought about it.

"No," she finally replied.

****

Jamie pulled away from his brother-in-law's house, the twelve foot johnboat in tow. He honked the horn in goodbye as he headed down the street, watching Kayla's brother, Jake, waiving as they left, shrinking away in the side mirror as the distance between them grew.

"Will this little thing actually make it out on the water?" Gavin laughed, questioning the tiny outboard motor and the lack of oars. "He said it had what, 18hp?"

"We're not going on a cruise here," Jamie smiled.

"It will do fine," Michael said.

****

Ashley finished fueling up the SUV and was just tightening the gas cap as Elizabeth and Cain returned from the station's restroom, "Ready to get back out on the road?"

Elizabeth nodded and took the keys from Ashley, climbing into the driver's seat and starting the engine. Cain settled into the back, playing with a toy his mother purchased for him inside the shop.

"You'd better use the restroom as well before we go!" Elizabeth warned with a smirk and a wink. "I know what it's like to be pregnant and travel with a full bladder."

Ashley did her business and quickly returned, taking her place in the passenger seat. The Mercedes lurched forward and they were on their way.

Within moments, Ashley's eyes, heavy from the hours behind them, blinked shut and she slept, resting in the hope that Gavin was at the end of their road.

****

The wind picked up steadily as thunder boomed in the distance. Slowly, the storm approached the city, its ominous black clouds blocking out the comfort of the summer sun.

Jamie pulled his BMW SUV into the driveway and hurried through the front door of his home, his iPhone raised, a weather report glowing on the display.

"What's wrong?" Kayla asked, suddenly realizing how dark it had grown outside as Delilah had shared her story.

"There's a huge storm coming," Jamie said, showing his wife the device. "There's a wave advisory for the lake. This could ruin everything."

Gavin and Michael followed Jamie into the house, closing the door behind them.

"What is a danger to us, will be a greater danger to Killion," Delilah explained. "We know our plan, we have our strategy. We can use the weather to our advantage."

"But it's a small boat," Gavin reasoned. "The waves could capsize us and kill us for sure."

"We have yet to hear from Killion," Kayla pointed out, "maybe the storm will pass?"

"I hope, but it's unlikely," Michael said, "It's a huge front moving in and there's no telling how long it will affect the water."

"Then it's a matter of faith," Delilah answered. "We will face the water when we must. If we arrive safely at the lighthouse, then it is meant to be, if not..."

"There's a big difference between acting in faith and acting stupidly," Jamie argued.

"This is my chance to get Killion," Delilah snapped back. "He will pay for killing my Saba!"

"Ok, just everybody calm down!" Kayla interjected, Marley now awake, but nuzzled close, at the sound of all the raised voices. "Let's think for a second. The weather can be used to our advantage: lower visibility, slower approach for Killion."

"We just have to make sure we're there first," Jamie replied.

"Delilah, he knows you," Gavin said, "and he's expecting me and Michael, but Jamie is our ace-in-the-hole. He can take up position from above, in the lighthouse itself if he has to. From there, he has a great vantage point and his shotgun will still be effective from that range: the lighthouse pier isn't more than fifteen feet above the breakwater."

"He has a point," Michael agreed. "An ambush is our best move. It allows us to be both offensive and defensive in our approach."

"Except that the key is gone. The ravens knew where to find it. Killion must have found out we had it here," Kayla sighed.

"Not likely," Delilah spoke up. "The ravens were something mystical, supernatural. They were not trained birds, and even so, Killion would have nothing to do with such things. If they were trained, such skill would not be his and he has not faith in anything other than his steady hand and a bullet's trajectory."

"Then where do the ravens even fit?" Kayla answered, her frustration clear.

"It's something I would have done," Michael said. "They were driven by demonic madness. The birds are like the physical eyes and ears of metaphysical entities."

"Like a witch's familiar?" Kayla asked.

"I guess you could say so," Michael explained, "but their purpose is pure evil, not witchcraft as you know it. Think of them like a manifestation."

"Ok," Gavin said, "the birds are your style, cryptic, dark...who besides you would use this method? The Tri-Six are gone. And I've never met anyone other than you who controls demons in the way you do, that can actually do more than just commune with the spirits. You actually manipulate their power, the power of their spiritual dimension, to warp the laws of physics in ours. You can stop bullets for crying out loud!"

Michael thought long and hard before answering. They stared at him in silence, waiting to hear what he had to say.

"This," he said, reaching into the inner pocket of his suit coat and removing the mask, "is all the power I have. In my possession, I can use it to do anything I want, anything I can imagine, even bend the will of nature. Without it, I am no different than any of you."

"And what does that mean?" Gavin asked.

"Triton used the power of the demon living within him to create a portal, a bridge to gap the chasm of the supernatural: our world and their world. The masks worn by the Tri-Six were that link."

"So if you died," Jamie questioned, "would the power of the mask die as well?"

"No, actually. The power resides in the mask, not the man. It is only his ability to wield it that unlocks its potential. The other members of the Tri-Six, though lost, their masks would still possess power to this day. But I mastered that power, learned to manipulate it, to bend it. That is why they fell at your hands when I was invincible. They hadn't unlocked their true potential. It is why Triton selected me out of all the men. He declared me *lucky*; fitting, seeing as how my surname, Laurent, means *lucky* in French. But only someone as powerful as Triton could enable such a thing."

Delilah quickly buried the look of confusion that had momentarily overtaken her beauty. Michael suddenly seemed so familiar, his stature, even demeanor, reminded her of someone she loathed.

"So who else is that powerful?" Jamie wondered.

Michael didn't reply. He seemed preoccupied, distracted by something in his head.

"The Frenchman could," Delilah smiled, her eyes fixed on Michael. "If Killion had nothing to do with the ravens, then it could very well have been the Frenchman, but that is all I can say for now."

"You have to tell us more," Kayla pleaded.

"The agreement was my information for Killion's life. When I get my revenge, you will get your answers."

30

"Lansing tower, this is Blackhawk November-One-Six-Niner-Eight-Alfa on westerly approach, requesting permission to land at heliport."

"Repeat tail, Blackhawk."

"November-One-Six-Niner-Eight-Alfa," Edward said.

-Radio static-

"Military or commercial?" the tower replied.

"Commercial."

"One moment, Niner-Eight-Alfa."

-Radio static-

"Continue on current approach, Niner-Eight-Alfa, you're all clear. Sorry for the delay. We don't see many privately-owned Blackhawks. The helipad is yours."

"Copy, tower...thanks, Niner-Eight-Alfa out."

Edward set the Blackhawk down on the tarmac at the Lansing Municipal Airport, the shadow of the craft blanketing the red *H* painted on the ground. His calculations were precise: they were right on time.

Killion slipped from the cockpit and headed for the rear of the Sikorsky as Edward began the post-flight shutdown. He peered out the starboard windows: dark storm clouds threatened to the north. Chicago was only a short twenty miles away, reachable in minutes, visible on the portside horizon as they had landed. He envisioned himself holding the key, handing it over to the Frenchman. Killion laughed to himself as he thought of how easy everything really was and that he was being paid for something so amateur. This mission was simple compared to his usual brand of counterinsurgent sabotage and geopolitical assassinations. There was no challenge when the players fell into place so predictably. True, he and his brother had taken some lumps along the way, Edward more than Terrance, but this was easy money and, his boredom aside, Killion wasn't complaining.

"Shut down the bleeding engines, will you?" Killion shouted over the noise reverberating in the cargo compartment. "I'm going to make the call."

****

Elizabeth looked over at Ashley, sleeping soundly in the passenger seat. They were already over two hours east of Denver and nearing Julesburg, CO. They'd be crossing into Nebraska a little before 8pm, leaving another seven hours of driving to Des Moines. From there, Ashley once again taking the driver's seat, they would be able to reach Chicago by 8am the next day.

The prepaid cell phone sat on the center console. Elizabeth picked it up and dialed Michael's number, waiting impatiently to hear his voice on the other end.

"Hello?" he said in answer, the sound of his voice overwhelming to his wife.

"Michael!" she nearly shouted as relief filled tears streaked down her face, trying to lessen her excitement so as not to wake Ashley or Cain.

"Elizabeth," he exclaimed, drawing the attention of all who stood in the living room at the Branson house.

"I miss you so much," she continued, the pacing of her words exhausting, "I wanted to talk to you so badly when we were in Vegas, but I didn't have the chance. And then, through most of the drive, we haven't had service. It was only by luck that I picked up the phone and saw it had two bars of service."

"Where are you?" he asked.

"We're in Colorado, almost Nebraska. We're taking turns sleeping and driving, stopping only for gas, food, and restroom breaks. We'll be in Chicago by morning if all continues as it has."

"And Cain...he's alright?"

"He's fine, sleeping now, as is Ashley. We were treated well in Los Angeles. He played video games most of the time." Elizabeth explained.

"But they didn't hurt you?"

"No, no," she answered, "we're fine."

"Alright," Michael smiled. "We're going to get the men who did this. We'll put an end to this once and for all."

"I love you," she said, hanging on every word her husband spoke, longing for his response.

"I love you too, Elizabeth."

She hung up the phone and set it back down on the Mercedes' polished wood console. The sun was low in the western sky. There was still another hour of light left and she knew that darkness would soon envelop them. But she had hope: she'd heard her husband's voice.

∗∗∗∗∗∗∗∗∗∗∗∗

"Was that Elizabeth?" Gavin asked, watching as Michael, his solemn face hinting a smile beneath, returned to the group.

"Yes," he nodded.

"Everything ok?"

"Ashley is asleep and they're crossing into Nebraska. They will be here by midmorning."

The words were followed by silence. Both Gavin and Michael knew that their wives would not truly be safe till they were there with them in Chicago, and only, but most importantly, if they were able to successfully remove Killion.

Delilah's phone cut through the silence. They all turned to her in anticipation.

"It's him," she said, looking at the screen, McNamara's number confirming the caller.

****

Killion stood just outside the helicopter, McNamara's phone raised to his ear, listening to it ring. Edward had excited the craft and headed to the airport's office to arrange refueling and hangar space for the night.

"Hello, love," he said after receiving a cold greeting from Delilah.

"So you're in Chicago, I assume?" she asked, ignoring his irritating pleasantries.

"Yes. I've called to collect, and the sooner the better. My client is expecting results."

"The Frenchman?"

"Who else, love? You know as well as I his desire for things rather...*unattainable.*"

"I don't think you know what you've gotten yourself into," she replied.

"I could say the same of you."

"Perhaps, but now to business. You are in Chicago and I have the key. If you want it you will listen to my terms."

"Oh, fun," he mocked, "you think you're holding all the cards. Fine. What are your *terms*, love."

She looked at the intricately detailed decorative clock that hung on the wall, "It is *7:35* pm now, we'll meet in one hour, twenty-five minutes.

"We? I assume you mean Thirteen and the hunter."

"Is that a problem?"

"I can handle myself."

-Silence-

"There's a lighthouse in the harbor, east of the Navy Pier," Delilah continued. "do you have a GPS?"

"Of course," he smiled. "But if I must reach it by way of water, it may take more time to secure a boat and the weather could be an issue."

"That's not my problem, Terrance," she said sharply. "I'll text you the coordinates. Remember, 9pm. If you're even a minute late, I'll disappear and deliver the key to the Frenchman myself. And then, you're good as dead."

His reply was cutoff. She'd hung up.

Killion leaned against the fuselage and grinned. He missed her so. The cellular in his hand buzzed, the small little icon noting the arrival of a new text message as it blinked fervently.

41°53'21.45"N   87°35'25.93"W   9pm

∗∗∗∗∗∗∗∗∗∗∗∗

"So are we good?" Gavin asked, the excitement in his voice high.

"Yes," she answered. "He acted as if there was not enough time to prepare, but I believe that was feigned. He expected us to have a plan and I know how calculating that man truly is. He would have already prepared several options and considered anything we may attempt. He'll be ready. There's no fooling him, he is very smart."

"Well with just a little over an hour, we need to move too," Jamie said. "Let's get our guns."

Michael was ready, his .50 cal pistols were already holstered beneath his suit jacket, as were his backup 9mm's. Gavin ran out to

Michael's Porsche and returned with a small canvas bag and the two steel plate-laden carrier vests. Rain marks splotched his t-shirt: the storm was near. Jamie gathered his 12 gauge Remington and a clear plastic container holding twenty red, plastic shells.

"Where's your bandolier, *Rambo*?" Gavin laughed at Jamie while reaching into the canvas bag..

"Very funny," Jamie sighed.

Kayla stood back, watching as they came together, armed and ready to meet the assassin. She remembered when she, Ashley, and Gavin had done the same, preparing to invade the fortress that was Tri-Corp. And then later, when Jamie, after being freed from Triton's make-shift basement prison cell, joined them in their assault on Thirteen at the old site of New York General Hospital. How ironic now, that she had been replaced by Thirteen himself, Michael standing before her, as Delilah, the envy of every woman, the desire of every man, stood in her sister's place.

Gavin handed Jamie one of the vests and then offered the other to Delilah as she opened her purse. She took her pistol from the exotic leather bag and checked the magazine, but refused the vest.

"It's not my style," she said, "you wear it; you brought it for yourself anyway. You would have never known you would be adding a companion."

"I brought two, just in case," he winked as he and Jamie then slipped into the vests, helping each other snuggly secure the side straps.

"Jamie, you've got your extra ammo," Gavin confirmed. "Do you want the Smith and Wesson?"

"Just in case," Jamie replied, taking the pistol and tucking it into the rear waste of his jeans.

"Delilah, our guns are both 9mm and I have extra subsonic 147gr rounds in the bag so we can both run suppressed. We'll load our extra magazines in the car. Are you good, Michael?"

"I have eight rounds per gun including the ones in the chambers. I won't need more than that."

"Then I think we're all set," Jamie said as he slung the pump gun over his shoulder. "Except for one thing...I'll be right back.

Jamie quickly bound up the steps to the second floor and stopped outside of Ethan's nursery, the door ajar. He peered into the room. His son was sound asleep, napping in his crib, his favorite striped *blanky* held close. Jamie sighed, fearing that this could be the last time he would ever see his son.

"I love you, Ethan," he whispered to the sleeping baby before heading back down the stairs, fighting off tears.

"Come home to me," Kayla said as Jamie returned to the living room, her arms wrapping around him tightly as she kissed him, fearful that this was his end.

Jamie whispered his love in her ear and held her close, then kissed Marley on the forehead before heading out the door with the team. Gavin hugged his sister-in-law as well and she kissed him on the cheek.

"I'll take care of him," he said, knowing that Kayla was hiding her fear. "You'll get your pretty boy back."

She stood in the doorway, watching as they all climbed silently into the BMW. That's when she remembered the most important thing, something they'd forgotten. Kayla raced to the kitchen then bound out the front door and off the porch, her hand clenched in a tight fist. Jamie rolled down the window as she hurried to the SUV, the rain now coming down harder, wetting her shirt and hair.

"Here," she said handing Jamie the decoy key, "you can't forget this."

Jamie took it and kissed her, hating to pull his lips away from hers. He carefully backed the vehicle out of the drive, skillfully maneuvering the johnboat on the trailer, then sped off down the road, leaving Kayla alone, standing in the pouring rain.

****

"Did you call her?" Edward asked, watching as a crew came out to fill up the Blackhawk.

"I did. She gave me coordinates."

"When are we meeting?"

"9pm," Killion replied.

"That only gives us one bloody hour!" Edward grumbled. "Is it close?"

Killion held out McNamara's phone, the message with the latitude and longitude open on the screen. Edward took the cell from his brother.

"I'll punch it up on the nav computer," he said, climbing into the helicopter.

"It's a lighthouse, east of Chicago, out in the lake," Killion yelled as he climbed aboard as well.

"I see it," Edward said. "We can easily reach it by nine. What's the plan?"

"You drop me off on the stone quay, then hover close. I'll get the key, dispatch the whole lot of them and you pick me back up. Then we fly back here, rest for the night, and then we're off to Paris in the morning."

"That simple, huh?" Edward laughed as he lit a cigarette.

"They couldn't have picked a worse location: deserted, far from safety or shelter...and the perfect place to dump bodies."

"Fair enough," Edward replied. "How many targets?"

"Three for sure," Killion said.

"You've bested more," he said after a long drag, "and what of the storm?"

"This bird will fly in a hurricane and I've got you at the stick."

"And your cover? I can't support you from the cockpit. Say they flank, or have others hidden in cover?"

"I'm aware. I'll threaten that there are snipers hidden in the chopper and I'll toss a smoke grenade or two after I have the key. They'll lose me in the chaos and we'll be gone before they know it."

"You could take frags," Edward suggested.

"No," Killion said, shaking his head, "too much risk I could blow the key into the bloody water. Flashbangs could do the trick though.

Flashbang, smoke, and we're gone."

"They'll be done fueling in about ten minutes," Edward explained, checking the instrument panel and getting the craft ready to return to the sky.

"Perfect," Killion smiled, "we're nearly done, mate. Good job."

31

Jamie carefully backed the BMW down the launch ramp at Diversey Harbor, the trailer and johnboat inching towards the small inlet. The wind was strong, the water already choppy. Heavy rain pelted the windows.

"I'm starting to think this may have been a bad idea," Gavin said, uncomfortable with the fact that his usually calm nerves were beginning to unravel.

"There's no turning back now," Michael stated solemnly.

"We should have life jackets though," Jamie added.

"No time," Delilah pushed, "let's move."

The SUV lurched to a stop. The boat was far enough down to ease into the water. Jamie and Gavin released the ratchet straps that secured the boat and slowly sent it splashing off the trailer. They then turned it so they could head straight out from the harbor. The rain was cold on their faces, but the shallow water was still warm from the day's hot sun. They quickly loaded their gear and the four climbed into the boat. Delilah unfolded a plastic tarp and they stretched it out over their heads, finally tethering it to retrofitted deck cleats that Kayla's brother had installed at the front and rear corners of the aluminum craft. Once fastened, the tarp provided a relatively effective makeshift roof, though Delilah had to hold it up in the middle to allow the rain and spray to roll off the sides. Jamie yanked on the pull starter for the motor; once, twice, and finally sputtering to life on the third try.

After carefully navigating their way out into Lake Michigan, they raced for the lighthouse as quickly as the weather would permit, the flat bottom of the aluminum boat rising up and over cresting waves, then splashing back down, shaking the passengers violently. The wind was vicious, ripping at the tarp, testing the strength of the carabineers that held it precariously in place. They headed south, parallel to Lake Shore Drive, then headed east as they approached the old stone wall that guarded the north end of the Chicago Harbor. Overcast and visibility limited at best, they could still see the Navy Pier, spotting the recognizable Ferris wheel. To the west, the towering buildings of downtown were already glowing, the lights eerily floating in the blackness of the storm.

"I don't know if this little boat will make it," Gavin shouted over the sound of the crashing waves and burbling motor, watching the small pool at their feet grow with every gushing influx of water.

"I've been in worse storms and rougher waters," Delilah smiled coolly, "the Baltic and Black Seas can be terrible, nearly died in the Aegean after my team completed an operation in Greece. It was strictly covert. A Libyan terrorist had been chased from Turkey and went into hiding on Samos Island. We eliminated him, used the storm to our advantage, but barely escaped with our lives."

The men all stared at her blankly, trying to imagine why someone so beautiful would have chosen such a dark and dangerous life. It seemed unimaginable.

"If we survive this," Gavin said, "I want to hear all your stories."

"I would very much like to tell them," she smiled. "Some weigh heavily on my heart. But it was unprofessional to ask questions. Besides, we knew the risks then, just as we know the risks now."

Jamie maintained a safe distance from the wall, using it as his guide, and followed it all the way to the base of the lighthouse. Their approach had hidden them from the interior of the harbor, giving them the advantage in case Killion had scouts watching from the shoreline.

The nose of the craft scraped against the rocks. Gavin quickly climbed out and managed to secure the small boat to the wall. Jamie was the last to step onto the slippery rocks, his shotgun in hand.

And there they stood, at the concrete base of the structure, their feet dangerously close to slipping into the churning water below. Gavin looked back at the light-weight boat as it was heaved about, so easily tossed by the crashing waves, and mouthed a silent prayer that it would still be there and intact when they returned.

They made their way around the north face of the tower and found an old rusty ladder that led to the level above. Once up, away from the deafening smashing of the waves on the stone wall, they could see the entire harbor and the skyline beyond. But there was no sign of any other boats. No one else was foolish enough to traverse these waters in this condition. But their cause was beyond foolishness. They were fighting for their lives and for the lives of their families, to end a conspiracy wrought from the evil intentions of men who hid behind closed doors and shadow organizations, behind corporations and governments, the men who indirectly guided the world.

"Let's check out the building, make sure all is clear," Gavin said, pulling a flat black suppressor from the small canvas bag he wore strapped over his shoulder and across his bulletproof-vested chest. "Killion still has approximately twenty minutes. Delilah, you're with me. We'll do a sweep. Jamie, Michael, you guys keep watch from this first room after we clear it."

Gavin twisted the suppressor onto the barrel of his USP. Delilah followed along behind him, her suppressed Sig 226 ready. The door was locked. Feeling along the jam, peering through the window, he saw no deadbolt, then stepped back and kicked hard, the sole of his heavy boot landing just beside the knob. The old, whitewashed frame splintered as the wooden door swung free easily. They were in. Delilah covered Gavin as he swept past the door and secured the room. As they'd hoped, it was empty: no sign of Killion.

Michael and Jamie followed Gavin's silent, beckoning wave and came in from the rain. From here, they could safely see to the south as well as the harbor and lake sides. The northern view, however, was hidden.

"Alright," Gavin whispered to the men, lowering his gun, "stay here, we're going to check out the rest of the building."

Gavin and Delilah disappeared deeper into the darkness within the lighthouse, heading for the metal spiraling stairs that wound to the top of the tower. Looking up, they could hardly see beyond the second landing, the rest obscured by blackness. Without flashlights, only sudden, flickering blue bursts of lightning illuminated the way, allowing brief glimpses of their ascent. The first step creaked as Gavin placed his weight on the aging iron structure. He looked back at Delilah cautiously, but continued on. They hurried up the spiral, the flashes of organic light erupting through the windows and the curvature of the walls creating an unexpected vertigo effect as they climbed, their pace dizzying.

At last, they'd reached the light at the top of the sixty-odd foot tower, the whipping wind whistling through the spindles on the railing. They could see in all directions, Chicago to the west, dark clouds to the north, east, and south. The wind was strong, but the rain seemed to be subsiding.

****

"Do you think he'll show?" Jamie asked, peering out through the hazy old glass of the windows.

"He wants the key; it's the object of his mission. If he believed what Delilah said, then this may be his only opportunity to get it before she disappears," Michael said.

Jamie nodded and looked back out at the lights of the city, "Looks like the rain might be done for a bit. The water's still very rough though."

"I'll be right back then," Michael said as he headed for the door. "I'm going to walk the perimeter, check on the boat. How are we on time?"

"Ten minutes."

"Fine."

Michael left Jamie behind and headed to the right, back towards the rusty ladder that led down to the break wall below. A voice over his shoulder caught his attention and he paused, lingering long enough to see if it repeated itself. It didn't, so he continued. Another five steps and he heard it again, this time from above, but he realized it must have been Gavin and Delilah at the top of the tower, the wind shifting and carrying their voices in its southeasterly course. He stopped and looked down over the edge, closing his eyes, listening to the unsettling sound of the water far below. The chaotic symphony brought back memories, memories thought forgotten. Michael reached inside his jacket and removed the rolled up bundle of cloth mask. He held it out in front of him, staring admiringly at the stitching: for all he hated the mask, what it allowed, encouraged, him to do, he also loved it, loved the power.

Slowly, Michael pulled the mask down over his face, immediately feeling the gratifying rush of strength course over him. He clenched his fists as if to hold on to the energy.

"Welcome back, master," a voice hissed from below as a horrid creature slinked up and over the chain guardrail.

Another black, leathery demon joined them on the cement ledge, "Yes. I was afraid the Christians had turned you. It would be such a pity to have to find a new master, one so...*imaginative*."

"You mean *sick*?" Thirteen smiled.

The demons cackled as well, one's laugh trailing into a sulfurous cough.

"Are you going to do it?" the first demon asked excitedly. "Are you going to kill them all?"

"You should," the other grinned, "you really should!"

"Yes," the first continued. "Kill them all and take the key. Then kill the one called Killion."

"Absolutely," the other wheezed. "Then deliver the key to the Frenchman yourself. Steal Killion's reward."

"The Frenchman wants nothing to do with me," Thirteen growled. "When last we spoke, he blamed me for losing the key in the first place, simply *toying with Triton's trinket*, he said. He called my choice to remain in the States exile and a just punishment for my failure."

"Triton honed you, but the Frenchman created you," the demons said in staggered chorus.

"I'm sure he'd greet you with open arms," the first spoke.

"If you returned to him with the key," the second finished.

"Enough," Michael spat. "I don't care about the Frenchman anymore. He was my past, Elizabeth is my future. All I wish for is the safety of my family, for us to go on as we have planned. If Gavin and the others die, then so be it. But it will not be at my hand, not anymore. Tonight, this mask is for protection, not aggression."

"You don't know what you're saying," the first demon chided. "The mask is nothing *but* aggression. Remember where its power comes from."

"Yes," the other spoke, "remember where *our* power comes from."

"Consider the consequences for Elizabeth if you fail," they cackled, again in unison.

Thirteen stood in silence, contemplating the demons' twisted words as they slipped away into the shadows. In his head, Thirteen understood the logic, but Michael pleaded from the heart, trying to convince himself of which man he really was: Michael or Thirteen.

"Everything ok?"

Thirteen gazed coolly over his shoulder. Jamie stood behind him.

"Yes," Thirteen said softly with a grin. "We're all clear."

****

"Maybe he's not coming," Gavin sighed in disappointment, "perhaps the storm scared him off."

"No," Delilah replied shortly. "He knows that I can disappear with the key. That's the last thing he wants."

Gavin looked down from the tower. In the darkness, he couldn't make out much detail, but he could see the shadowy figures of Michael and Jamie below.

"Looks like they're patrolling the perimeter, good thinking," he said.

Delilah nodded, but didn't respond: she was concentrating on the southern sky, watching intently, listening for the sound she thought she'd heard.

"What? Is it Killion? Do you see a boat?" Gavin asked excitedly.

"No," Delilah answered, the navigation lights flying low in the sky confirming her assumption as they grew near enough to hear the rotor blades chopping through the air, "helicopter."

****

"We're almost there," Edward said, pitching left to begin his approach on the western side of the lighthouse. "I'll hover low over the breakwater and let you drop out. I'll then pull back up and circle low around the tower. That way, it will keep them on their guard. One of them will have to focus on me, reducing the attention they can give you. Get the key and take them out quickly. We don't know when this storm might pick back up."

Killion smiled. He truly loved his brother. Together, they had tackled jobs that would have sent most other professionals fleeing in the other direction.

"The smoke will be useless out here with the wind, but I'll toss a flash grenade as soon as I'm out of the heli," Killion said.

He slid his pistol from his holster and checked the magazine, chambering a round as the helicopter swooped down, pulling level with the lighthouse pier. Killion watched as two figures scrambled from the building's door and met the two others who stood overlooking the break wall. They'd shown their numbers. He was ready.

Edward hovered, steady and low, above the breakwater. Killion watched out the port cargo window as Delilah and two men, one in a mask, climbed down the ladder to meet him on the stone wall. The third man remained above on the pier, a tactical shotgun aimed at the helicopter. Killion opened the door to the cargo hold and looked down at them, calculating his drop and readying to attack, his gun in one hand, the flash grenade in the other.

32

The lapping waves crashed against the old weather-worn stone at the base of the lighthouse, splashing up and over the breakwater and then receding in gurgling fits, retreating back to the swirling water below. The rotors on Killion's helicopter made the conditions worse, the down force from the blades disheveling their clothing, their hair, blocking out any other sounds. This was it.

Gavin and Delilah raised their suppressed pistols, focused on the helicopter's cargo door. Michael stood casually, his hands at his sides, Thirteen's mask shrouding his face. Jamie tried to define the faint movement from within the Blackhawk, but the darkness was a disadvantage; still, he pumped a 12 gauge round into the chamber and steadied his aim.

A small glint caught Gavin's eye, but there was nothing he could do, his movements not quick enough, his cry of warning no match for the sound of the helicopter. The flash grenade landed at their feet and exploded. The sudden burst of pure light in the blackness of the storm, mixed with the disorienting bang of detonation, pushed Gavin and Delilah back against the wall, shielding their eyes, their ears ringing. Jamie was less affected, but orb like spots marred his vision.

Killion dropped from the cargo hold, landing athletically, his gun pinpointed on Thirteen. He watched as Gavin and Delilah struggled to regain their senses, but Thirteen was unaffected, something he couldn't have predicted.

"Your friends seem to be having a rough go, mate," Killion taunted, the noise of the helicopter's rotors lessening as Edward climbed and began to circle the lighthouse.

Thirteen cocked his head to the side, focusing his strength, his will.

"Strong silent type, I see," Killion said.

Thirteen just stared on in silence, refusing to answer. He knew that the longer Killion was distracted; his companions were afforded another opportunity to recover.

"Suit yourself, mate," Killion smiled, squeezing the trigger.

Thirteen shifted slightly, the bullet whizzing past his left ear and smashing into the cement pier behind him. Killion fired again, and again, Thirteen, with just the faintest movement, dodged each deadly bullet. The assassin's aim was true, but Thirteen was faster.

"Franklin warned me about you, Triton's puppet," Killion frowned. "They said you'd bollix it all up. But I know you have a weakness, everyone does."

Thirteen reached beneath his jacket and slipped the matching .50 caliber monsters from beneath his expensive suit coat. Killion, realizing that Gavin and Delilah were regaining their awareness, switched his aim and leveled the gun at his lost love.

"So to business then," Killion said slyly. "I am rather disappointed in you two, bitter enemies. I had hoped that each of you would blame the other for the disappearance of your loved ones, and in turn, eliminate one of you in the process as you waged war against each other. But alas, that was not the case and here we are. So then, which one of you does in fact have the key?"

Gavin angrily reacquired his aim, "Why did you take my wife?"

"Are we really going to have this conversation?" Killion asked. "I just told you that it was a ploy, plain and simple, nothing personal I might add. And honestly, she knows how to handle herself quite well, gave my brother a rather good beating."

"I wish she'd have gotten her hands on you then," Gavin barked.

"It was a *lamp*, actually."

"You're outnumbered. Why shouldn't we just kill you and keep the key?" Gavin said.

"Because I can guarantee that your precious little wife will never be bothered again. If you kill me, there will just be another man sent. Kill him, and there will still be another. It will go on and on until the Frenchman gets his way; and I promise, the Frenchman *always* gets his way. If we can reach an arrangement, we can all end this quite happily. Besides, I have snipers at port and starboard. If they even think they see your trigger finger flinch, they've been ordered to put a bloody bullet in your head."

"You killed my Saba," Delilah said, hatred burning in her eyes.

"Yes, a regretful requirement of the contract to be certain, love. But you know how it is: we can't pick and choose what parts of the job we like, it's all or nothing. If it makes any difference, Franklin is the one who killed Leroy. He was technically dead when I killed the rest."

"Is this funny to you?" she screamed.

"Not in the least, love," Killion frowned. "Now give me the key and we can all go on with our lives."

Thirteen had yet to speak, his guns trained on his target. He understood what Killion had expressed. The Frenchman *did* always get what he wanted.

"Give him the key," Thirteen urged Gavin. "The Frenchman is more trouble than he's worth. We can end this now."

"Your friend is smart," Killion said, "a poor sense of fashion, but smart. However that is a fine suit, would be a true pity to spoil it with blood."

"I say we listen to him," Jamie said, calling down from above as he stepped towards the ladder, watching the helicopter come back around the southern side of the tower.

Killion watched as Jamie slung the shotgun over his shoulder and quickly descended the ladder. Edward had nearly completed his pass, the helicopter moving behind him, the blades again kicking up a spray that showered down on all of them.

"So do we have an agreement," Killion questioned as soon as he could be heard once more, "the key for your lives, your families' lives?"

Jamie reached in his pocket and removed the key, handing it to Delilah, then taking hold of his shotgun and pointing the barrel at Killion, "Let's end this."

Delilah looked at Gavin for an answer, but she knew they were all in agreement, "Fine. Come and get it."

"Sorry, love, but that's not happening," Killion laughed. "I want you to bring it here."

"It's too dangerous," Jamie reasoned. "We'll toss it to you."

"And risk losing it to the depths?" Killion laughed again. "I don't think so."

"Then toss your gun into the lake," Gavin said.

"I would be at your mercy then. Can I trust you not to simply kill me? And remember what I said: the Frenchman *will* send another."

"Fine," Gavin conceded. "We'll lower our weapons once you've disarmed."

Killion shook his head and lowered his aim. Quickly, he removed the full magazine and tossed it into the lake side of the wall, then racked the action and ejected the round in the chamber before sending the gun splashing into the harbor on his right.

"Satisfied?" the assassin asked, his hands raised submissively as he stared at the useless bullet that had landed at his feet.

As promised, they lowered their guns and Delilah stepped forward slowly. She did her best to steady her shaking hands as she approached her former lover, but she couldn't hide the look of disgust that dirtied her beautiful face. Her hate for Killion grew with every step. She wanted nothing more than to place her gun against his forehead and scatter his brains into Lake Michigan, but there was always the Frenchman, his shadow looming over them all.

"Check him," Gavin called out when she reached him.

She placed the key in her pants pocket and, with her pistol still in hand, she patted his chest, first the left, and then the right, then down to his waste, slipping her hand beneath his jacket, feeling across the line of his belt, her fingers trembling as she felt his familiar body beneath his shirt.

"Cheeky," he whispered, leaning in close to her ear, his lips grazing her cheek playfully.

And then they watched helplessly as he lashed out with his left hand, his fingers wrapped tightly around her left wrist, then whipped her around in the same continuous motion so that she now faced her companions, but locked in the assassin's firm hold, his hand slipping from her wrist and over her hand, forcing her to aim the suppressed pistol at her friends. He locked his finger over hers, placing pressure on the trigger. For the first time in her life, Delilah was paralyzed with fear.

Killion caressed her body with his right hand beginning at her neck, then pausing at her breast. The three men took aim once more, but they knew they couldn't fire, the risk of killing Delilah too great.

"Come away with me," Killion whispered, kissing her soft neck, his eyes still locked on the men. "We'll have more money then we'll ever be able to spend. No more contracts, no more killing; just you and me. We can disappear. We'll make love like we used to, on the beach, the boat, beneath the stars. I'll buy you any house you want, from Europe to the Mediterranean, just come with me. Love me again."

Delilah felt his body pressed closely against her back, his softly groping hand unwelcome. But she couldn't move. She wanted to scream, to turn and stomp his foot, then strike where he'd hurt the most. But she couldn't. Tears streaked from her eyes as Killion moved lower, his hand slipping inside her pants.

"I never stopped loving you," he said sweetly, his longing for her suddenly, frighteningly real.

"Let her go," Gavin shouted, angry that he couldn't line up a clear shot. "Just take the key and leave her be."

"Is that what you want?" he asked Delilah. "Do you want me to leave you be?"

"I hate you," she managed between shallow breaths.

Killion removed his free hand from her pants, the other, still forcibly around her hand and the pistol, tightening, her fingers crippled, pale, and numb. His eyes burned in rage.

"What life could you possibly have without me that would be better than what I offer you?" he said angrily.

"A life in which my Saba lives," she smiled, closing her eyes.

"So be it," Killion sighed.

He thrust his hand violently into her pocket and retrieved the key, looking only briefly at it in his palm before hiding it in his own pocket. Edward was again completing another circle, hovering low above the wall behind his brother.

Killion cupped his hand over her mouth and began moving backwards towards the helicopter, dragging Delilah along as a shield. There was still nothing that Gavin, Jamie, or Thirteen could do without risking her life.

"Can't you use your magic, or...or...*whatever*?" Jamie yelled at Thirteen over the helicopter's roaring engines. "He can't hurt you!"

Thirteen raised his guns and charged. Killion was ready. He tightened his grip on her hand, Delilah's finger pulling the trigger.

The bullet slammed into Thirteen's shoulder, a splatter of blood following as it passed clean through. He stopped, confused. His mind hadn't yet realized the pain. His power should have stopped the bullet. What had happened?

Killion smiled. Thirteen was vulnerable. He forced Delilah to fire again, but his aim was unsteady and the bullet missed. Gavin and Jamie now charged as Michael stood in shock, fingering the bloody hole in his jacket.

But it didn't matter: Killion had reached the aircraft. In the same quick motion as before, Killion spun Delilah back around, now face to face, and pulled her trembling body tight to his, feeling her warmth one last time. He forced his lips against hers and stole a final kiss. Wrenching her wrist, he pulled the gun free then jammed the muzzle of the suppressor into her ribs.

"Goodbye, love," Killion whispered as he pulled the trigger.

"*NO!*" Gavin screamed, watching as the killer boarded the helicopter, leaving Delilah deliriously gasping for air, her legs growing weak as the coldness of death consumed her.

Jamie's shotgun boomed. He pumped the action and fired again, the 00 buckshot pelting the cargo door on the chopper. Gavin also opened fire, his suppressed 9mm barely an audible whisper compared to Jamie's thunderous rounds. Jamie fired again and again furiously, shell after shell, till his magazine was exhausted. They knew their guns were useless against the armored helicopter, but it was their desperation that drove them so.

Gavin tried to catch Delilah as she slumped to the ground, the stone wall crunching beneath them as they landed on the pier's rough surface. He located the bullet wound in her side and applied as much pressure as he could, hoping she could hold on.

"Delilah, stay with me," he pleaded, her blood flowing through his fingers, staining the stones of the breakwater as her life fled with each red drop.

She trembled in his arms, coughing up blood as she struggled to breath, "I'm so sorry, Saba. I'm so sorry."

"Please, focus," Gavin begged.

Again, she coughed, her chest heaving as she struggled painfully for air.

"His name, Delilah, what is the Frenchman's name?"

Her long lashes fluttered as her eyes rolled back into her head. And with her dying breath, Delilah whispered one last word…*Laurent.*